SLOTH

A DEADLY SEVEN NOVEL

SLOTH

LANA PECHERCZYK

also by lana pecherczyk

A Labyrinth of Fangs and Thorns

A Symphony of Savage Hearts

Game of Gods

(Romantic Urban Fantasy)

Soul Thing

The Devil Inside

Playing God

Game Over

Game of Gods Box Set

CARDINAL CITY MAP

← ------- MISHA'S HOUSE

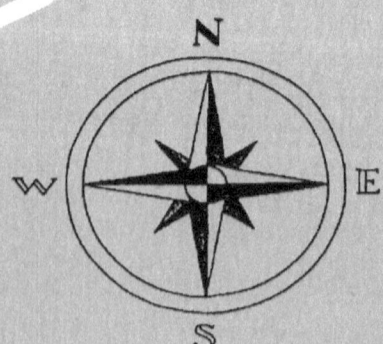

AIRPORT

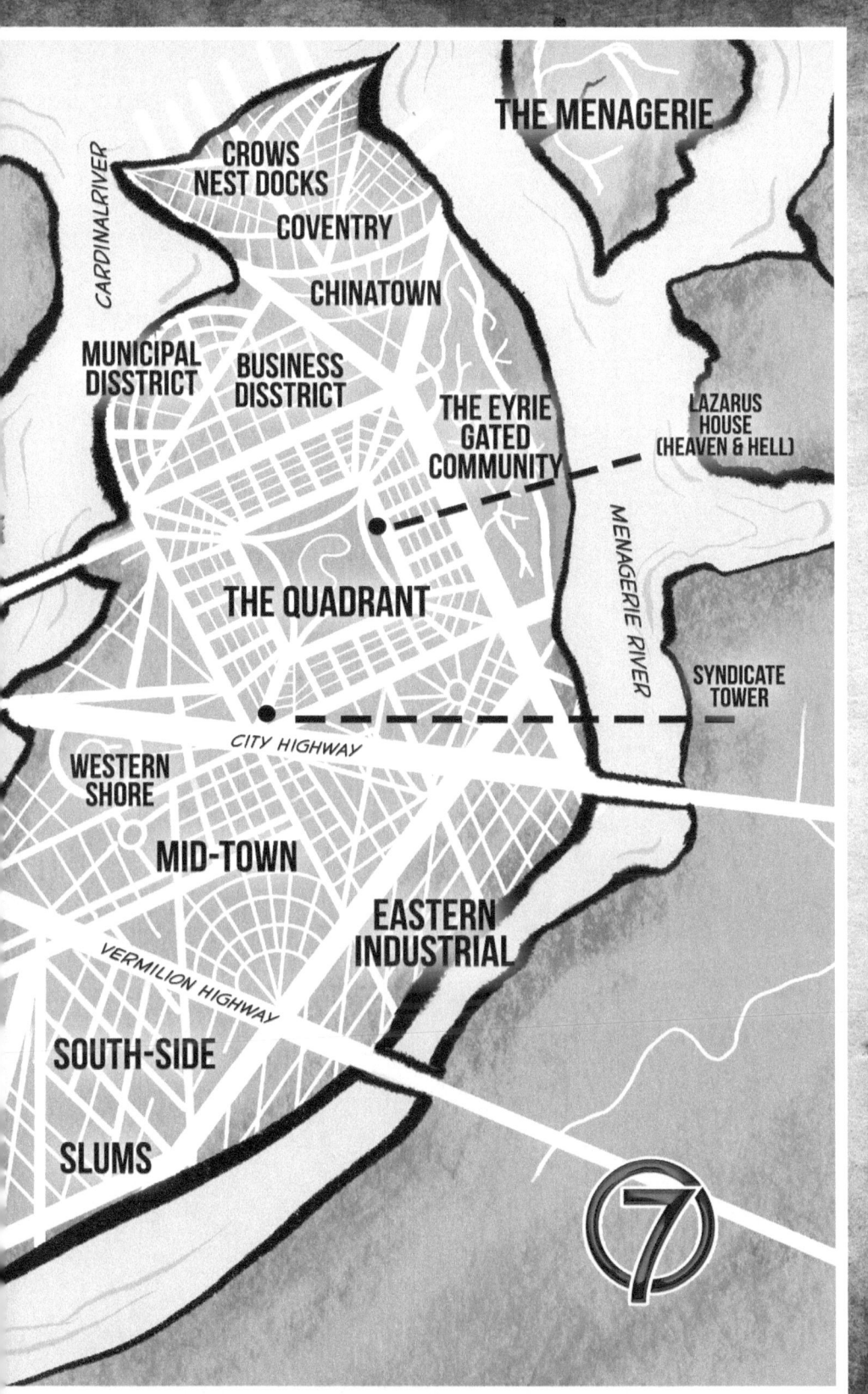

"What is right is often forgotten by what is convenient."

BODIE THOENE

prologue

WALKING down a dark hallway of the Syndicate's base of operations, Despair was a world away. While her father chatted with a scientist about the progress of their latest project, she found it hard to maintain focus. Memories tugged at the shadows of her mind.

The sound of giggling children swam through her head. The phantom smell of daisies wafted by.

"All is not lost, Julius." The British scientist stopped outside a lab door barely containing the vicious growls of animals. "We may not be able to stop our human clones expiring so soon after birth, but we may have found another solution."

"I'm listening, Barry." Julius's hands clasped together.

"You may remember the sin serum we made."

"The one that turned Doppenger into a raving beast before killing him. That one you mean?"

Barry tugged at his lab coat collar. "Yes, that one."

"Have you managed to control its effects?"

"Not on humans." Barry opened the door and led them inside.

"We're still waiting on blood samples from the rest of the Deadly Seven group."

"Eight," Despair blurted.

"I'm sorry?" Barry frowned. Her father also looked down at her.

Tall, feared and sophisticated, he was a man not many interrupted. But Despair wasn't one of the many. She was one of eight. The first.

"Eight," Despair repeated. "There are eight of us."

"Right."

Julius pursed his lips. "Please continue, Mr. Pinkerton. A little louder so you can be heard over the din of animals."

"Right." Barry pointed at the wall of cages filled with frothing beasts resembling dogs. "It's the animals we've managed to control. To a point."

Julius's lip curled. "Animals?"

"Animals injected with the sin-sensing serum, yes."

"These mindless beasts can track down sin?"

"Yes."

"And then what?"

"Their instincts force them to eliminate the sin. We might not need to trigger the Deadly Seven after all."

"Are the animals ready for the field?"

"Not quite. We still can't keep them from distinguishing the worst of the sinners from those who can be redeemed."

"We don't care anymore. We just want the sinners gone. All of them."

"But...." Barry gaped. "What about the children? They don't know any better."

"This is the area where Gloria and I disagreed. She believed evil is a learned behavior." Julius crouched and peered intently at the beast closest, unworried about the snapping jaws behind the metal grate. He cocked his head and studied the animal. Breaking under the scrutiny, the beast broke eye contact with Julius and cowered, whining. "I believe the rot starts in the seed," Julius murmured, gaze never wavering. "It cannot be unlearned. It is why I stand before you today, and Gloria does not." He stood and continued, "If they're not evil, they have nothing to worry about. Are you saying your beasts can't tell the difference between good and evil, Barry? Are you telling me you haven't done your job?"

"No. I mean. I have. But..." His protests failed to gather weight.

An itch at Despair's palm buzzed with a ghostly echo of her brother's blood. *Brothers. Sisters.* She had seven of them. They'd named her Daisy. They'd thought she was dead.

Maybe they were right. Maybe this emptiness inside her was as good as dead.

Somewhere deep in her soul, emotion stirred but retreated when the scientist's despair flared, casting a wedge of sin in her gut and blocking all else out.

Hidden danger was everywhere—such was the nature of sin. Even these scientists who boasted and preened to Julius about their latest breakthrough, even they had sin, festering away in their hearts and minds. Their despair revealed more truth than words. None were confident their project would succeed. Rid the world of sin, so those free of it could flourish.

The thing was… it was getting harder and harder to ascertain who was without sin.

Perhaps that's why the scientist despaired. Perhaps he already feared the future shape of the world.

A world with no one in it.

Let he without sin cast the first stone.

Except...

She looked down at her tickling palm. No one was without sin. Especially not her.

IT ALL BOILED down to zeros and ones. A no or a yes. That was how computers thought. It was how humans *should* think. It would make life a hell-of-a-lot easier for Sloan Lazarus, but, no. Humans didn't think in binary. They thought in the vast gray, messy expanse that laid in between: Life.

And Sloan was about to serve up a bucket load of messy life to one poor, unsuspecting ex-army officer she used to date—Maximilian Johnson.

She snorted. Her sister Liza was right. The guy was a big dick. Giant. But she couldn't tell him that. He'd probably just wink at her and say *thanks*. So instead, she pranked him.

Earlier that day, she'd tapped into the closed circuit video feed of Nightingale Securities across the street. It wasn't hard to hack, considering they shared a network, and the company worked for the Lazarus family. So it was almost like he'd asked for what happened next.

Sloan tapped the "up" button on her keyboard, remotely increasing the temperature on the thermostat in Max's office. She'd picked this day to exact her revenge because the weatherman had forecasted record summer heat. She'd picked this day because it had been long enough since her previous prank that Max would most likely fail to connect the dots, leaving her open to commit more prank crimes. Any minute, he'd be sweltering.

Nothing to do now, but sit back and wait.

Wait for the suffering to be unleashed.

She grinned and scooted her wheelie chair to the next monitor where a countdown ticked over, tracking her pizza order. Four minutes and it would arrive by drone to her fire-escape. Four minutes. She thrummed her fingers on the desk.

Waiting sucked.

Three minutes and thirty-five seconds.

Waiting.

God. *Why is waiting so hard?*

Two months ago, she had been the queen at waiting. But ever since that jackass turned up, she'd been reinvigorated with the sole purpose of making his life a living hell. Now she had more energy than she could contain. It was almost like she'd been intravenously hooked up to an energy drink.

Sloan wheeled to her third monitor where she created a program that converted binary code into abstract visual patterns, making a code that took months to crack, decipherable in hours. This kind of project was precisely why she couldn't afford to waste time on efforts that would give her no gain or pleasure.

She had learned that lesson in fifth grade when her eldest brother, Parker Lazarus, also known as King-Know-It-All, or King Pee, had been caught manipulating another child in his class to sit the history exam for him. It wasn't as though he didn't know the answers, in fact, he was too smart. While his chosen student sat the exam, Parker had been creating his own experiment in the science lab. He'd recognized his time was precious and more efficiently spent in the lab, so paid someone to do the other.

Now Sloan was the queen of misdirected effort. She wasn't too lazy. She was too smart. She saved herself for more important things. That's what she kept telling herself, anyway. There was no one else to tell because she hadn't left the haven of her apartment in the Lazarus House complex for weeks. No one came in. Only she went out. Sometimes. Occasionally.

Rarely.

It had been two months since Sloan left the security of her room. Two months she'd spent holed up, updating algorithms in her personal computer queendom, tracing money trails left by a recently discovered affiliate of the Syndicate, hoping to crack their investigation. Two months since she'd discovered her ex had somehow weaseled his way into her personal life.

Whatever.

A beep sounded at her fire escape.

Delivery. *Yes.*

She hopped from her seat, almost tripped on a fallen bathrobe, an empty packet of Skittles and a few other items she'd failed to put away since the housekeeper had been there.

Sloan lifted the window pane. The sound of traffic blasted in, and a wall of heat slammed into her face, making her stagger. Whoa. *Yeah, that heat.* Sweat prickled her skin and dampened her camisole. She also wore boy-short undies and knee-length socks but, hell, it was hot. She retrieved the pizza box—*thank you pizza drone*—from her landing and retreated to the icy comfort of her apartment.

A meow came from outside and a black cat with white feet launched onto the metal landing.

"Luna," she muttered. "You shouldn't be out there. Come in and have some pizza."

Once the cat scampered in, she shut the window, letting the cooling system do its job.

Glancing down, five levels below to the busy Cardinal City street, the entrance to Nightingale Securities gleamed in the afternoon sun. A small modest place, it housed not only Max, but a collection of ex-military orphans looking for a purpose now their official gig was up.

Turning, she lifted the box lid and wafted steam into her face. *Mmm.* Ham. Cheese. Best thing ever.

Wait a minute.

Pineapple. On her pizza. Gag. She had deliberately ordered it without.

Max had loved pineapple on his pizza. The great pineapple debate had raged between them for five years, since they'd met during an online gaming tournament. She'd always said that if, *when*, they'd met in real life, she would shove that pineapple up his ass. He'd always said he'd find a way to make her love it. She would reply that she already loved his ass, and on it went. Of course, being an online relationship, they'd never physically been in the same room to make the other eat the aforementioned pineapple or touch said asses.

Never been in a room together until two months ago.

Suddenly, she frowned at the pineapple with suspicion. Could Max somehow have changed her pizza order to include the pineapple?

Nah.

Sloan picked a piece of pineapple and held it to Luna as she made her way back to her computer desk.

"Here you go, ladyface. All yours."

The cat scrambled after her. She lifted onto her hind legs and nibbled the fruit from Sloan's fingers.

"Let's go see how our thermostat is doing."

With a wicked grin, she settled into her desk chair and watched the monitor. The camera angled from behind Max on the ceiling, giving her a view of his entire office floor. Four desks with computers, a couch in the corner. Fridge. Kitchenette. That even looked like a flat screen hooked to a gaming console. He was alone in the room. The rest of his staff must be on assignment.

Max's tawny hair had gone dark around his face—stuck down with sweat. He had that sun-kissed surfer look about him which was understandable. He was from Australia, had lived by the beach and surfed throughout the year when not on tour with his regiment. His perpetual bronzed tan was now turning red, but good ol' Maxie-boy wasn't retreating to a cooler place. Nope, the man continued to stare at his computer.

With the thrill of the chase licking up her spine, Sloan checked the temperature. One-oh-four degrees. She chuckled and took a bite of pizza. A chunk fell and landed on her stomach. She glanced down and grimaced at the pudgy pale flesh poking out from beneath her camisole and underwear. Frowning, she flicked the chunk off for the cat, and then returned her attention to the screen.

Any minute now he was going to lose his shit.

"Fuck you, Maxie-Pad."

A ping on her cell made her jump. Six siblings lived in her building, and without a doubt, one of them was constantly in her hair. It was a message from her brother Wyatt. Today, it was his turn to harass her. She'd missed her last two martial arts training sessions with him. The man had been on a relentless crusade to get her back into shape. At the start it had been awesome. She really did need the extra motivation. But now…

The phone pinged again. She ignored it, instead, settling in to watch the Max Show.

Max fanned his hand in front of his face. He got out of his chair and went to the fridge to pull out a can of soda. Huh. Would you look at that. Diet. *Since when did he drink diet?*

Another ping sounded in her periphery, but her eyes were glued to the screen, watching Max's brawny but graceful body as he tipped his head back, chugging the drink. His throat worked, Adam's apple bobbing as he swallowed. Sweat ran down his temples, but he didn't leave in a huff. No. He went back to his damned desk and continued to work.

"AIMI," she asked slyly.

"Yes, Sloan," came the feminine computer voice from speakers hard-wired into her apartment ceiling.

"What's the highest external temperature a human can sustain before receiving permanent internal damage?"

A pause, then, *"This is the entry I found on the internet: Human cells start to die at one hundred and six degrees Fahrenheit, but a healthy person can survive up to one hundred and forty degrees providing he has access to water."*

Max got up from his desk, and Sloan leaned forward. Was this the moment?

"Are you healthy, Max?"

Max retrieved a second soda can and rolled it over his handsome face, a face she knew well. Had seen it virtually every night for almost two years, unless he had been on tour. She knew those cut cheekbones, his cheeky lips, sparkling brown eyes... except they weren't sparkling anymore, and those lips were often pressed hard together. The man who had recently turned up in her city wasn't the man she once knew. He was a humorless stranger with haunted eyes.

Movement caught her attention. She gaped, a mouthful of pizza fell out and dropped with a splat to the floor.

Max had taken his shirt off, leaving nothing but a sweaty, sculptured chest. Washboard abs were carved into his stomach from the fine chisel of relentless core work. Veins bulged down his arms from the heat. Another change in him. He used to have a thick, muscled physique. If she had to pick a word to describe him then, it would have been solid. Now his body took the shape of someone who lived in the gym, someone who wouldn't sit still.

Damn these high-resolution monitors.

Suddenly, Max leaned forward, squinting at his computer screen.

"Shit." Sloan ducked, as if he could see through her monitor which was impossible. The camera was behind him in the ceiling. It wasn't a two way. Still, she hid beneath her desk, cheeks heating, heart pounding. Maybe she'd imagined the tension tightening his shoulders. But... she'd changed the configuration of the CCTV monitor network to include his office. His monitor also displayed the same configuration. There had been no way about it. He'd know a picture of his surroundings wasn't supposed to be on his interface, and since he was the only one with admin access... he'd know the only person with up-to-par hacking skills was her.

"Shit." She dared a look at the monitor again.

Max craned his neck to view the camera in the ceiling. Narrowed his eyes. Looked right through her soul.

"Shit. Shit. *Shit!* AIMI," she shouted. "Change the user interface for the CCTV on user account—" but she had no time to finish her directive. While she watched helplessly, Max typed with murderous intent, and one by one, all her camera links of footage winked out until only one video stream was left—his office. His muscled arm whipped out in the direction of the camera, then his fist, then his middle finger—aimed at her. The screen winked out to black, reflecting Sloan's surprised and beet-red face.

"No," she whined, flopping to the floor dramatically. *Backfire!* So stupid. He knew she was there. He knew she watched him! He was half naked. He must think...

The front door opened and she rolled to her feet, faster than her cat. Heart thumping in her throat, she looked for something to throw, something to ditch at the head of the jackass, but all she could come up with was a slice of pineapple pizza.

Perfect.

But it wasn't Max. It was Wyatt, holding a box of personal items in one arm. He ran a hand through the shock of black hair on his head, frowning at her attire.

"Ever heard of knocking!" Sloan stomped her sock covered foot.

"You weren't answering my messages."

"That's because I'm seriously busy, bras."

"Someone has to be serious about getting you back to fighting shape."

Sloan looked down her body. As far as she was concerned, she was good enough. A few months ago, the call of her slothful sin had overwhelmed her. She'd spent too much time sleeping, never eating, never doing anything. When each of her siblings sensed their sin, it produced a trickle of unease. This sense became unbearable the closer they got to a deadly sinner, urging them to end the offending cause of their sick sensation. The Lazarus family preferred to help sinners redeem themselves before a crime was committed. The thing was, low level exposure to sin was also tricky. Over time, if not balanced, she could fall under the influence of her sin—either become sloth incarnate, or the opposite. Whatever that entailed.

Sloth had a strong call.

Her bed had a seductive voice.

But those days were behind her. For the past few months, she'd felt like a new woman. She worked out, sort of, she ate better and she had goals. Sure, she didn't have a six-pack like her eldest sister Liza, but she was okay with that. For her, this was good.

"Why do I have to be buff?"

Wyatt arched an indignant eyebrow. "Because lives depend on your strength, that's why. Do you really want to put yourself in a position like last time, simply because you decided you've had enough training?"

By "last time" he referred to when Sloan had hid beneath a dead body and let their mother do all the hard assassin work. It sounded worse than it was. Yes, she had been unfit at the time, but she was also out of practice, and got a case of slothful feet.

"So, why are you here?" she asked.

Wyatt held out a box. "This is the last of Sara's things I had at my place. Her old phone is in there, and some other bits and pieces I found hidden under the couch."

"Why are you bringing them here?"

Wyatt shrugged. "Don't want them, and you might be able to crack the phone. Get inside and snoop around."

Curiosity piqued, and Sloan looked in the box. Next to the old smart phone was a small red jeweler's box. Sloan picked it out. "Why do you think I'll want this?"

Expecting the engagement ring he'd given Sara, Sloan opened the box and gasped with delight.

It was a replica of Usagi's and Mamo's engagement ring in Sailor Moon—her favorite Manga. Pink heart diamond center surrounded by little clear diamonds on a platinum band.

Wyatt laughed. "That's why."

She shot him a wry, arched brow. His laughter took some getting used to. Being with Misha had done wonders for his mood. Having a baby on the way also changed him. The jury was out on whether she thought the new change was for the good. He was the last of her siblings she would ever have thought to catch the love-bug, but he did. So had Evan and Griffin. They were dropping like dominos.

"I didn't know Sara was into this geek stuff." Sloan's fingers hovered over the ring. She snapped her hand back to her side. "But it's weird. I can't wear anything that psycho woman touched."

Sara was Wyatt's ex-fiancée from a few years back. She had also been working with the Syndicate and had tried to murder Wyatt. It had taken him a long time to get over the betrayal, but he'd found Misha, his lifemate, and he knocked her up. They were happy. Misha was the happiness to his wrath. She balanced him perfectly, and it showed.

Sloan collected the box of items. "Maybe I'll hack the phone."

"Are you coming down then?" Wyatt asked. "You've missed the past two workouts."

She groaned and dragged her feet to her kitchen bench, laying the small box on top. He was probably right. This was her sin talking. To prove her point, she lifted her inner wrist and inspected her Yin-Yang tattoo. Instead of being equal parts black and white, it was three-quarters black. The ink reacted to her biology, giving her a visual marker for how saturated her blood was with the sin of sloth. Too much sin, and she was in danger of blacking out and murdering any slothful sinner in proximity, even if they were redeemable, or just having a lazy day. Not enough sin in her system, and too much white showed on her tattoo. If this was the case, then the same outcome applied. She would blackout and enter a berserker sin-ending frenzy.

A shudder wracked her body.

Her computer beeped with an alert and they both looked over.

"Holy hack," she breathed. "The algorithm got a hit."

Wyatt watched over her shoulder as she investigated the new information. She'd followed the money trail from The Kremlin night-club bank accounts and had been bounced around from dummy corporation to an offshore account. Finally, she'd found something: GPS coordinates. Typing them into the public Google Earth mapping system, she cursed at the mass of black area blocking the bird's-eye view of the land. "Double shit. It's a black site. You think this is their base?"

"That's got to be the Syndicate." He patted her on the shoulder. "Good work. Let's go tell the others."

Sloan enjoyed the warm rush of endorphins from the praise. It felt good to be useful again. Good to stack up next to a family of muscle bound heroes she could never physically compete with.

"I'll just put some proper clothes on. Be right behind you."

"See you downstairs."

After Wyatt left, Sloan went to her closet and peered inside. For the first time in a while, pride straightened her spine. Instead of putting her robe on over her underwear and heading down in her slippers, she put on jeans and a blouse. Hell, she even brushed her slightly ratty long hair and tidied the locks into a single braid. But as she opened the door to leave, she found she couldn't cross the threshold.

"Come on, Sloan." Her hand wouldn't let go of the doorknob. "You can do it. Let go of the handle. It's only downstairs. Not like you're going across the street. It's not like *he'll* be there."

She closed her eyes, took a deep breath and counted to ten. When she got to eight, she let go.

"You've got this."

THE NIGHTINGALE SECURITIES office was a furnace even after Max Johnson wrested control from Sloan's evil clutches. With the outside temperature still in the nineties, the cooling system struggled. Sweat dripped down every dip and cranny of his body. He received no relief, despite being shirtless and using a folded sheet of paper to fan his face.

He scanned the space of the small business he'd started. Only four worked there, but the tight-knit crew was all he wanted for the time being. It was hard to trust these days. He wouldn't have taken anyone on, except he owed his mates, Daymo and Tom-Tom. It was Max's fault they'd needed a job.

The fourth person in their crew, Bailey, had found them. Don't ask him how. The ex-CIA agent was a wonder of mystery. He'd been suspicious of her intentions at first, except the pain on her face when asked about her agency history was real. The only reason she'd let it slip about her past employment was an olive branch of trust. She needed out, and she needed a job. For that to happen, she had to build trust with Max. There was a reason the CIA were often called spooks. You weren't meant to know who was one. He respected that. When he caught the pain in her eyes, the first time he'd asked, he didn't push for more details. He knew that look well. Saw it in the mirror daily.

In two months, he'd turned the washed out, run down retail space into a neat, respectable little operation. Kitchen, office and entertainment room out the front. Locker room and showers out the back. Storage room with a cot. It was all he needed.

The sound of the door opening came just before the voice. "*Phew.* What cooked and died in here?"

"Me." Max turned to greet Bailey Haze. "Back so soon? How was the job?"

After dumping her bag on her desk, she pulled her sweaty, curly black hair into a top knot and fanned her face with a hand. Despite the heat, she still wore smart business attire. Bailey believed you had to dress for respect. Black tailored pants hugged her hips, and a classic white button-down shirt complimented her brown skin.

Once, he'd made the mistake of suggesting the woman relax a little and dress down. Her response had been to purchase them all matching navy wool jackets with the Nightingale Securities emblem on the breast pocket. It made them look like a bunch of pansy-assed Prep boys rather than the rugged ex-soldiers they were. The tailored piece was itchy and as uncomfortable as hell. It was also currently hanging in his locker, waiting precariously for the day Bailey decided they should all "dress up" again.

He shivered involuntarily.

He'd stick to his fatigues, T-shirts and bomber jackets, thanks.

Admittedly, right then, he felt like a half-naked oaf next to her slick style, but she barely spared a second glance at his lack of shirt.

Already her head was shaking as she thought back to the question Max had asked.

She peeked inside her handbag, searching for something. Found a compact mirror and took it out before landing her chocolate eyes on him. "Would have been a lot easier if it weren't for the damned clowns needing an escort. Remind me again why we took that job?"

Because they needed the money. He retrieved her firearm and went to the weapons cage on the wall. "You'd rather go back to the CIA?"

The tendons in her jaw flexed. "What crawled up your butt?"

He sighed, unlocked the cage and put her gun inside before locking it back up. He flicked his gaze back to his desk and the screen where he'd caught the CCTV video footage mixed up earlier. It must have been Sloan messing with him. She thought he had no clue about her meddling in his life, but he knew her style. He wouldn't be surprised if the intolerable heat in this office was her doing. Sarcasm dripped from his tone. "Maybe you'd rather join the Lazarus Babysitters Club."

She jerked back, eyes widening. "You sassing me now? Because a gig like this is what you get when you're dishonorably discharged. Wasn't me who made you come here."

"Why *are* you here?"

"You know I have my reasons. Now, you got any more lip for me, or can I leave for the day? There's a Cosmo with my name on it waiting for me."

"Boys will be back soon. You don't want to wait?"

"No. Any other jobs?"

"Nah, mate, I'm good. You can go. Thanks for your work."

The look she gave him said "Damn, straight I can go" but the actual words out of her mouth were, "All right then. See you tomorrow, sunshine."

"Prop the door open on your way out, will you?"

After she left, he sat down at his sweaty desk chair and opened the Lazarus family dossier he'd created for the team. As far as the Nightingale crew knew, the Lazarus family were rich, spoiled brats and their women in need of protection. Even though Daymo and Tom-Tom had served with three of the Lazarus brood: Parker, Wyatt and Tony in the Australian Army, neither Daymo nor Tom-Tom knew about the Deadly Seven. Neither did Bailey. They didn't need to know. The only reason Max knew was because Sloan let her secret slip before… well, before his life went to shit.

The Lazarus secret was what brought Max across oceans to Cardinal City. He was done with the military and their brand of by-the-book justice. He wanted a brand of justice a little more effective, especially after Gale.

Unable to stop himself, his gaze tracked to the large service photograph on the wall under the Nightingale Securities sign. Four of them dressed in army fatigues, desert behind them, dirt in their faces, squinting at the sun. Smiling. Max, Tom-Tom, Daymo and Gale. Only three were left. None were smiling now.

Half his life—that's how long Max had spent with those men. It was more with Gale.

As if conjured by his thoughts, the sound of two men conversing filtered in from the back door. Max looked over in time to see them come in. Daymo, the big bearded man, and Tom-Tom—the smaller, tattooed man with a shaved head—shouldered through the door, still armed and wearing their Nightingale Securities black ball hat and uniform: black fatigues and a black T-shirt with a logo.

"Man, if it were any hotter out there—" Tom-Tom started, paused and looked to them all for effect. Picking up the cue, all three of them finished with: "I'd be roasting."

They all shared a moment of silence, reflecting on their absent friend who would say that exact phrase every morning they'd wake up sweltering in the Middle Eastern desert. Max's eyes drifted to the service picture on the wall again.

"Boss?" Daymo took off his hat and dumped it on his desk. He scratched his red-tinged beard and then scrubbed his dark hair.

Tom-Tom unclipped his firearm from his holster and plonked it on his desk. "What's going on?"

"Nothing," Max replied. "Waiting for you two slow pokes to get your shit together." He gave a pointed look to where Tom-Tom had laid his gun. "That needs to be in the cage. You too, Daymo. Put your things where they belong."

Not one, but both men, rolled their eyes at Max.

Daymo grumbled, "Yes, mum." But he did it with a smile.

Max ignored them. He was used to it. He was the boss and had a responsibility to make sure these fuckers kept safe. The last thing he needed was an accidental firearm discharge... or worse.

He cleared his throat.

When both soldiers returned from the weapon's cage, they strode over to Max's desk.

"You coming out for a drink tonight?" Tom-Tom asked.

Daymo jerked his chin toward the front door. "We found a place about a half a click from here. Serves the best barbecue chicken and actual beer. None of this sissy shit they drink here."

Max half-smiled. "You go. I want to stick around in case—"

"Yeah-yeah," Tom-Tom said. "In case you've forgotten to dot the i or cross the t."

Daymo glanced at the service picture on the wall. "You know he wouldn't want you sitting here brooding over things."

"That's not what I'm doing," Max snapped.

"Then why haven't you called his parents back?"

The energy left Max's body, and he slumped. "I'll do it soon."

"Whatevs, boss." Tom-Tom fished out a business card from his wallet and dropped in on Max's desk. "That's where we'll be if you change your mind."

Ten minutes later, the temperature still hadn't dropped, and Max was starting to regret his decision to stay, but he'd given his crew the night off. It didn't mean he would have it. Security jobs came in at all sorts of times.

To prove his point, the shrill sound of his desk phone echoed in the empty room. He picked up the handset. "Johnson."

"You're needed."

"Tell me something I don't know."

"Your pride always did make me want to puke."

"What's up, Parks? I mean, besides your puke."

A low masculine chuckle. "How soon can you get over? We've had a break."

Max checked his watch as if he had somewhere to be. "I could head over now."

"Good. See you soon."

Bounding out of his chair, he went to the locker room and found himself a fresh shirt to put on. He considered having a shower, but decided against it. Parker usually let him use their state-of-the-art gym, and with nothing left to do at the office, he needed to keep busy.

If he stopped, his demons would come out to play.

FIVE MINUTES LATER, Max found himself outside the private elevator door in the Lazarus House lobby across the road. With his position in the company, he had full security clearance to the multi-story building. After Sloan's latest onslaught of pranks, he half expected his biometric scan to be denied.

When the elevator doors opened, the car was empty, and he breathed a sigh of relief. The scanner read his face and thumbprint to activate the artificial intelligent interface. She was a new security upgrade in the building since they'd discovered Wyatt's ex-fiancée had worked for the enemy.

"Welcome back, Maxi-Pad," came the feminine computerized voice over the intercom. *"What level would you like to go?"*

He closed his eyes, trying his patience. "Basement."

"Stand clear. Doors closing."

Bloody hell. Maxi-Pad? When was she going to let up? Probably never. The two of them used to spend hours planning pranks on anyone they'd perceived had done them wrong. From her brothers, to Gale, to the gamer who'd once decided to drop into their game after tracking them on a live stream only to one-shot them. Bad form. Point was, when Sloan set her mind to do something, she followed through. That's why he was surprised with how she'd ended things between them. *Not even a goodbye.*

The elevator slowed, then stopped. As the doors opened, the voice came over the speaker again. *"You have arrived at the basement level. Have a nice day, Maxi-Pad."*

First the heat today, then the name. If he didn't know any better, he'd think this was Sloan's version of foreplay. But he did know better, and she hated his guts. This was animosity.

Hoisting his duffel bag over his shoulder, he stepped into the secret underground headquarters of the Deadly Seven. The first time he'd seen the place, he'd been blown away. Years ago, when Sloan had told him what she did in her spare time, he'd never imagined the magnitude of the operation. Well funded, well planned, and well run. Grateful for the opportunity to help in any capacity, he didn't even care if that meant being a glorified babysitter for their public identities. At least he was being useful and not waiting for red tape to clear before making a difference, however small. By protecting the identity of the real heroes, he could save lives that counted.

Raised voices came from the operations room, getting louder as he approached. He passed the med room, weapon's room, gym, and a few other closed doors before arriving at the big open space that consisted of the communications room and conjoined workshop.

"Yeah, but I told you it's a closed loop network." His chest tightened at the sound of Sloan's familiar voice. "We can't get access unless we're inside the building, logging into a hard-wired computer. And even then we'd have some hardcore encryption passwords and biometric authorizations to bypass."

A few of the Lazarus clan stood around the central operations table, watching over Sloan's shoulder to her laptop screen. As he stored his duffel bag next to a wall, he counted heads. Seven in total. Evan noticed Max first and broke away from the group, sauntering over.

"Yo, bud." He gave Max a fist bump. "How's the tatt doing?"

When Max had arrived in town, and Evan had discovered his virgin skin, he'd busted his balls to get Max down to his tattoo shop. The man was covered in full sleeves himself, so when he'd prompted the issue, Max felt like he couldn't say no. The man could also fry Max where he stood, with self-made electricity. Sometimes Max was sure he could see lightning gathering in the man's green eyes.

Scary as fuck.

"Yeah, it's good, mate." To prove it, he showed Evan the inside of his forearm where the man had inked the nightingale bird and a stunning freehand geometric black line design around the two dates Max had asked for.

"What's *he* doing here?" Sloan's voice cut through the room with a razor's edge.

She sounded different in real life. Over the internet, her voice had a tight, tinny quality, but standing a few yards from her, it held a warm, smooth timbre—even when she was pissed.

All heads swiveled his way. The room became exponentially crowded.

"He's here because I asked him to come." Parker, the eldest and largest, broke away from the group. Long auburn hair brushed past his collar. The bloke was at least a head taller than anyone else in the room, and when he came to stand next to Max, it was hard not to be intimidated. When he'd first met Parker, he imagined, not a wolf in sheep's clothing, but a wolf dressed in a tuxedo, with a cane and monocle. He looked like a smart, rich man, but if you spent too long staring into his amber eyes, there was something wild and daunting staring back at you. Good thing he was a friend.

Parker shook Max's hand with a firm grip and then shot his sister a bold look. "I'm not the one who slipped our secret to him. I'm just the one capitalizing on the opportunity. Max is an intelligence-gathering specialist. We can use him."

Sloan mumbled something under her breath.

"What's that?" Max asked, his voice coming out scratchier than he intended.

"I said, you're a specialist asshole, so gather *that* intelligence."

Someone laughed—Liza, the detective.

Mary slapped Sloan on the head, mumbling for her *mija* to have respect, then she gave her other daughter daggers for laughing. Mary was a fit, black-haired woman in her fifties with death in her eyes. Her husband Flint had balls of steel to sleep next to her every night. The man, also in his fifties, worked in the workshop behind her, a half-interested eye on his wife's reprimand to their daughters. He adjusted his spectacles and swung his ball cap around to face backwards before refocusing on the tiny mechanical object on his cluttered bench.

Max drew his attention back to Sloan. It had been hard to retaliate when he'd first arrived in Cardinal City. She'd been a mess. Ratty black hair. Clothes hung off her bony hips. He'd actually felt sorry for her. But over the past few weeks, the color had returned to her cheeks, and mischief had returned to her eyes. She'd put on weight and looked healthy. She'd once been his only link to the civilian world, and he'd immersed himself in her uplifting presence to help deal with the aftershocks of battle. He'd had no idea she'd been using him for the same reason until she'd confessed about the Deadly Seven.

She was the woman he fell in love with all those years ago. And now she hated him.

Yeah. Definitely not friends.

Max caught Sloan's older brother Wyatt watching him with the same wariness. Not friends with him either. They used to be once, but the man had changed since his stint in the army. The quick to anger warrior had become invulnerable—literally. Max did not want to get on his bad side.

Max folded his arms and turned to Sloan. "How would you know what I'm a specialist in unless you looked me up? I'm flattered."

"You wish."

"Why would I wish? You already did it."

A berry stain hit her cheeks. "I don't know what you're talking about."

"Of course you don't." Hell yeah, she did. The guilt was all over her face. A satisfied swell bloomed in his chest.

"Oh, get a room already." Liza moaned. The tall brunette rolled her eyes, but slammed a deadpan look on when confronted with

Sloan's raging intent. "Ugh. Can we get back to the task at hand? Some of us actually have a real job here and some dickhead's been leaving bodies in the river. Captain's asked for me to go canvas."

"You need help?" Evan perked up.

"In broad daylight?"

He shrugged. "You won't even know I'm there."

"Nah, we're good. Thanks though, bro. Maybe tonight if we haven't had a break. So… back to the task?"

"My thoughts exactly." Parker waved Max over to the table.

As Max approached, he noticed Mary stood with a dagger in her hand, twirling it expertly between her fingers. Immediately, he went on high alert. Muscles locked. Adrenaline buzzed. But the woman didn't seem to notice him. She was lost, frowning at Sloan's laptop screen.

Jeez, that woman freaked the shit out of him. Fifty-five and with more kills on her belt than his old squadron. He'd best be staying on her good side, and she already distrusted him because of the bad water under the bridge between him and Sloan. He shifted to stand to her right. The side without the dagger in her hand.

"So," Parker started. "Sloan was asked to look into the financial records of a company we recently discovered linked to the Syndicate through Misha's connection. It took some time, but she's traced the payments to a location. This is it. Sloan. Bring it up. *Sloan.*"

Sloan sat there, hunched and still fuming, hands fretting in her lap. Part of Max preened to see her uncomfortable around him, the other part still felt empty. She gritted her teeth and brought up the relevant satellite footage. Zooming in, the map quickly filled with black space.

"Black site. Military protection," Parker said.

"History?" Max prompted.

"Google Earth dates the restriction back twenty-five years."

"That's about the time we destroyed Biolum Tech," Flint said, coming from the workshop to stand next to his wife. He placed a steadying palm on Mary's shoulder and squeezed. "Wasn't there a military officer who came in to speak with Julius the day we extracted the kids? You think they're still involved?"

Mary nodded. "And an Asian business man."

Max fumed. He'd dedicated years to the military, and no matter where he was in the world, there were still corrupt assholes using their service positions for power. From what Parker had told him about their history, the Syndicate experimented on children. They manipulated and brainwashed vulnerable people into becoming suicide bombers or members of their *Faithful*, promising them rebirth as clones healed of their genetic deformities or inflictions. He doubted these people followed through with their outrageous promises.

"Have you searched the current whereabouts of these old contacts?" Max asked.

The condescending look Sloan sent his way could melt stone. "What do you think?"

"I think you did a quick search. But, people change their names. They get sloppy."

"Well, Akiko Ito and Amare are alive and kicking. Nowhere near the site. Akiko is in Kyoto, and Amare is randomly in Alaska. I have no idea what for."

But Max's gut was telling him something. Not to be dissuaded, he addressed Mary and Flint. "You both worked at this Biolum Tech?"

Flint's voice was a deep rumble. "Yes."

"I know it was a while ago, but have you searched for old known associates who live locally to the black site?" Max asked Sloan. "Anyone your parents used to work with. Janitor? Lunch lady? I know the black site is a fair way from the city, but it looks like it's under an hour's drive from the closest town. If anyone is living off-site, it would be there."

"Like you said," she replied. "People changed their names. Moved on. That sort of thing. At a site like this, most employees live on base."

"How would you know if you haven't looked?" Hot frustration crept up Max's neck. How could she expect success if she assumed so many things? "Leave no stone unturned."

"I thought you were supposed to check all of them," Daymo asked Max, deep in the Middle Eastern desert.

"I checked four out of five containers. None of them held armor-piercing bullets. It's sweet. Don't stress. She'll be right, mate."

Max shook the memory away before it took hold of him. He did not need to go down that rabbit hole today.

"Have you looked, Sloan?" Parker asked.

"Yes!"

"Really?"

She paused. "I checked a few."

"Actually," Flint said gingerly, cutting through the thick silence. "There are some names of technicians and scientists I've not given you. Mary and I can get together to brainstorm a few others. See if we can come up with a list."

"Good idea," Mary added.

"Start with Barry Pinkerton. He was another geneticist who showed promising potential, but he was never allowed into the main lab so I assumed he was ignorant like me."

Parker tapped Sloan. "There you go. Start there."

Grumbling, Sloan's fingers hit her keyboard with dizzying speed. She whipped through programs—secure government programs she should have no business accessing—like they were a fourth grader's computer system. Damn, he knew she was good. Just didn't know how good. She'd kept a lot from him when they'd dated. If you could call their online relationship dating. They'd never once touched in real life, but online, over video stream, they'd done plenty.

The memory of her lush, half naked body flashed before his eyes. He wondered what she would look like today under those clothes. How much had changed?

His cock stirred.

Shit. He cleared his throat and forced himself to think of footy. Aussie rules. Essendon versus Carlton. Grand Final. Last five minutes. He mentally replayed the match, play for play, until his blood cooled.

Sloan's search stretched into minutes. Flint and Mary retreated to the workshop corner where Flint continued to pull apart a small gray drone. Mary spoke to him in a hushed, urgent tone.

Parker soon retreated to a row of glass cabinets containing their combat suits on mannequins. He had one cabinet open and a soldering iron ready to use on inbuilt tech.

The Lazarus family was one talented mob.

Evan was the warrior of envy, so it made sense when he shot Max a quizzical look, and went to stand next to Parker. Max must have let his envy flare.

"Call me when you get a hit," Liza said, gathering her leather jacket and slipping it on. She tugged her long brown hair from the trappings of her collar. She also cast Max an odd stare before flicking her gaze back to Sloan, and then to Max. Then she rolled her eyes. "I gotta go to work."

No secrets in this family.

He had to remember to guard his emotions. Conjuring up a compartmentalization technique he'd learned in the army, Max put all his lust, envy and other inessential emotions into a box, locking up tight. He'd unpack later that night. Maybe.

Soon, it was just Max and Wyatt standing behind Sloan. From

the way she glanced daggers over her shoulder, she didn't like it, but he'd be damned if he stepped away first. She'd already demonstrated she liked to cut corners.

Max stood back, hands folded, and watched Sloan do her thing. Wyatt stood arms folded, watching Max.

The longer the search took, the more his gaze strayed away from the screen and back to Sloan. She still wore the same expression when she concentrated. Her little wet tongue tip stuck out the side of her lips, giving him just the hint of pink. Her nose scrunched up. Black eyebrows flicked up every few minutes, as though she'd come across something surprising, then puckering with a frown when she hit a road block. The only thing he hadn't seen her do recently was chew her hair. When they used to game together, her hair lived in her mouth. And when she'd shout something, it would pop out. At first, he'd thought it was disgusting, then, he'd come to associate it with her, and everything he'd associated with her back then came with the warmth of dopamine.

"He's alive," she said, screen footage coming to rest on the face of an older man of Indian descent.

"This the bloke, Flint?" Max asked, waving him back from the workshop.

Parker and Evan rejoined them.

Flint came back with Mary and peered at the screen. "Yeah, that's Barry."

"And where does he live?" Max asked, even though he could see on the screen. He just wanted Sloan to say it, to admit she was wrong.

"Twenty clicks from the black site," she mumbled.

Damn straight. "It can't be a coincidence."

Parker rubbed his designer stubble, scratching up the jaw. "What else did you find out about him?"

Sloan tapped a few keys, bringing up the man's private email and social media accounts. "Well, you can see he's a Leftie in public, but —get this—he's a closet Trump supporter, decidedly right-wing. Barry doesn't want to admit it, but he likes all the appropriate political candidates' posts. See?"

"Something useful, Sloan," Parker rumbled.

"What? I thought that was funny. Okay, fine. Here. Let's take a look at his RSVP'd events." She scrolled through some information Max was sure only this Barry dude should know. "Looks like he's going to a charity gala supporting science in the environment this weekend. He's scheduled to speak."

"That's your man," Max stated. "That's your vulnerability. Get to him at the gala. Grab his biometrics. Get into the site."

Evan whooped. "All right. Road trip."

"No," Parker said immediately. "You stay behind."

"What?" Evan groaned. "Why?"

"You and Griffin have flashy powers. If you're not here, and you're seen there, people will put two and two together. We need a good cover story and stealth. Sloan, you're obviously in."

Her face paled, but she said nothing.

"I'm happy to help," Max offered, hoping to piss off Sloan even more.

"We need you here," Wyatt replied. He'd been quiet the entire time, but with this, he spoke up. "Misha is three months pregnant. She'll start to show soon. If the Syndicate find out she's carrying my child and I'm not there..." He trailed off, shaking his head.

"Got it," Max said. "Security on her will need to be increased."

Wyatt gave him a curt nod, but gratitude blazed in his eyes.

"Does that mean you'll go?" Parker asked Wyatt. "Having a super on the team will be beneficial in case we run into trouble."

"How long will it take?"

31

"Well…" Parker glanced at the map on Sloan's screen. "There's a national park on the east side of the black site. What if we plan a hiking trip there?"

Wyatt pointed at a spot. "That's near the mountains."

"Base jumping. Nice," Evan added.

Even from Australia, Max had heard about Parker's cliff climbing and base jumping exploits.

A slow grin formed on Parker's face, showing a glimpse of that wild beast within. "It's all coming together. I'll get Tony on board and we'll go to the charity gala—show our faces, donate some cash—act like we're stopping by before heading off on a boy's weekend."

"Boy's weekend is fine with me," Sloan said. "I'll just stay here."

"It was a figure of speech. Your presence is not up for debate. You'll be required to install the back door program into the closed circuit system so we can access the Syndicate data from here. Then we can take our time searching through their files from a safe distance. You're coming."

Wyatt added, "How long will it take to hike to the site from the national park?"

"Two days, give or take," Max suggested. "Maybe do it in less if you don't stop to rest."

Wyatt's hard blue eyes met Max's. "You'll have around the clock security on Misha while I'm gone?"

Max nodded. "Whatever you need."

"Good. I'm in."

"Great. It's settled." Parker clapped his hands. "I'll go apprise Tony. Wyatt, you make arrangements with Misha. Sloan, you…" Parker's brows lifted in the middle as he took note of his sister, now with the end of her braid in her mouth. His top lip curled in distaste. "You need to clean up. You can't go to a high-priced ticket charity gala looking like that. Get your hair cut. Buy an outfit. It's black tie."

She spat her hair out. "You're an asshole, too."

Parker flipped her the bird and then left the room.

An awkward silence filled the space Parker left.

Max turned to Evan. "Do you mind if I use the gym?"

"You gotta stop asking, bro. Just use it."

A short nod, and he left, scooping up his duffel bag on the way.

three

THE SECOND MAX left the room, Sloan rounded on her dumbass brothers. "You let Parker talk to me like that? *Ooh, get a haircut, Sloan.* Get a life, Parker, right?"

"You know"—Evan folded his arms, giving Sloan an exaggerated once over—"He's not half wrong."

"What's that supposed to mean?" Hackles raising, Sloan slid off her stool and straightened her spine. The top of her head came to Evan's nose. Damned male height. "I'm not that bad. I've improved plenty in the past few months. Check it, the tattoo is virtually balanced."

He snorted. "No, it's not. You've been sitting on your ass all day."

"And you've not left your apartment in weeks," Wyatt pointed out, again.

"Now you're joining in? Ugh. Whatever. That's not the point. The point is, there's nothing wrong with my hair." God, men were so stupid.

"No offense, Sloanie, but you could do with a bit of a..." Evan waved his big hand around Sloan's face.

She gasped, shocked. She was perfectly fine. What did they know about personal presentation? Evan had black lines all over his body. He wore frickin' flip-flops, and Wyatt... Wyatt... well, he wore black all the time. Boring.

"Is this what you think, too?" Sloan asked Wyatt.

He made an awkward face. "Maybe just a little."

"Mama?" Sloan shouted to get Mary's attention in the workshop. "Pops?"

Flint ducked his head, clearly not wanting any say in the matter, but Mary's eyes softened and she held up a finger and thumb, pinching. "You could do with a small haircut, *mija*."

Oh sure. Pick on the slothful one.

Emotion hit her in the throat. It tightened. Burned. Was she so terrible?

She swallowed it all down.

Don't be a pansy. Just go look at yourself in the mirror.

Sloan walked to where tall glass cabinets housed Deadly Seven battle suits on mannequins. Behind each suit was a mirror. She'd brushed her hair today, but the truth was, they were right. Her hair was split, ragged and down to her waist. It was a weakness in battle. Their Art of War sensei had taught them better than this.

There was power in appearance. The ancient Spartans terrorized their foes by dressing dramatically and with intimidation. This tactic ensured their enemy's knees buckled before any battle began. It was one of the reasons why the Deadly Seven had a uniform. They wanted criminals to cower when they saw her brothers and sisters coming for them. Saved a hell of a lot of pain when the criminal simply turned himself in rather than face the terror of the Deadly Seven.

Right now, Sloan's appearance said, *Walk all over me. I'm useless.*

A ball of anxiety grew in her stomach.

It was entirely possible her last haircut was a home job using manicure scissors in her bathroom. A glance toward the gym. Max hadn't let himself go at all. He'd buffed up. If anything, he looked better.

Screw him.

She could look better, too.

But she had no idea where to go. Sloan wasn't a girly-girl. She was a Tom boy. The very thought of having to go into a salon made her heart palpitate. Just imagine, hairdressers swooping in to force opinions on her. *Oh, yes, sweetheart. Those bangs look lovely on you.*

She almost threw up in her mouth.

As if hearing her thoughts, Wyatt suggested, "Why don't you ask Misha to take you to her salon? She loves all that—" He waved around his face with a perplexed look.

Sloan chewed her lip. "You think she wouldn't mind?"

"Not in the least. But you'll have to let Max or myself come along for protection. I won't let Misha head out on her own, not in her condition."

"She's not an invalid. She's pregnant."

"With a Lazarus child. Who's saying what kind of DNA secrets the baby will give the Syndicate if they take it. Considering when we were children they wanted to cut off our limbs to test our regeneration, I'm not taking the chance."

Sloan's anger swiftly morphed to defense. "You don't think I have what it takes to protect her?"

A slow arch of Wyatt's brow.

Evan tried not to laugh. "I'm not touching this one with a ten-foot lightning rod. See you two later." And then the coward left.

"Wyatt?" she prompted. "I can look after Misha. I helped at The Kremlin when you needed me. I did good." Okay. Maybe she didn't do good. The Kremlin was the nightclub Misha used to work in. Her boss was an A-grade Bratva psycho who worked with the Syndicate, and Wyatt had needed Sloan's help to save his woman from hench-men. The Faithful were as fanatical as their leaders. Worse. They believed they had nothing to lose.

Thinking back on the battle, Sloan knew her words were a lie. She didn't do good. Maybe Mary did all the work while Sloan hid under a dead body, but she had fired a few good arrows from her bow. It was months ago, but damn her if she let Max or Wyatt watch while she went in for a makeover. No fucking way.

Wyatt sighed and looked to the workshop for help, but both Mary and Flint kept their heads down, pretending not to hear. "Look," he said. "I'll tell you what, how about if you can get one over me on the mat, I'll let you go on your own with Misha."

"Elaborate."

"We spar. You get me down, submitting, you get to go with Misha on your own. You can't, I win. You take a security detail."

"You're powered. That's not fair." Clearly he was at an advantage. The dude could punch through a wall. She was strong, but not that strong.

He took a deep breath, raked his hand through his black hair and stared intently in the direction of the gym. "Okay. How about this, you get Max down."

"No." Her hand cut through the air. "I'm not fighting him. I don't want him anywhere near me."

"All the more reason he's a good pick to test your skill. Unless you want to go against Mary, that's my final offer. Take it or leave it."

Seriously considering their mother at that point, Sloan looked over to her. The petite, black-haired woman was insanely lethal. Trained as an assassin for the Hildegard Sisterhood, Mary could kill you before you knew she was there. And, while she passed on many secrets to them, she was the master. Mary didn't care that Sloan was a woman. She gave no quarter. Sloan was certain there had been a broken bone or two over the years. Definitely a nose. She rubbed it when the phantom pain of the past echoed.

Max wouldn't be used to fighting a woman. He might hesitate before hitting her. She could use their history to her advantage. He also didn't know that her advanced physiology made her stronger than a normal man. That was one secret she'd never confided. It had always made her feel less of a woman. She shouldn't feel bad for being stronger than her lovers, but she did. It always made things awkward in the bedroom. In a fight it could be advantageous.

She could take Max, no problems. She would also get to kick his ass.

A slow, devilish smile lifted her lips. "Okay. Deal. I'll fight Max."

Mirth sparkled in Wyatt's blue eyes. "Good. Let's go find him."

Together, they left the operations room and entered the gym. Sloan's attention went straight to Max on the treadmill. Dressed in baggy black basketball shorts and a gray muscle shirt, it was hard not to be impressed with his physique. Long legs moved with graceful, fluid strides. Blood pumped in his veins, shaping his body into sharp relief. Sun-bleached hair darkened with sweat. He ran that treadmill with a single-minded focus. If he screwed like he ran… Feminine places in her body clenched with desire.

Maybe this was a bad idea.

Too late. Wyatt already stood before the man, asking him to slow down. Shit. Sloan huddled by the door, watching their interaction. Stopping his machine, Max's brown eyes darted her way then went back to Wyatt with a nod. He slipped his towel from the treadmill and wiped his face. Yep. This was happening.

It's fine, Sloan. Kick his pasty Aussie ass. Now she had images of his ass in her mind. Crap. Definitely not pasty. Tanned and tawny as fuck. He also had two dimples on the cheeks. She knew because he'd teased her once over a private video chat—shaking that derriere like he just didn't care.

Heat inundated her body and sweat prickled her skin.

Nerves. Just nerves.

Sloan toed her shoes off, rolled her shoulders and then walked to the plastic covered foam mat at the center of the gym. She flexed her arms, pulling back, popping her chest out—hoping to distract him with her feminine wiles. *I got wiles that last for days, jackass.*

Max and Wyatt met her there. Max's chest rose and fell as he caught his breath, but he looked inspired. Not distracted. Her confidence faltered.

I got this.

Her atoms came alight as he drew closer. Heart rate pounded. Hairs on her arms lifted. His coconut scent mingled with his sweat and she caught a full breath of heady masculinity. This was the first time in months, hell, the first time ever she'd been so close to him. All those years they'd spent conversing over online video, all those years she'd spent yearning for his touch to be real, and now it was too late.

Because he'd fucked up.

Don't forget that, Sloan. He was the one who came to meet up with her, to take their relationship to the next level, and then bailed without a word. He was the one who believed the hype in the news about the Deadly Seven being terrorists. She had no time for a man who had little faith in her. He didn't deserve a second chance.

"You understand the drill, Sloan?" Wyatt asked. "Just get him down. That's it."

Perhaps Wyatt had caught the murder in Sloan's gaze as she eyed Max. She shot Wyatt a mischievous smile. She'd damn well do what she wanted, *bras.*

Max's brows lifted at her attire. "You're going to fight in that? I can wait if you want to change."

"O ye, of little faith." She wore jeans and a stretch camisole with a sports bra underneath. This outfit was a walk in the park compared to what they'd all fought in before. Full heavy combat gear, sometimes underwater.

So has he.

Shut up, inner voice. I got this.

Max shrugged. "Just don't crack the shits when your movement is impeded."

Both Wyatt and Sloan gave him a blank look.

"I meant, don't get angry." He grinned, flashing a dimple that probably made most ladies swoon.

Dimple. Dimples everywhere. Damn it.

"You Australians talk about poop a lot."

Max snort-laughed.

It wasn't supposed to be funny. Sloan circled Max, eyes narrowing. "The only person 'cracking the shits' around here will be you. So... I hope you're wearing a diaper because you're about to go down."

"You know my thoughts about going down, Sloan." He winked salaciously.

Grr. He was trying to rile her up, and it worked. A blush hit her cheeks so hard her eyes blurred.

It wasn't fair. He shouldn't be having fun. It was supposed to be him faltering over her wiles, not the other way around. The heat riding Sloan's circulatory system increased. For a moment, she thought she'd somehow messed with the thermostat in the gym by mistake, but no one else was affected. She shook her arms out and then held her fists in front of her face, boxer style.

"Bring it, Maxi-Pad."

A flicker of—*something*—behind his eyes, then it was gone. Max bounced deftly on his toes, fists hanging loosely at his side. The smug asshole wasn't nervous in the least. Probably thought those bulging biceps were going to save him. Ha! Even if Sloan was a little out of form, she'd been trained by Mary—a small, fiery, un-powered assassin who was still the deadliest person Sloan had ever met.

Wyatt harrumphed and moved to lean a shoulder on the concrete wall, as far as he could get from the mat.

Just as well, Sloan didn't hesitate. She took two steps forward and jabbed relentlessly, driving for Max's face.

He bounced back each time, darting out of reach. "That all you got?"

A frustrated sound came from the base of her throat.

Mary always said, when fighting someone bigger, go for the vulnerables. Eyes. Groin. Throat. Incapacitate him from the word go. He was bigger so supplied the energy. She'd have to be smarter and control the force. All she needed was to get Max down on the mat and she was sorted, but you'd have to excuse her for wanting to make this last. She had a broken heart to defend.

Circling, she jabbed a few more times and took note of his reactions, cataloging each twitch, flinch, step, breath. They danced around each other, feinting, but never connecting.

"Come on, Sloanie. Show me some of that skill you've always bragged about," he teased, but she only gave him a secretive smile.

When she was sure she knew his tells, she dropped her fists as a decoy. She intended to confuse him, to surprise him with a feint, and then go in for an uppercut—

Max rushed her. *Shit.*

He jack-hammered strikes to her head. She jumped back, arms out, blocking his fists with her palms before they hit her face. Damn that man, trying to use brute force against her. Trying to intimidate her. She knew how he played. She knew his battle strategy. They didn't get to become one of the leading *Call of Duty* teams without learning how each other's minds worked. He was a smash and grab guy. She preferred to use her brain. Anger spiked, turning her defense to offense. Spotting an opening, she planted her hind foot, bounced back, cut under his arm, pivoted and roundhouse kicked him in the face.

Max's head snapped back from the force, a spray of saliva or sweat bursting in the air.

Agony!

Pain in her face, so sharp, she could barely draw breath.

Every muscle locked rigid. Suffering became her world and all she could think was, *That's not right*. Why am I hurting when he was kicked? Then the pain became so intense, she couldn't think.

Max didn't get the memo.

He reset and came at her again. He grappled. Without control of her body, she went down hard, screaming from the blinding torment emanating from her nose to hammer behind her eyes and temples.

This isn't right.

Something is wrong.

Max wrestled her down with a joked, "Looks like I'm on top."

She curled into a ball, clutching her head. "Hurts."

"Sloan?"

Hurts so bad. Like someone reached into her brain and squeezed with an iron fist. Even her nose screamed in pain. "Oh my God, it hurts."

The weight on top of her suddenly disappeared, and a crash shook the room.

"What the fuck did you do to her?" Wyatt bellowed.

Sounds. Fists. Crashes. All in her periphery, beyond the veil of pain blinding her.

Wyatt was hurting Max.

"Stop," she tried to say. "It's not his fault."

Her pain had come before Max had hit her.

It came… when she touched him for the first time. When *she* hit *him*.

She gasped. What could that mean? What…

Whimpering, she peeled her eyes open. Wyatt had Max checked against the wall, fists at his collar… and Max, he was horrified. Wide brown eyes full of regret and hurt and worry speared her way.

"I didn't…" he said, blood dripping from his nose. Had she made him bleed?

"Not his fault," she gritted out. The pain was subsiding. "It's not his hit that caused my pain."

How could it be?

Wyatt shoved away from Max and came to Sloan. "Then why is your nose bleeding?"

"I'm what?" A nose wipe came away wet. Red liquid stained her fingers. "I'm bleeding."

Why was she bleeding?

Max stepped toward Sloan. Wyatt gave a warning growl.

"Pipe down, Wyatt. It's not his—" she hissed as pain stabbed her brain again and she clutched her head. "I've got a headache. That's all." Headache, and nose ache. Weird.

The sound of feet pounding down the hall got louder. It reverberated in her head. She winced. Mary rushed inside, Flint not far behind her. Now everyone knew. Everyone knew she couldn't handle herself against an ordinary human.

"What happened?"

"Jeez, you're all acting like I'm a baby. I'm fine." Fuck, this was embarrassing.

"I'm sorry." Max crouched and touched her foot. The instant he connected, lightning flashed in her head and she cried out. Something was happening to her brain.

"Just get out of here," Wyatt snapped at Max. "I'll contact you if we need you."

Max worked his jaw, clearly wanting to retaliate with a retort, but he bit it back. He gathered his duffel bag and went for the door. Just before he left, he turned, shot a ferocious look at Wyatt, then said to Sloan, "I'll check in later."

Flint walked him out, speaking soft words, but Sloan missed what they said. She was too busy coming to terms with the fact that her headache was linked to Max. The further he went, the more her pain abated until it was gone all together.

"You don't get headaches, Sloan." Mary looked down at her, shrewd eyes picking up what Wyatt had not; Sloan's Yin-Yang tattoo had moved from its unbalanced marker to complete equal parts black and white. The only time any of their tattoos moved so swiftly back into balance was when one of them met their lifemate—a person who embodied their sin's opposing virtue.

Was Max... was Max her mate?

SLOAN KEPT her revelation to herself for two days. Two days of hiding out in her room, staying away from people, and dealing with the odd flash of pain in her head. Something had happened to her brain after connecting with Max. Whether it was TV, or in real life, any time she watched someone get hurt or receive pleasure, she felt it in her own body. If this was her power manifesting, what kind of fucked up one was it?

Evan could control electricity. Griffin could manipulate metal. Wyatt was invulnerable. And Sloan? She could get a fucking headache when her enemy went down. Whoopdie-doo.

She wanted to cry.

Instead, she hid out in her room, working out using stupid things like Thigh-masters and Sit-up machines, or hiding under her covers until Thursday came around and a loud knock banged at her door. When the pounding failed to abate, anxiety crept into her system and she lifted her covers higher on up her body. She'd deliberately ignored all text messages and phone calls. What happened with Max shook her to the core.

45

The black cat at the foot of her bed released a low warning growl.

"My thoughts exactly, Luna." They could go away.

The door clicked, and Sloan swore. They must have the master key. A surge of panic and fury washed through Sloan as the door opened. "Go away!"

Luna lifted on her paws, back arching with a hiss.

Sloan sat up. The cat never got aggressive. Sure, she made the odd growling rumble from time to time, but she looked down-right murderous and ready to pounce at whoever walked through the apartment door. It was almost as if the cat felt Sloan's emotions—or vice versa.

Sloan gathered the kitty into her arms and stroked her back. "Shh. It's probably just Wyatt. I was being stupid."

The gala was tomorrow night, and she had run out of time to get her hair done or to buy a dress as per Parker's instructions. King Pee was a jackass for telling her what to do. He may be the leader of their team, but he was a snob.

She'd not always been ratty-haired and sloppy-clothed. She used to like funky clothes, and gamer themed accessories. She used to tie her long black hair into high pigtails with buns on the top, tails streaming down her back, just like her favorite manga character. She wore cosplay themed clothing and cool T-shirts. Sloan was part of the nerd herd and she loved it.

"Yes, it's just Wyatt." The man in question stopped at her open bedroom door. Misha's blond, curly hair poked in from behind.

"Hi, Sloan!" Misha waved. "We've missed you. You okay? Wyatt —*oof*. Move aside man." Misha tried to push the big warrior of wrath, but he wouldn't budge until he gave Sloan's room a furtive once-over.

"Jeez, bras. No baddies in here," she teased. "Misha's safe to enter."

"No baddies. Just stale air." He scrunched his nose. "When was the last time you opened a window?"

"Last night when I ordered pizza." Sloan poked her tongue at him as he moved to her bedroom window, brushing aside the drapes so he could get to the pane.

Misha looked good. Glowing, as they often said. Her yoga-trim, well looked after body, barely showed the tiniest of belly bumps. Sloan could only tell because she knew how super flat Misha's stomach was before. Misha grew the first of the next Lazarus generation and she couldn't be happier. Then again, she was always happy.

She bounced over to Sloan's bed. "Ooh. Kitty cat."

Both Sloan and Luna tensed with the sudden approach. Sloan forced herself to calm, and the cat did too.

Wyatt snorted. "It's true what they say."

"What's that, Wyatt?" She scowled at him, very conscious of her two-day-old appearance. He better watch what he said next.

"Like owner, like pet."

She'd give him that. It *was* true. Luna had been mimicking Sloan over the past few days. She slept when Sloan slept, moped when Sloan moped. Whatever.

"Why are you here, Wyatt?" She pouted at him.

It was Misha who answered brightly. "I've made us an appointment at my salon. You and me. Girls morning. Yay!"

"Really?"

Misha nodded excitedly, and Sloan couldn't help connecting with that excitement, just like she had every time she watched someone get an answer right on *Jeopardy* last night. Damn it. The flood of Misha's endorphins rushed Sloan awake, pushing out the worry coating her thoughts. She supposed she could go outside. Staying locked up would only cause her more problems. She should expose herself to strangers and test out her new emotional limits.

"Come on, Sloan. You did say you wanted this, right?"

Thinking back to how she'd felt so inadequate around Max and his new buff physique, she nodded.

"I'm coming too." Wyatt folded his arms. "You still failed to put Max down first."

In other words, she wasn't good enough. "Technically, I did. But, fine, whatever."

"Speaking of Max, um—*koteczek*, can you give us a minute?" Misha asked.

Wyatt moved to stand outside Sloan's room, but she could faintly sense him somewhere near the kitchen. Her sin sensing capability gave her the power to know when someone was still, relaxing, or remained unmoving. Sloth was a strange sin. She could feel it like the ghost of an illness in her stomach, almost there, until it became a sickening pain when the sin became deadly. She'd often lamented over how their creator should have made their sin radar something fun, like a tingling in her loins instead of a sickness. But then, where would be the urge to stop the sin?

"I heard about what happened with Max at the gym," Misha said quietly. "Do you want to talk about it?"

"No." Sloan pushed her blankets away. She wanted to avoid thinking about Maxi-Pad and the intense feelings he provoked.

"How about we do a few Asana poses? Banish the brain fog, and—"

"God, no." Sloan was not a yoga person. "Just let me get dressed, and I'll come. I'm feeling better now."

"And you'll feel much better once Angelo gives you an extra long Ayurvedic scalp massage." Misha wiggled her brows and Sloan couldn't help smiling. Yep. She'd definitely been cooped up way too long if that sounded appealing.

AFTER SITTING NEXT to the happy-go-lucky woman on the ride to the salon, most of Sloan's jitters had abated. Relentlessly, Misha had chatted away, while Sloan brooded out the window.

Wyatt dropped them off at the door with strict instructions not to go anywhere until he arrived after parking the car. By the time Sloan followed Misha to the big glass doors of the modern salon, she was almost back to her old, feisty self.

"I'm sorry about my attitude earlier," she said to Misha while they waited. "I shouldn't take it out on you."

"Oh," Misha laughed. "Trust me, I get it. No woman wants to change appearances just because an arrogant man tells her to. Believe me, I get that. Just say the word and we'll go home."

Sloan guffawed. *Arrogant.* "You know Parker so well."

"Do you know he forced my yoga studio closed once? Didn't even ask. Just assumed he knew better and refunded my customers their tuition fees. As if money can solve all problems. I had to do some major damage control customer service after that."

"I hope his mate is someone who says no to him. A lot."

"Now, I'd pay money to see that!"

The two of them chuckled until they fizzled out, looking through the glass doors into the salon. Despite the warm summer breeze tickling her skin, Sloan hugged herself. Inside, the decor was clean and white. The only splash of color came from the beauticians' and hairdressers' outfits. And the horde of customers.

So many people. So many emotions and feelings.

Her heart pounded in her throat. She put her hands in her pockets to avoid fidgeting. "You're right. I need to do this; I'll feel better afterwards."

"Awesome." Misha linked arms with Sloan. "And we can have a

proper sister gossip session. I'm dying to rant about my darling brooding—oh hi Wyatt. Back from parking so soon?"

He glared at them with suspicion.

"Hon, you're not coming in, okay?" Misha said sweetly. "You can do your thing from the café across the street."

He checked the salon. "I'll take a look around. Survey the back entrance. How long will you be?"

"Could be hours, babe."

Exasperated, he frowned. "Hours?"

Misha shrugged but gave Sloan pleading eyes.

Sloan added, "I'm getting my hair dyed, so hours."

"All right. After I check it out, I'll be across the street." He went inside and walked straight past the receptionist who trotted after him, flagging him down.

God, her brothers could be alpha assholes when they wanted to be. The word arrogant applied to all of them.

Misha rounded on Sloan. "He's driving me nuts! Do you know he sits in my yoga classes now? Doesn't join in, just watches my students like he's some kind of crazy stalker man."

"Sounds like Wyatt."

"Like, I get it. There's danger and all that, but ugh." She took a few deep breaths, mumbling a mantra about the past and future. When she was done, she brightened again. "It's all good. If I let him win this level, then it means I get to be bossy in the bedroom later on, if you know what I mean." She waggled her brows suggestively. "Last chance I'll get to jump his bones before he leaves for a rare weekend away."

"Ew. That's my brother you're talking about."

"But he's so hot. His bones are very jumpable."

"Double ew."

"Okay. Let's go inside. I really need a scalp massage."

Wyatt returned from whatever dark spaces he'd assessed. "All good. You know where I'll be." He waved his cell phone and bent to kiss Misha tenderly on the cheek, using his big palm on her face to hold her there a moment.

The man who used to be in a perpetual foul mood, softened and relaxed at contact with his mate. The sight made her insides ache, and it had nothing to do with sensed emotion. This was all her. She was jealous. Thank goodness Evan wasn't around, or he'd call her out on it.

As soon as Wyatt left, a short Italian man in a bright yellow suit rushed up to Misha. His two front teeth prominently poked over his bottom lip, reminding Sloan of a chipmunk. "Misha, darling. Give me a hug."

"Hi Angelo."

Angelo patted Misha's curly hair with a few disapproving sounds. "That regrowth needs attention, sweet thing."

"No dye for me today, Angelo," Misha said.

He gaped, horrified. "But, sweetie. The regrowth."

"We're here for this tall drink of water." She waved at Sloan then leaned toward Angelo. "Her hair has never been dyed."

That was all Angelo needed to perk up. "Never?"

"Never."

"Fabulous." He pursed his lips and inspected Sloan with shrewd eyes. "And you darling, what are you wanting today?"

"Whatever says 'Fuck you. You gave all this hotness up, and now you'll never get it back.' Can you do something like that?"

Angelo blinked back at her, then his face split into a grin that made his nose lift and teeth show. "Girl, I like you. I've got just the thing."

He snapped his fingers and two stylists came running over. "We want the Revenge Package ladies."

51

Three hours later, Sloan sat in front of a mirror, staring into the face of a woman with slashes of red through her newly trimmed black hair. Shoulder length and healthy. A little weird with the style, but she could work with it. The strands still fit snuggly in a tie if she had to enter battle. Her nails were red. Eyebrows waxed. Lady parts waxed —don't ask. It seemed like a good idea at the time. Even if Max would never see her goods, she knew she was in babe territory. It was like wearing sexy lingerie for her own joy. It empowered her.

Misha sat next to her jabbering about something Sloan had missed over the roar of the hairdryer.

But it was all done now.

No bangs.

Sloan grinned. She could deal with this.

"You look hot, Sloan," Misha leaned in, chewing on gum. "Max is going to seriously regret whatever he did. What did he do, by the way? Wyatt won't dish and it's driving me nuts."

"This isn't about Max." Sloan scowled.

Misha snorted. "Yeah, okay. Revenge Package for the doorman then?"

Damn it.

Angelo's fingers ran product through her hair. "Don't ruin all my good work with that frown, sweetheart."

When Sloan turned her scowl on him, he made a hasty retreat, leaving Sloan alone with Misha.

"You okay, Sloan?" Misha asked. "You're scaring away the staff."

"Fine. I'm fine." She rubbed her temples. "Just getting another headache."

"So... Max? What's the deal?"

She wasn't going to let up, was she? Sloan sighed, fingers moving to tug on her hair, wanting to put the end in her mouth, but she resisted.

"After years of online dating, we decided to make a go of our relationship in real life. He made the first move. Said he was quitting the army. He booked flights to come here. We were going to get married. Have babies. Live together forever. All that vomit stuff—no offense. It was such a huge commitment, that I told him my secret. He got cold feet."

"Oh. That's... yeah. That's rough."

They were both silent for a moment, and then Misha piped up. "Are you sure nothing happened to him? I mean, what if he didn't show because something happened, you know?"

"Oh, he came." And that was the hurtful part. Sloan understood if he couldn't deal with the vigilante crime-fighting, but it was the fact he believed the media before asking her for the truth. That betrayal hurt most of all. "I checked the flight records. He was in Cardinal City the day Sara blew herself up and killed a building full of people. The flight records also showed he left the city the same night. So... he believed the hype, I guess."

"What do you mean?"

"He must have seen what the news stations were saying about us and decided it was too much."

"But he's here now. If he didn't want to be with you because he believed the lies the media spread, why did he come back?"

Sloan had been avoiding asking that question herself. Was it as simple as he'd changed his mind? Decided *not* to believe the media?

"Ow." Misha's hand went to her mouth.

Sloan hissed as a stab of pain sliced through her tongue.

"I bit my tongue instead of the gum," Misha whined. "I'm such an idiot."

The tang of metallic blood filled Sloan's mouth, and she held her finger there to inspect the flavor. It came away stained with red.

When Misha spat out her gum, covered in red, she spotted the matching red on Sloan's finger. Misha's head cocked to the side as she studied Sloan. "Did your mouth just bleed when mine did?"

The urge to confide in someone was stronger than Sloan's will to deny. "Yes."

"Are you serious? Did you bite your tongue too?"

"No."

"Then how?"

Sloan stared at her new short, sparkly nails. Somehow, she couldn't keep the truth from Misha. She was family. "I think it's my power. Stupid as it is. I feel pain when others do. Sometimes I bleed. Not all the time... but... yeah. I think it's some sort of empathic ability. I'll be holed up in my room forever at this stage. I mean, I can't even go to the salon without hurting myself when someone else does. This is hopeless."

Tears burned in her eyes. It was too much.

Misha's hand came over hers and squeezed. "Why haven't you told anyone? Your family can help."

"Have you met my brothers?"

"What about your mate?" When Sloan kept silent, Misha understood. "It's Max, isn't it? It's Max and you hate him."

She couldn't hold it back any longer. Tears spilled over. "Why me? Why do I get the asshole? Why do I get the power that hurts so much? And why do I give a shit?"

It's bad enough she had to prove she was as good as her macho brothers... but now this?

Misha's face crumpled. Tears welled in her eyes too. "You're making me cry."

"I'm sorry." Sloan wiped her eyes, but couldn't stop. This breakdown was a long time coming.

"Let it out, Sloan. Just release it all," Misha said, nodding emphatically. "You'll feel better. Go on."

She was right. Sloan had this pressure building inside that she'd been holding onto for so long. She needed to let it out. She closed her eyes, took a deep breath, and then... just released.

Something weird happened.

Invisible energy whooshed from her body, lifting strands of her hair.

Angelo started crying over the hair of the customer next to them. Then the customer started crying. Like dominos, everyone in the salon teared up.

The entire salon was crying.

Shocked into silence, Sloan's jaw dropped.

Misha whispered, "Oh my God, you're *really* making me cry. You're making all of us cry."

"Wh-what?"

"Come on. Deep breaths. In. Out. You need to calm down."

Panicked, Sloan did what Misha said. Refusing to focus on her blotchy face in the mirror, she forced herself to breathe. Misha came to stand behind her and gave her shoulders a massage, coaxing her to relax.

"That's right Sloan, focus on your breathing. This will help you anytime you feel overwhelmed. Inhale the future, exhale the past. That's right. Keep doing it." With each intake of air, Sloan felt her strength returning. With each exhale, peace eased into her body, spreading to loosen her limbs. When she was done, Misha locked eyes with her in the mirror. "Do you know what this means?"

"No."

"You can affect the emotions of others. And... if you can bleed when others bleed, you might be able to make them bleed. Sloan. You have to tell your family about this."

She shook her head. "No. I'm not ready. If I do, they'll piece together about Max, too. I don't want him to feel that pressure. I don't want him to know."

Misha's phone pinged for the millionth time, but she ignored it.

"It's probably Wyatt," Sloan pointed out.

"He can wait. I need to say something first. It may be none of my business, but I think you shouldn't write Max off without speaking with him. For the record, I don't think he hates you. You should find out what happened to him. Get the whole picture about his cold feet and then make a decision. I'm not saying you have to be with him, but... I know how having a lifemate helps Wyatt, and it's more than just having the powers. Our connection keeps him sane. He visibly relaxes when he steps into my orbit." Misha's eyes softened. "You're sad, hon. You shouldn't be. Maybe this thing with Max was a misunderstanding. Maybe he thought you did something."

"Why? Has he said something to you?"

"No. I'm just thinking aloud. The whole situation is just a little bizarre, you know? Why work for the very people you hate?"

"Maybe he's working for the enemy, and he's spying on us."

"You don't really believe that, do you?"

"No."

"So, if he hates you, why come back?"

That question again. It burned in Sloan's stomach like the effects of sin. She couldn't ignore it. Misha was right, Sloan was missing something.

"You know," Misha continued. "Having someone you love by your side could be good. How much better have you felt these past two months, and that's only with Max walking around your proximity. When Wyatt and I touch—wow. And the sex... next level. That pheromone business you guys have going on... wow."

"You said 'wow' two times." Sloan frowned at her brother's girlfriend. The pheromones were a reaction programmed into their biological systems, supposedly to help entice their mate to their side… and keep them there. That's how important it was to have your mate close by.

"All I'm saying is that, if you want Max, he'll have a hard time saying no to you. The ball is in your court."

Sloan didn't know what to think.

The phone pinged again. While Misha checked, Sloan chewed her new red nails.

"Wyatt. Again. Wants to know how long. What should I tell him?" Misha asked.

"Not ready yet. Can we, I don't know, do something else?"

"Yeah, I'm not ready to have him looming over me again." After thinking about it for a moment, Misha jumped up and clapped her hands. "I know. We still need to get you a dress for tonight, right? Let's sneak out the back and give Wyatt the slip. I know a store just a few streets away."

"Wyatt will be pissed."

"He'd let us go on our own if he knew about your new power. We'll be fine. If someone attacks us, you can make them—"

"Cry?" Sloan said wryly.

"Sure. Let's go with that." Misha tugged Sloan out of her seat, whining. "Come on. Nothing will happen. He's an overprotective father-to-be, that's all."

There was definitely something wrong with her brain, because Sloan nodded. "Fine. Let's go."

She did kick Max's ass, after all.

"Yes!"

But before she left, Sloan swiped a pointy metal nail file. Just in case.

IN THE BACK of an unmarked van parked somewhere on the streets of Cardinal City, Barry Pinkerton sat under the watchful eye of a member of the Faithful, and Despair—the Syndicate's enforcer and the boss's right-hand woman. Most others called her Falcon, because of the birdlike battle mask she wore to hide her identity. But lucky Barry had been privy to her secret for many years. She was the boss's daughter, the only one of the eight experimented on children who burned in the fire at Biolum Tech almost thirty years ago. She was left behind by the others.

The Faithful was a white robed and masked man holding a semi-automatic. Barry was more afraid of Despair, even though she had no weapon. She only needed to watch him with those unblinking violet eyes, and he trembled inside.

Like it had almost thirty years ago, the feeling of wrongness festered in his gut. He'd started this genetic engineering project thinking he was helping humanity become better. He could regrow arms and limbs in a petri dish. What better way to help the victims of war or disease?

Give him two years, and he could replace your broken limb with a new, tank grown one out of your own cells. But a few years ago, he'd learned his research wasn't going to save humanity, not in the way he'd hoped. The Syndicate had lied to him. And now he was here, in a van with a caged rabid beast he'd created from a few cloned cells. A beast that had no other purpose in life but to hunt down sin and eliminate it.

He felt sick.

"I'm not sure this is the right thing to do," he said to Despair.

The white-robed man with the white faceless Halloween mask lifted his weapon and pointed it at Barry's head.

Despair lifted her hand, and the Faithful lowered his gun. "It doesn't matter what you think," she said.

"But we've only tested the beasts against other animals with deadly sin." Not around chaos like a city park. Not around children. What if it was his daughter out there? What if they were testing in another neighborhood? Or at her school? This wasn't what he signed up for.

"That's why we are here."

"And what if something goes wrong?"

"If the Deadly Seven don't stop the slaughter?" Despair reached into a tool box and retrieved a canister filled with acid. Her solution was to destroy the evidence?

Barry's stomach rolled. The Syndicate were constantly pushing the buttons of the Deadly Seven. It was an obsessive game of theirs. The ultimate goal was to push them over the edge, get them falling prey to their sin, and becoming insatiable beasts themselves. Becoming unstoppable.

Barry wasn't blind. He wasn't stupid. He knew the boss was trying to prove that he could still manipulate and control the Deadly Seven,

even though they weren't in their grasp. But the real question was, who was he trying to prove it to?

"Need I remind you who will suffer if you don't do this, Mr. Pinkerton?"

Stuffing his doubts deep inside, he adjusted the dosage on the drip feeding into the sleeping beast's vein. Immediately, the animal awoke and snarled at them, knocking against the cage.

Despair opened the door and released the beast.

six

MAX JOHNSON

MIDDAY HEAT REFLECTED off the sidewalk as Max walked along, tracking the GPS on his cell. He could have stayed at the office where Wyatt had ordered him to remain, but he'd been hired for security, and he took orders from Parker. Security was what he'd damn well provide.

Protect the Lazarus brood during civilian activities was his goal. If any of them gave away their powers or abilities, their identities would be compromised, and they wouldn't be able to fight to protect those the system failed. He'd gone against his better judgement once, and a life was lost. A life very important to him.

Never again.

Sometimes these Lazarus siblings were their own worst enemy.

Coming up to a block of retail stores, Max checked the tracker. Looking up at the street sign, he knew he was close. This was the Quadrant, the lifeblood of the city. Four shopping and cultural districts surrounded an enormous park enjoyed by many, especially on a clear summer day. It was the perfect place for Sloan and her usual brand of hijinks to ensue.

AIMI's voice came across his ear-piece, directing him as he walked. *"Turn next right and you will find your destination in twenty feet."*

Max packed away his cell, stuffing it into the pocket of his fatigues. Despite the heat, he wore a denim jacket to conceal his Glock. It still amazed him how easy the license had been to obtain. In Australia, it was unheard of to walk around with a gun strapped under your arm.

He approached the shop window and stopped, pretending to be enamored with the mannequins dressed in evening attire. He searched beyond into the store. Sloan was in there with Misha, somewhere. Unless this was one of Sloan's pranks... *nah*. He dismissed the thought immediately. Sloan had been conspicuously silent since the incident on the gym mat. She was as rattled as he was. A fact that tugged at his curiosity, and concern.

His heart clenched at the memory. He still had no idea how he'd made her nose bleed. Didn't even touch her there. That first kick she'd planted on him had been professional and ruthless. He was surprised she didn't break his nose. She wasn't fragile. She was strong. He liked strong women. Strong, funny, and with long black hair.

The question now was, should he go inside and let them know he was there, or keep watch from a distance? He used his cell to check the map displaying all the Lazarus GPS signals. Wyatt's location had him at the café across the street from the salon a few blocks away. It was odd that he'd let Sloan and Misha go without him. The dude had been savage with his protection tendencies lately.

Max had better go inside.

Pushing the door open, he almost sneezed from all the perfume in the air. Racks of expensive-looking dresses lined the walls. A chandelier hung from the ceiling. Pastel blue patterned carpet lined the floor. *Bloody hell.* Looked like a sherbet candy had puked in there. Women drank champagne on pink velvet ottomans, laughing and talking as their girlfriends came out of dressing rooms to show off their latest clothing acquisition.

Where are the girls?

A few of the champagne-drinkers stopped laughing and eyed him. He moved to the far end of the store. Misha's curly blond hair was hard to miss, but the woman standing next to her... it took him a moment to recognize Sloan. Her usual messy nest of hair was cut just below her shoulders. It shone in a glossy stream, vibrant red tips at the end, almost as if they'd been dipped in paint. Instead of the usual blunt cut, the baseline of her hair was an arrow—shorter on the outside, longer down the middle as it kissed between her shoulder blades. She did love her arrows. She always picked the bow during their online games. He wondered if she knew how to use one in real life.

Probably.

He still had a lot to learn about her.

As he drew closer, their conversation came into earshot. Should he interrupt?

"... he's not always going to be like this, right?" Misha asked Sloan, who only seemed to be half listening. A small frown and distant look marred her face. "Sorry, Sloan," Misha continued, "I usually vent to Lilo but she's been so busy with this latest story. All that stuff you uncovered on the you-know-who has really got her journalist instincts firing."

"All good," Sloan replied. "Vent away. I'm happy to hear about someone else's problems rather than mine."

"You're amazing. I'm so glad we did this. It's nice to feel independent again, if only for a few minutes. Oh, wow. That dress is simply stunning." Misha gushed over the dress the attendant folded into a bag. Rubbing her belly, she added, "I'm so jealous. Soon I won't be able to fit into something as sexy as that. You're going to look incredible."

What would Sloan need a sexy dress for?

Unease flittered in his stomach when he remembered how he'd looked her up after his discharge, hoping to reconnect, only to discover she'd been dating someone else. The online picture showed some wanker at this gaming convention with his paws all over her. The image had burned into his memory. He could still remember the sick feeling when he'd realized she hadn't waited for him. At a time when he'd needed her like no other, she'd moved on with her life like he'd meant nothing to her. Like she never cared about him.

That cut deep.

"Well, you can go to the gala instead of me, how's that?" Sloan's dry humor leaked through her voice.

The gala. Of course.

He cleared his throat.

The two women turned around, surprise lifting their brows.

"What are you doing here?" Sloan's blue eyes narrowed on him.

Misha sighed, resigned. "Did Wyatt send you?"

"No. But he's going to be spitting mad you left without him."

"Please don't tell him," Misha begged. "We're going to go back to the salon, and he'll never know. I promise."

That far off look had returned in Sloan's eyes. She gazed toward the window. He pivoted, tracking her line of sight. Nothing out there.

"You okay, Sloan?" Misha asked.

"Something… isn't right," she murmured. "I sense… negligence. Someone is feeling mighty guilty about *not* doing something."

She reached into her jeans pocket and pulled out something long, silver and pointy.

"Is that a nail file?" he asked.

"Shh. Something's out there."

They all turned to the window again. This time, a low black shadow darted past. Alarm jolted through Max. "Did you see that?"

Too big for a dog. Too small for a person.

Brows puckering, Sloan eased toward the window, watching as she passed the giggling customers. When a scream shook the window, she turned to him with alarm in her eyes.

"Stay here," he said.

"No. You stay here." She mumbled something Max couldn't quite catch, but it seemed like she was trying to convince herself. She flexed her fingers. "Yeah, I got this. You need to stay with Misha."

Before he could stop her, she pushed through the glass doors and ran down the street.

"Shit." That was *his* job. Shit, Sloan. He turned to the shop keeper. "Lock the door after me. Misha, stay here."

Max burst onto the sidewalk. He pushed past people running in the opposite direction and followed Sloan and the black blur. A feeling. A creeping feeling of foreboding hammered inside him. All he needed to do was follow the screams.

His jog slowed as he came to his first blood stain, two shops down.

Blood splattered the street. A sidewalk tree had been cracked in half, like a car had run into it, but there were no tire marks. No damaged vehicle. He unclipped his gun from the holster and proceeded with caution. Where was the screaming coming from?

Bloody hell, Sloan.

Gritting his teeth, he pushed on, following the trail of evidence to the next store. The front window was smashed in and shards of glass had sprayed the inside. Clothes were ripped from racks and littered the floor. People screamed and huddled against the wall. A body lay ripped open on the floor. It may have been female. Viscera and blood and gore assaulted his senses. For a moment, his memories of other bloody scenes flashed before him.

Gale's pale eyes a shock of blue against a bath of red.

He winced. Not now.

You wanted to feel useful again, Max, well, here you go, mate.

He kept moving.

A snarling growl rumbled from further in the store where a flash of black tumbled around with a human attached to its mouth. The human was Sloan. With the dog-thing latched onto her leg. She tried to pry its jaws open. Sloan was strong. If she had trouble unlocking that jaw…

Heart in his throat, Max aimed his gun, but couldn't risk shooting. They rolled too fast. One minute, Sloan was on top, the next the animal twisted to the side. He might shoot Sloan by mistake. Instead, he lifted his weapon and shot into the ceiling, hoping to draw attention.

The dog lifted its head. Sniffed.

Fuck me.

That's not a dog.

Maybe it was—once. Resembling something like a Doberman, its short black ears pointed skyward, but it was huge. The sharp fangs and roped muscles belonged on a dragon. Lethal claws flashed. It twisted and wrestled in Sloan's hold, getting loose, trying to come at him.

He fired the gun again. *Come on beastie. Come to Maxie.*

It snarled and broke free from Sloan's grip. Teeth and saliva came at him. He froze, petrified. But it didn't attack. Its sights were on something else. It launched past Max, through the window and onto the sidewalk. Shit.

Shaking himself from his stupor, he aimed. It wove through the street, making it hard to get in his sights. Max leaped through the window and pounded after it. Sloan's footsteps thudded behind him. She soon overtook him, running faster than he thought her capable. They passed the store Misha was in, and the dog—beast—suddenly stopped, skidding as though it caught a scent. Snarling, it turned its attention to the shop's glass window.

It battered the glass window, using its head as a ram. It wanted something or someone inside.

"Shoot it, Max," Sloan shouted. "Now."

Max trained the animal in his sight. He fired.

The crack echoed in the street and the beast jolted—shot, but not down. It didn't even slow, but launched at the window with single-minded viciousness.

He fired again. This time, the beast moved too fast. He missed.

Sloan darted forward.

"Out of the way, Sloan!" he roared.

But she didn't listen. *Fuck.* She was going to wrestle it down, to attack with her fists. Darting a glance around, he noticed they had spectators. She could reveal her secret if she wasn't careful. There was no way a normal woman had the strength to fend that beast off.

"Sloan." He moved around the animal, to get a better shot. He lowered his voice. "Don't compromise your identity."

"I got this, Max."

Once again, it sounded like she was trying to convince herself, more than anything else. What was she trying to prove?

As they moved closer, the animal stopped attacking the glass and snarled, aware the two of them were circling, surrounding it. Sloan darted forward, and it ran. Right toward Max.

"Run!" Sloan shouted. "Run, you dumbass."

Adrenaline surged through him. He pivoted, boots pounding the pavement, muscles pushed to the extreme. It chased. He had to get it away from the public. He darted into an alley, hoping the animal would continue its pursuit of him. With Sloan chasing its tail, it did.

Breath burning his lungs, he ran, jumping over fallen crates, nearly tripping. Hot beast breath tickled his neck. Paws pounded the pavement. Slobbering snarls snapped. *Panting, panting. Slobbering. Snarl. Snap.* Jaws clicked perilously close.

And then he came to a brick wall dead end. There wasn't enough time to climb. Turning, he pointed his weapon and fired as the black blur launched at him. In the space of a blink, he caught two black demon eyes, white fangs, slobber. It didn't stop coming. The bullets did nothing.

Jaws locked onto his wrist, over his jacket. They careened into the wall, hitting hard. The gun went flying. Panic swamped him, and he thought, *This is it. This is the end and I haven't had a chance to tell Sloan…*

A piercing squeal came out of the dog like he'd never heard before. Its body seized, paralyzed, as though being stunned. For a moment, Max thought perhaps Evan was there with his electricity, but when he pushed the beast off, he only saw Sloan with her furious gaze intent on the beast. Alley wind buffeted her hair as she stabbed the nail file into her palm, blood dripping onto the pavement. Max's gaze darted to the beast, whining in agony, then back to Sloan. She was doing something. Something supernatural.

"Sloan?"

"I don't know how long this will last. Whatever you can do, do it now."

His gun was too far, kicked out from their collision, but he had a knife strapped to his leg. He reached down, released it, and launched onto the beast, driving the blade deep into its heart. Two-seconds later, the animal stopped seizing. It stopped all together.

Panting hard, the two of them looked at each other, eyes wild. *What the holy fuck?*

Max stepped toward Sloan. She still had the nail file pierced into her palm. "Sloan. You're hurting yourself."

Her gaze whipped from him to over his shoulder. "No!" she shouted, suddenly panicked. "Daisy, no!"

Who was Daisy?

Max turned to see a woman in white leather perched on top of the brick wall. A stream of long white hair billowed behind her head, eyes and nose concealed by a birdlike mask. She poured liquid from a canister onto the beast's corpse.

A sizzling sound joined a new acrid scent, fumes so strong, neither Sloan nor Max could breathe. Coughing, they ran toward the alley exit, toward fresh air. When they looked back, the beast was a bubbling mess of black fur and viscous liquid. And the woman in white was gone.

Tires screeched as a black SUV came to an abrupt halt on the main street next to the alley. Wyatt barreled out, jogging down the cobbled alley floor.

Great.

"Where's Misha?" Wyatt demanded, whites of his eyes dominating.

"She's in there." Max pointed to the shop a few feet away.

Wyatt's gaze snapped to the mess behind them, then to the shop. "And why is no one with her?"

"Because we were chasing down a rabid beast, fucktard," Sloan snapped.

Wrong words to say, because Wyatt's face reddened. A vein popped in his forehead and he pointed at his sister's face. "You *fucking* messed up."

"Hey." Max tried to get between them, but Wyatt shoved Max.

Aw, hell no, he didn't. Not this time. It was Max who pointed back at Wyatt, getting right in his face. "If you weren't being such an overpowering prick, your missus wouldn't be sneaking off to get five minutes peace. So, don't blame this on Sloan."

"Fuck you both." Wyatt slapped Max's hand away and went to the dress shop, leaving him standing with Sloan.

And she still had that damn nail file in her palm.

"Sloan," he said softly.

"What?"

"Your hand."

Blinking, confused, she looked down at her palm. "Oh."

Her adrenaline visibly let down; her shoulders dropped, her eyes fluttered, she exhaled.

"What's going on?" He reached for her hand, but she snatched it away.

"I'm a fast healer. Why did you lure the animal out of the shop?"

Blinking at the sudden change of direction, he answered honestly. "To save you."

Hell washed over her features. Darkness poured from her eyes. Her voice came out low and deliberate. "You think you need to save me?"

"Well, yeah. The demon mutt was chewing your leg off."

"This leg, Max? *This leg?*" She lifted the hem on her jeans. The skin at her calf was a little pink, but otherwise fine.

"Don't bloody give me lip for trying to help. You kept flashing your abnormal strength about. People were going to put two and two together that you're different."

"Unbelievable. This is just like the time we were in that gamer tournament and you swooped in and took my kill apparently to save me from the big bad monster. All you did was steal all my XP, level up, and boot me out of the tournament entirely."

"It was a bloody computer game, Sloan. I was trying to impress you. It backfired."

"You men. You're all a bunch of assholes who think you can do better than me. None of you trust me to do my fucking job. I'm a fucking super—"

"Shh." He waved her down. Had the woman no sense of self-preservation? Drawn by their shouting, a crowd had gathered.

As though a bad taste filled her mouth, her lips twisted in disgust. "I don't need you to rescue me."

And then she strode away, nail file still lodged in her bloody hand.

seven

SLOAN LAZARUS

SLOAN'S ALARM woke her at a fresh five a.m. the day of the gala. She'd spent most of the previous evening giving her family a rundown of the beast attack. Much of what they'd talked about was conjecture considering Daisy had destroyed the evidence, but they'd surmised the animal had been injected with the same serum that Lilo's ex had been months earlier. That man had turned into a superhuman beast, able to sense greed, like them. He'd also had extraordinary strength, but in the end, he'd become so mindless with sin, and drunk on the serum, that he'd killed himself from taking too much. It burned through his insides.

As Sloan switched on the faucet in her shower, her mind inevitably turned to her lost sister. Daisy had been left behind when Mary and Flint rescued the family from the lab that created them. They thought Daisy had perished in the fire their biological mother set to destroy the lab. Obviously, they'd assumed wrong. If they'd only checked to see if she had survived the fire…

Sloan dunked her head under the hot stream and let it wash away her worry. It was stupid to get caught up with ifs and maybes. At the time, Sloan was only a baby, and Mary and Flint had their hands full running from the Syndicate with seven children. They couldn't change the past.

But that niggling feeling was still there.

Last night, Sloan set a plate for Daisy at the family dinner table. No one said a thing as they all sat down at their seats in their private dining room in Heaven. Without saying a word, each and every one of them knew who the setting was for, and at the end of the meal, Mary had requested that Sloan do the same thing at every meal until Daisy was brought home to them. It was a start. A dinner plate today, an olive branch tomorrow, a rescue the next. They would return Daisy to their family. Sloan's heart clenched and she wrenched her mind back to working out why the Syndicate had experimented on animals instead of humans.

They'd been after the Deadly Seven for years, trying to get samples of their blood, especially the members who had leveled up with abilities.

Maybe they weren't getting what they needed, and the animals were a back-up plan.

Regardless, moving to animal experimentation was another level of depravity from the organization, and this break in their hunt for the bastards couldn't have come at a better time. *Her* break, she had to keep reminding herself. It was *her* work that gave them this lead with the gala.

Anger still fired in her blood from the way the men in her life seemed to think she wasn't capable of fighting her own battles, or doing her damned job. In the back of her mind, she kind of got it. She was a slothful bitch sometimes, but it wasn't like none of them hadn't danced with their sins before. Typical.

She tutted to herself the entire time she showered, dressed, and then packed her bag. When she was done, she gave her purring cat a rub on the head.

"AIMI, I'll be away from home for a few days. Can you look after Luna please?"

AIMI replied, *"Yes, Sloan, oh Masterful One. I'll arrange for Luna to be fed. Will you be checking in while you're away?"*

She grinned. That last software update she'd given AIMI was so that she would address her by her new exalted title. "Yes, I want to keep working on that binary code to visual pattern algorithm, and I also want to develop some communicator watches. Something we can program with an SOS."

"Similar to the system we have in the suits?"

"Yes, but something normal enough we can wear during our civilian lives."

A pause, then AIMI said, *"You're wanted down in the garage. Should I tell them you're on your way?"*

"Yes, thank you."

Sloan hoisted her duffel bag, collected her dress bag, and went to the exit. But she couldn't leave. Something stopped her.

This was it. No more hiding out in her room. No more waiting for someone else to do the job for her. And no more waiting for respect from her family. She had to earn it. But... maybe they were right. Maybe she needed saving. Maybe she wasn't good enough to get the job done.

No. Fuck that shit. She was good. She was a badass. She single-handedly—sort of—stopped that beast from killing anymore people. *Her.*

She may have even saved Max's life.

"Sloan?" AIMI prompted. *"Oh, Masterful One? Shall I tell them you're running late?"*

"No. I'm going." She took a deep breath and pushed open her

door. Just before she left, she cast a glance behind her. Luna stood watching her, yellow cat's eyes blinking.

I've got this.

She closed the door.

SLOAN FOUND Parker and Tony in the Lazarus House private garage, playing a game of luggage Tetris in the back of Parker's custom built Bugatti SUV.

So they were traveling in style. All the better to maintain their cover, she supposed. She would have much rather gone on their recon mission completely incognito, but Parker was right. They needed his and Tony's affluent identities to get them into the gala.

All this cloak and dagger business was silly. The Syndicate knew who they were. They knew their true identities and where they lived and worked. The fact the Syndicate failed to move on the Deadly Seven meant they were waiting for something.

Walking up to them, she watched, amused, as they bickered over who had the best idea for storing their rock-climbing equipment. It seemed obscene to taint such a luxury car with dirty supplies, and chances were they'd never use it considering their mission wasn't actually rock climbing. She wondered if she should point that out.

Dressed in khaki shorts and a stiff-collared polo shirt, Tony looked every bit the entitled movie star he was. Aviator sunglasses rested on his forehead, not fully up, as though he were too cool to push them on top of his head like the common people. They all had good bone structure, but Tony's was perfect. He only had to smile at a lady—even a man—to get what he wanted. But, it was a mistake to think the man didn't work. Just like Parker, the cocky rich boy was the public persona the world knew. The more they believed Tony was a dumb, pretty-boy actor, the less they suspected his lethal night calling. Although, lately, the two personalities seemed to bleed into one.

Parker wore cream chinos and a linen collared shirt that barely contained his brute musculature. Some sort of leather moccasins graced his feet, and his long, auburn hair was scraped back into a masculine bun tied at an angle that accentuated his barber-shaved stubble. Honestly, how could women find that walking shampoo commercial attractive? Probably had something to do with his He-Man size and savage strength.

I have the power, Sloan recited in her head, imagining her brother with the power of Grayskull in his hand. She should make AIMI scrap the King Pee and call him He-Man from now on.

"You just going to stand there staring?" Parker glowered her way.

"Yup. This is entertaining."

Tony, whose head had been deep in the back of the car, pulled out. His gaze landed on her vintage T-shirt.

"Something's different," he noted, scanning her body. Making a show of it, he put his fingers under his jaw in the classic Thinker's pose. "No, don't tell me. I'll figure it out."

"Nothing's different. You're still a dickhead."

"So... not a new attitude, then. Hmm. Something else... the shirt?"

She glanced down at her chest. "What?"

"Fight like a girl?" He snorted at the inscription. "In case you missed it, you *are* a girl."

"Aw, Tony." She went up to him and knocked him on his head, checking for hollow feedback. "You're not *really* dumb. You just act it, remember?"

He flashed his megawatt Hollywood smile. "How else would you feel so smart?"

"Jerk." She punched him in the arm, but he didn't budge.

He just laughed. "I get it. New hair. Jeez, Louise."

"If you two are finished acting like children, we're done. Weapons and suits are buried under the rock climbing gear." Parker slammed the back hatch closed. "Get in."

Tony took the front, Parker drove—of course—and Sloan sat in the rear. She buckled herself into the plush leather seat and asked, "Where's Wyatt?"

"He's not coming." Parker adjusted the rearview, meeting her eyes. "He's not happy leaving Misha after the stunt you two pulled."

She bit her lip. "That guy seriously needs a chill pill."

"His child could be worth its weight in gold to the Syndicate. I don't blame him. We protect our own."

"Of course you don't get it," she mumbled. Bunch of macho chauvinistic poop heads. Misha was perfectly fine. In no danger whatsoever. As they pulled out of the lot and into the side alley, she raised her voice. "Just us then?"

Silence greeted her. Fine. Stupid question. Got it. She reached into her backpack and pulled out her iPad and headphones. Expecting a long drive, she was surprised when the car slowed down almost immediately on the main street.

Confused, she lifted her head from her screen to check for traffic, but the other passenger door opened. Max folded his long body into the car, bringing the scent of sunshine and coconut. Her stomach flipped.

"Thanks for coming on short notice, Max," Parker said before pulling back onto the road.

"No dramas." Max brought his fist to the front as Tony brought his back for a bump.

"Road trip!" Tony whooped.

This was officially the day from hell.

The groan that came out of Sloan couldn't be helped, and when

Max looked her way with the faintest of smiles, dimple in cheek flashing, she wanted to be pissed. She really did, but she couldn't avoid the fact she felt more energized sitting next to him. They weren't even touching. When—if—they touched, she was told it would be an enormous relief; her reaction to sensed sin, the constant queasy stomach, would just disappear. Poof!

As long as they held that connection, she would be immune to sensing sin. She'd be almost human.

She put her cat's ears headphones on and scowled at her screen. Normally, she'd pull up a game, do a few Fortnite battle royales, increase her skill points. But feeling unusually productive, that binary code to visual pattern program called to her.

Sniffing, she turned the music up and did her best to ignore the two-hundred-plus pounds of hot male next to her. Damned mating-bond. It was enough to make her question her beliefs about him.

eight

MAX JOHNSON

MUCH TO MAX'S ANNOYANCE, Sloan ignored him the entire four-hour drive. He was grateful for their arrival at the luxury hotel where the gala was taking place that evening. The four of them had separate rooms in the penthouse suite. Upon arriving, Sloan had immediately retreated to her room, avoiding him and her brothers like the plague until she was called out for a briefing session.

It couldn't go on like this.

How could they work together with all that unresolved tension between them? By the end of the night, he would work out what her problem was. If anyone had the right to be pissed about how things ended between them, it was him.

The four of them spent the latter part of the afternoon going over the plan. Sloan was to lure Barry to the bar while Max did a shifty on his fingerprints and biometrics. Tony and Parker were to make a show of their celebrity, drawing attention away from Sloan and Max in case they needed to improvise. Tomorrow, the four of them would head into the wilderness for their alibi adventure trip. Parker had already had his assistant schedule fake social media pictures of their trip—making it look like they were nowhere near the black site.

Max had never met Parker's assistant, but it sounded like she was his go-to woman. It must be one hell of an NDA contract she'd signed for Parker to be comfortable giving her tasks that could potentially put their identities at risk. Probably similar to the contract he'd signed. In that case, it was iron clad. One slip of the tongue about any of the secret goings on of the family Lazarus, and Max was severely in breach.

Putting the finishing touches on his tuxedo and bow tie, he checked his watch. Five to six. Time to go.

He joined the other two men in the central living area between the penthouse bedrooms. Cream brocade and gold graced the decor, from the sofas to the lampshades and cushions.

Both in custom tailored tuxedos, Tony and Parker looked suave and sophisticated as they sipped on expensive champagne. Parker's outfit caught the eye with its deep maroon and satin lined jacket. Tony's was edgier with leather lapels. Max wore the standard type you rented. They'd offered to purchase him one, but after seeing the fashion style they had in mind, he declined.

Jeez, he felt out of place. He was just a surfer kid from the south-west of Australia. A town with a population of five thousand. Both parents dead by the time he was eighteen, he'd joined the army as a means to travel the world. His squad had become his new family. Gale had become his brother. Max still remembered spending summers at Gale's family farm, catching yabbies in the dam and riding ATVs down the dunes. They'd thought they were invincible. How times had changed.

Parker poured another glass of champagne and offered it to Max, but he declined. Alcohol might burn through their system quickly, but not his, and he didn't drink on the job.

"How long do you think we'll have to wait for Sloan?" Tony mused, draining his glass.

"She's been better lately. She'll be out soon," Parker replied.

"Better?" Max queried. Was she sick?

"She's sloth, you know?" Tony poured himself another glass, but held onto the bottle. "For a few years before you arrived, she'd hardly left the building. Was usually late, slept all day, that sort of shit."

"I've not noticed it." Much.

Parker's cell phone rang and he dipped his hand into his pocket to check it. Giving the two men a swift look, he held up his finger. "I need to take this. Won't be long." Then he disappeared back into his room, leaving Max alone with Tony.

Tony poured himself another glass.

"Slow down, cowboy," Max joked. "We've got all night."

"Ugh. Sorry." Tony rolled his eyes. "These things tie me up in knots."

"Really? I thought you'd be a pro at it by now. You always seemed to love the attention."

Tony shot Max a derisive arched eyebrow. "Love the attention?"

"Don't you?"

"You think I love being trailed home by paparazzi, or having women maul me at the grocery store?"

"You buy your own groceries?" Max mocked. "Never thought Agent Danger did much other than blow up city buildings, go on car chases and—"

"And you can shut up. You know what I mean. Wait. You saw Agent Danger?"

Max smirked. "Of course. Me and the boys have seen all your movies."

"Huh." Tony nodded. "Cool."

Max gave a grunt in return.

"For the record, the attention wasn't what I liked. It was the anonymity."

"Paps chasing you is anonymous?"

"No, the acting part is. I get to play whoever I want on screen. No pressure. No"—he flicked his gaze Parker's way—"no demands. Anyway, that's how it started. Now… it's just the same fucked up shit I get everywhere."

"Well, I think you're good at it. Better than good." He nodded solemnly. "What you do is hard, both sides of you, but you do it. Proud of you, Tones."

Tony's eyes widened. "Thanks."

Yeah. The hero gig was tough. None of them had down time. For Tony and his siblings, it was their day jobs, and then nightly missions out to the city trying to save people from themselves. On top of all that, they now had the Syndicate to worry about. At least in the army, Max had time off after tour. Heading out into the bush or the beach for some R and R was the highlight of his year… until he and Gale got antsy and wanted back in on another mission. In the companionable silence that followed, Max couldn't help looking in the direction of Sloan's room, and Tony noticed.

"She'll come around," Tony said.

"What do you mean?"

But Tony just smiled cryptically from over his champagne flute as he tipped it for another gulp.

"Think I'll take that drink now," Max said.

SIX O'CLOCK, on the dot, Sloan's door opened and a vision stepped out.

Her red dress clung to her curves from breasts to ankles. Shoulders glinted from some kind of jeweled body cream. Red lips he'd never realized were so full, pursed with irritation, or with nerves.

When she shifted the dark fall of her hair over a shoulder, exposing delicate decolletage, Max caught a whiff of fruity perfume and went hot. Couldn't think. Just knew he was screwed because, despite the animosity between them, his body reacted with passion, hardening in all the wrong places. He blew out a slow breath through his teeth. He still wanted her. More than ever now that she was more than a pixilated picture on a video screen.

She was real.

"What?" she snapped. "What are you looking at?"

Tony gawped. "You look like a girl," he murmured.

"No shit, Sherlock. Have you forgotten already?" She rolled her eyes.

"Um." Tony shut his mouth. "Nothing."

"I think what he's trying to say is, you look beautiful, Sloan." Parker returned from his room and strode over to kiss her suavely on the cheek. "Now, let's get this show on the road. Max, Sloan, you have your earpieces in? Hidden microphones?"

Max nodded, still unable to speak, still unable to tear his eyes away from Sloan as she busied herself, searching inside her red clutch. She smelled mouthwatering. He already mentioned that. Shit.

All business, Parker looked to Max and Sloan. "When we get there, Tony and I will do our thing. You two find Barry. Activate your mic when you're speaking with him."

"Why?" Sloan frowned.

"So we can stay on top of things," he replied.

"So you can micromanage, you mean."

"Don't take it personally, Sloan. Just activate your mic."

"Whatever." She pushed her finger behind the strap of her dress and pressed. After giving Parker a stare, she exited the suites.

Max went to follow, but as he got to the door, an arm blocked his way. Jerking to a halt, he turned to find Tony's scowling face, inches from his.

Max frowned at him.

"I know I said she'll come around, and I don't know what happened between you two, but you two need to sort it out."

"Got it."

"I don't think you do, but I have an idea on how to fix that."

"Oh?"

"Just wait for the opportunity."

Now Max was getting suspicious. "You playing match maker, Tones?"

"If I was playing matchmaker, I'd say something like, break her heart again, and I'll break you." A few seconds of charged silence passed between them and then Tony's lips split into an impish grin. "Just kidding." He deadpanned again. "But, seriously."

"I get it."

"Good man." Tony pushed through to the hallway, taking his champagne bottle with him despite Parker's scowl. "Now, let's have some fun."

Max turned to Parker and almost wished he hadn't. He'd caught every word of the exchange. The wilderness stared out of Parker's eyes, promising many dangerous and violent things without words.

Max nodded and stepped into the hallway, following the first two down to the elevator. Message received, loud and clear. *Don't fuck it up this time.*

THE GALA WAS WELL underway when Max walked into the ballroom behind Sloan. Music from a string quartet softly rolled over him as he surveyed the room and checked for exits. For an environmentally conscious charity, the wastage was obscene. Plastic plants hung from chandeliers. Fake pink flowers frothed at the center of tables. Sparkling butterflies dangled from fishing line. There was a bar to one side, a big screen and stage at the front of the room, and a few hundred people gliding about, laughing, drinking and eating their fill.

Tony blanched. The corners of his mouth went white. For a moment, Max thought Tony would hurl, but the man snatched a glass of champagne from a passing waiter and downed it in one gulp. Parker shot him judgmental eyes, then immediately replaced his exasperation with fake excitement. He clapped his brother on the shoulder and shouted for another waiter. Of course, upon catching the celebrity faces of one of the country's richest men, and his movie star brother, nearby heads swiveled their way.

Operation Distraction was a go.

Max sidled up to Sloan and leaned close. "How you want to do this? You do east, and I do west?"

"No need," she said, eyes shrewdly locked in one direction. "I know where he is."

Really? So soon?

She nodded toward the bar. Max followed her gaze. When gaps in the crowd parted, he spotted Barry looking morose, nursing a glass of Scotch.

"How did you know?" he asked.

She took his elbow and drew him to the side, out of the path of commotion her brothers caused, and near a wall where bored husbands and delinquent teenagers sat.

"Remember when I felt that negligence at the clothing store?" she whispered.

"Before the... uh... dog thing?"

"Yeah. Well, it seems like Barry has the same sin-signature. He must be the one I felt."

"What does this mean?"

"It means he's not happy working for the You-Know-Who. He had something to do with that animal attack and he feels bad."

Max rubbed his chin. "We might be able to turn him to our favor."

"Exactly."

Impressed, he looked down at her with a sense of pride. A small smile tilted his lips. "So, what now?"

"You're not going to convince me to stick to their plan?" She tugged on her hair.

Their plan, meaning Parker's plan to gather Barry's biometrics surreptitiously. Max pondered the opportunity presented. There was always the risk that Barry's guilt wasn't strong enough to supersede his loyalty to his employer… but if Sloan had a strong feeling about it, he had to trust her. This was what she was made for, besides, he was a cover-all-bases kind of guy. If they turned one of the Syndicate's lead scientists, it would be a major turning point for the Deadly Seven. "I trust you. You got this."

A small hitch in her breath drew his gaze downward. She looked at him as though she didn't know him. Some unnamed emotion passed over her features before morphing into something he hadn't seen in a long time: hope. It was only for a fleeting moment and then her guard went up, shuttering. She turned away, eyes intense in the direction of her brothers.

Had that flicker of hope meant what he thought it did?

A raging inferno sparked inside his chest and every feeling he thought locked away came rushing to the surface. She was all he could see and scent. Fruity and musky at the same time. It was as though she climbed inside him and unfurled herself, warming his every cell. Enamored, he couldn't look away. Her delicate nose. Red, juicy lips.

Kiss those lips.

Licking his own, a yearning like no other captured his soul. Unbidden, his fingers lifted to trace her smooth jaw with a feathered touch. She shuddered, full body, but didn't pull away—she leaned into him. That little movement told him more than words. He lowered and breathed deeply. Her musk grew stronger until arousal washed through him. Hot, heady and drugging.

Cupping her nape, he tilted her head back and like a moth to a flame, his mouth dipped to hers and hovered. Somewhere, a part of him bellowed—*what am I doing?*—but it was distant, and the moment her lashes lowered, fanning her cheeks, he no longer heard a single protesting thought. He craved her in every cell. His body was all in.

"You miss us," he whispered against her lips. Wanting. Hoping. Begging. "Admit it."

Those lips pressed together.

Stubborn. So stubborn.

He missed her. He wanted to roar, to shout and scream it. To show her that he'd never stopped thinking about her, never stopped missing or wanting her in his bed. His one true love, she had been. His confidant, his best friend, and the woman he still fantasized about in his dreams.

"Do you remember what I said you'd do to me if you ever wore red lipstick?"

A low moan slipped from her lips. Her hot breath tickled his face. Oh yeah, she remembered. And she wanted it, too. At least her body did. Unmissable hard nipples pushed at the fabric of her dress. Together with the pulse rabbiting in her neck, the flushed tinge to her cheeks, and her quickening breath… there was no denying it.

But she shook her head, and it cut his heart like a knife.

"This isn't you," she breathed. "Your behavior right now is my fault."

He opened his mouth. Shut it. "Sloan?"

"It's the pheromones." She shook her head again. "Later."

Right. Later. Confused, he stepped back, putting some distance between them. The lust-filled haze that had drenched his mind cleared a little. Bloody hell. He'd been so distracted. They were on a mission.

"What do you need me to do?" His voice came out low, rough.

"I'm going to talk with Barry. Feel him out. You need to get his glass for the fingerprints, just in case."

Then she pushed off the wall, and walked away, hips swaying seductively. That cute new haircut brushed between her shoulder blades, drawing his gaze down to her perfectly round ass. He liked that she had some curves on her and his fingers itched to explore. He blew out the breath he'd held and tugged his collar for air. The minute this mission was done, the second they were alone, they'd sort this thing out between them.

He wasn't done with her.

nine

SLOAN LAZARUS

FANNING HERSELF WITH HER HAND, Sloan strode across the ballroom, making a beeline for the bar. Somewhere to the right came the high pitched squeals of women no doubt being flattered and ego-stroked by the Wonder Twins, Tony and Parker.

Utterly failing at keeping her thoughts on track, she kept veering toward Max's words. *"Do you remember what I said you'd do to me if you ever wore red lipstick?"*

Oh, she remembered all right. Both she and Max had been very open about their sexual fantasies with each other. When you could only communicate with sound and picture, you had to be honest and clear. Words were their erotic foreplay. Their video calls were as vivid in her memory as if they'd happened yesterday. They'd start off innocent, a shared game or movie, and then the friendly banter and ribbing would turn sexual. Sometimes they'd play a game of strip poker… then… well, you can imagine how *that* ended. At the end of the call, they'd always kiss their fingers and raise them to the camera at the same time, imagining touching across the vast cyber expanse.

"I trust you. You got this," were Max's other words.

She forced a lungful of air in, and pushed her nerves out. Focus. Barry is there. The same Barry with whom Flint worked alongside for eight years. The same man who once thought he could save the world with his brain. On a flash of genius, she pulled out her cell from her clutch and dialed Flint.

Two rings, and he picked up. *"Sloan. Is everything okay?"*

The deep voice of familiarity grounded her. "Yeah, but... we found Barry, and I don't think he wants to work for the You-Know-Who. He's got the same sloth-signature as the one I sensed right before the animal was loosed on the city. I'm going to try to turn him. Can I patch you into my earpiece while I talk with him? Maybe you can offer insight."

As she spoke, a hushed, urgent voice hissed through her earpiece. Parker had been listening, and he wasn't happy.

"Just a sec, Flint. There's some white noise in my ear I need to clear."

"Sloan," Parker snapped. *"What are you doing? Turning him is not the plan."*

"It is now," she said. Her gut believed Barry could be swayed.

"We haven't discussed it."

She huffed a sardonic laugh, shaking her head. "Doesn't matter if we discuss it. You do what you want anyway, right? I'm on another call, bras, please... shut up."

He tried to speak some more, but she brought her cell back to her other ear. "Sorry Flint, you were saying?"

Parker was hard to ignore while simultaneously listening to Flint, but her brother would soon get the message. If not, she didn't care if she was in full view of the room, she'd pull the earpiece out.

"Flint?"

A pause. *"Sloanie, you know I want Barry to be on our side more than anything in the world, but the fact is, if you're right about the sloth-*

signature, he's been making those beasts. He's probably the one who made the clones and the Greed serum. None of that is good. I don't know if you can get through to him. It might be too late."

"We should try, though, right? Redemption is what separates us from those beasts." By "us" she meant her and her siblings. They were created in a lab, just like those animals. If they weren't careful, they'd turn into the very same thing... or worse, like Daisy.

There had to be a way back.

Another pause, then: *"You're absolutely right. I'll be here."*

"Patching you through now." Despite King Pee sounding like he was having a conniption, she cut him off and transferred Flint's call to her earpiece before slipping her cell back into her clutch. "You there?" she murmured.

"I'm here."

Another deep breath, and she stepped forward. Her palms felt clammy, her heart fluttered, but her gut was never wrong. Negligence was a version of sloth. She knew this. They had to trust her.

Plastering a smile on her face, she went to sit next to Barry, and flagged the waiter down. "Two more of what he's having."

Barry shot her an uninterested sideways glance, dark eyes inspecting from underneath dark brows.

"You're barking up the wrong tree, love. Married." He waggled his finger with the gold ring and then went back to his drink. "Plus, I'm old enough to be your father."

He's British, she realized with a jolt. Flint had never mentioned that.

Behind Barry, Max arrived, pretending to wait for the barman. He didn't show it, but she knew he kept one eye on Barry's almost empty Scotch glass, waiting for the opportunity to scan it for fingerprints. Seeing Max there, looking calm and collected, gave her the confidence to continue.

"Oh," she laughed softly at Barry. "This isn't a line. I'm a fan of your work, Doctor…" Shit. What was his name again?

"Pinkerton," Flint said.

"Pinkerton," she finished.

"Well, that makes one of us."

The barman dropped two glasses in front of them and poured the Scotch. Sloan dragged one to Barry, and lifted her own, tipping it toward him in a salute.

"Tell me, love. What exactly about my work do you like?"

She paused. Should she talk about his current work? There wasn't much about that to like. Which meant… Flint saved her by adding, *"Tell him, although you were never a fan of the smell, you're a huge fan of the way he preserved his Hairy Frog."*

She almost spat out the Scotch. Hairy Frog? Gross. She wouldn't be saying that. What kind of nonsense did Flint and Barry get up to when they were younger?

Barry watched her expectantly.

"Say it, Sloan."

"Um." She felt the blood drain from her face. "I can't say I'm a fan of how it smells, but I'm a huge fan of your work with Hairy Frog preservation."

"Hairy Frog!" he exclaimed. "Haven't touched one of those in decades."

"Remind him about how the frog's bones extend from its digits when under attack. Tell him. Also, it's highly carnivorous and territorial. Tell him."

Good Lord, Flint was getting excited. Sloan repeated his words. When she was done, Barry had forgotten his old drink, and swiveled on his stool to peer at her with clever eyes. "What else?"

With Flint's guidance, she mentioned some sort of underwater slug that could withstand boiling and freezing temperatures, and an amphibian that could grow its brain back. While Barry gawped at her, Flint muttering about how his little round ball that could disrupt three floors of tech was much better than any slimy invention of Barry's.

Sloan handed the man his fresh drink and casually nudged his empty glass back toward Max.

"Impressive," Barry said, accepting her drink. "I never thought anyone was interested in that line of research anymore."

"Well," she snorted. "It's nowhere near as good as a little silver ball that can disrupt three levels of tech."

Silence.

Both in her earpiece and in front of her. Barry's eyes narrowed, his voice lowered. "Who are you?"

"I'm someone who knows you don't belong with your current employer."

"You better start talking before I call security."

"I'm hoping you won't, Barry. I'm hoping that the sin I sense churning in your gut tells me otherwise."

His eyes widened, he paled, and a sheen of sweat broke out on his shaved upper lip. "Which one are you?"

She lifted a shoulder. "Doesn't matter. What matters is whether you want to make things right."

"I-I can't. It's not possible." Barry's wide eyes darted about the room. "They're everywhere. They could be listening or watching now."

Sloan opened her clutch and pulled out a business card with a single number on it. No name, nothing else, just her number. "In case you change your mind."

He took it, fingers trembling.

"Before I go," she asked. "An old friend would like it very much if I get a picture with you. Do you mind?"

She pulled out her cell and activated the camera. Standing next to him, she aimed so they were both in the shot and smiled. Stunned, the man stared into the lens as she took the snap. She took the shot from two more angles, feigning a complaint about the lighting. Packing her cell away, she went to leave but he stopped her.

"Did he find his nun?"

Sloan almost laughed. Back when they worked in the lab, Mary had disguised herself as a nun to work with the children. They'd had no idea she was one of the world's most dangerous assassins. Possibly still didn't. Flint had fallen in love with Mary—even when he believed she was a nun. To be fair, she sort of was a nun, but one allowed to sin in the eyes of the church.

Flint still joked about how Mary had taunted him back then.

"Yeah, Barry. He got the girl, and they're happily married. They saved our lives. Because of their sacrifice, the Deadly Seven protect the innocent and the redeemable, every day."

Barry's eyes glistened and he gave a curt nod.

"Instead of destroying them, you can save lives too, Barry."

Walking away, Sloan knew she'd done the right thing. Barry could be reached. He'd call. And if he didn't, they had his fingerprints, and a high definition photograph of his face. It was all she needed to create a synthetic match to fool the biometrics at the black site. They'd get into that black site one way or another.

When Sloan left the ballroom, she disconnected the call with Flint and made her way to the elevator. She checked to make sure no one was around, then said loud enough so Parker and Tony could hear. "We got what we came for."

Crackling feedback was her response, then Parker's: *"And more. Risky, Sloan. Not happy. Not happy at all. You could have completely taken away our anonymity. If he snitches, they'll know we're coming."*

"They know our true identities. And if he snitches about us being here, we'll know by the morning," Sloan added. "But he won't."

Parker cursed. *"You're done for the night. Go back to the room."*

She opened her mouth to protest, but shut it, heat flaming her cheeks. Why was she defending herself like a child? She was a grown woman, a part of this team, and he was sending her to her room like a naughty kid. This leadership role was going to Parker's head.

"Good," she said. "I don't want to stay out here with you losers anyway."

"Harsh, Sloanie." Tony's voice was punctuated by some feminine giggling. *"You should use the time to work out your shit."*

Work out my shit? Oh, now she was definitely pissed. "I don't know what you're talking about."

"You will soon." Tony laughed. *"Don't wait up. I'm off to do what I do best."*

Ass-wipe. While he got to have fun, boozing it up and no doubt satiating his desire for gluttony with women, she was told to relax and work out her shit. Riled and irritated, she stormed toward the lobby. *Damn these heels.* And the thong giving her an eternal wedgie. She was dying to get back into her Converse.

After a few moments, the elevator doors opened. Empty. Thank God. She entered and swiped her card for the top level. Just as the doors were closing, a tall, lithe body slipped in on light feet.

Max.

He waited for the doors to shut before speaking. "You and I need to talk."

"Yeah, well, I don't want to talk about the mission. Had enough from my jerk brothers." She pulled her mic at her strap and growled into it: "Jerk. Jerk. Jerk."

Max's wince of pain made her smile. If Parker and Tony still had their pieces in, they would feel the shout in their ear too.

She plucked the little instrument from her strap and stuffed it into her clutch, along with her earpiece. She made the gimme sign to Max until he did the same. Damn her brothers listening in on every word she said.

"You know what I meant." Max untied his tie and popped his collar. "You and me. I think we need to get it all out in the open."

She blinked, looking at him properly for the first time all night. She hated to admit it, but he worked that simple tuxedo like a model. The understated charm suited her much better than the flash of most gala attendees. His hair, as usual, was trimmed and simple. Still always somehow lighter at the tips, as though years of time in the sun and salt water had ingrained in his DNA.

"Sloan?" He angled to face her. "I swear to God if you avoid this conversation—"

The elevator jerked to a halt and she stumbled, palm flying out to his hard chest for support. What the hell?

They both stilled at the contact, and then Sloan jumped back until her shoulders hit the cold press of the mirrored glass around them.

Max swiped his room card at the security fob, and hit their floor button, but the elevator wouldn't move.

"Are we stuck?" he asked. He pressed the emergency call button, but it didn't connect. When his wary gaze met Sloan's, she knew something was up. For a second, she feared Parker was right. Barry had gone straight to his employers and this was their doing. They were trapped in an elevator, half way up a multilevel hotel building. Shit.

"Give me a minute." Sloan pulled out her cell and dialed. "AIMI, it's Sloan."

"I've been expecting your call."

"Hey, I said maybe I'll check in. Not definitely." Sloan put the cell on speaker so Max could hear.

"Tony said you would call."

"Tony?"

"You are stuck in an elevator."

Narrowing her eyes, she met Max's.

"How does she know?" he whispered.

"AIMI?" she prompted.

"Tony said, and I quote, 'Debbie Downer needs to sort her shit out before we go on this hike.' Then he ordered me to stop the elevator until you had. Debbie Downer is you, Sloan."

"Very funny, AIMI. What happened to Oh, Masterful One?" Sloan laughed nervously. "Joke's over. Start the elevator."

"To answer your first question, Tony changed your salutation. To address the latter comment: Unfortunately, this is not possible."

"Are you kidding me? You're not supposed to do anything unless I tell you. How did he manage to override my access?"

"It's perhaps best I play you his response."

Two-seconds later, and Tony's smug voice came over the speaker. *"Who's the dumbass now, Sloanie?"* he laughed. *"Now, you two sort out your shit. We're not going on this mission tomorrow until you have. I expect rainbows and unicorns the next time I see you both."*

Then AIMI disconnected.

"When the hell did he find the time to do this?" Sloan ground her teeth.

"Must have been planning it for a while." Max folded his arms, fighting a smile. "That Tony is a sly one."

"He's a dead one. Tony just moved up to numero uno on my hit list." She tapped her cell, trying to access the app which gave her access to AIMI, but it wouldn't open. She expected this level of tech

97

savvy from Parker, but not Tony. This was why he'd gotten one over her. She'd underestimated him.

"Well." Max removed his jacket and lowered himself to the floor, resting an elbow on his knee. "Knowing how stubborn you are, this could take some time. May as well get comfortable."

"No." She paced. "There must be some way to get out of here. Surely the hotel will notice an elevator has stopped. What about the cameras?" She looked up at the ceiling and squinted, then checked the instrument panel with a groan. "No cameras! How can a luxury hotel like this have no cameras? Wait." She stopped. "What do you mean, stubborn? I'm not stubborn."

Max huffed. "You kidding me? Woman, you're the most stubborn person I know, including Bailey."

"Am not. I'm totally easy going." She pointed at herself with two thumbs. "Sloth, remember? It's not in me to hold a grudge."

"So why have you been pranking me from the moment I arrived in the city?"

"Pfft. Tss." She snorted incredulously. "I am not."

Clearly not fooled, he arched an eyebrow. "So, the cooling in my office magically switched to heating the other day. On its own?"

She tried not to smile. "That's the first I'm hearing of it."

"And, then I suppose you know nothing about AIMI calling me Maxi-Pad."

She shrugged.

"Or switched my pizza order to remove the pineapple? Oh yeah, I noticed."

"Not me."

"Or the fact someone was logged into my internal office CCTV the other day."

Heat flushed up her neck as she remembered how little clothing he'd been wearing when he'd caught her. "Look, sometimes AIMI does things I can't control."

"You just said AIMI isn't supposed to do anything unless you tell her to."

She punched the emergency button again, but no response. *Dammit.*

This was hopeless. She leaned her forehead against the cool mirror in an attempt to abate the sweat prickling her neck. Her reflection wavered, the air in the room disappeared and she had to gulp in a few breaths from underneath the shroud of her hair. It was all too much. The room too small. She hated being forced into a situation she wasn't ready to face. She hated it. Damn Tony. Damn Parker. She should have stayed in her nice cozy little apartment.

She missed Luna.

Max got up and stepped toward her. "Hey. It's fine. We'll get out of here."

"When?" she asked. "When Tony decides he's played enough games?"

"I guess when we've sorted our shit out, as he so eloquently put."

She sighed. Right.

The two of them leaned on opposite ends of the elevator, staring at the other, neither willing to take the first step. The man in front of her had broken her heart. She'd had so much anger for so many years and, yet, she found none in her now. No fuel to light the fire, nothing to start the conversation. The man in front of her was exactly like the one she'd fallen in love with. Kind, attentive, supportive.

"Do you remember that time we camped out in our rooms for a twelve hour video-chat?" he asked.

"Which time?"

"The first one. There was that special event on with that game we were playing"—a crease deepened between his brow—"I can't even remember which one, but it all started because you got it in your head that between the two of us, we'd win. You'd just received that light-up cat's ears headset and wanted to test it out."

"You bought me that headset." She realized with a start, remembering how random she'd felt to receive a gift in the mail from this guy she'd been hanging out with online. "I remember thinking the first time I used it should be with you."

He smiled affectionately. "The call started out with us playing the game, but eventually, even when it was over, we kept talking, telling each other our secrets. You liked playing games because you felt like a different person in there, that your gender wasn't a factor in your success."

She frowned. "Why are you saying this?"

"I want to know if you miss us. I want to know if I meant anything to you at all."

"This is not the time, Max."

A cruel laugh huffed out of him, and he glanced around the elevator. "I'm pretty sure now is the perfect time."

What was his problem? Why was he pushing this? *He* was the one who broke up with *her*. Yes, of course she missed him. She ached from being in the same room as him. Her lungs burned from breathing the same air. Her heart felt bruised and squeezed. Her body wanted him back. It remembered that night everything changed between them. That twelve-hour long video-chat.

Yes, you stupid man. She'd yearned for him for years. She'd cried herself to sleep because she'd wanted him so much.

Max pushed off his side and came to stand next to her, shoulder to shoulder. He took a deep shuddering breath. "After how things ended, I know I shouldn't, but I've missed you, Sloan."

She squeezed her eyes shut. Don't cry. Don't give him the satisfaction.

She ground out, "Are you trying to rub salt in my wounds?"

"You're the one who started dating someone else."

"Dating someone else?" Was this guy for real?

"That loser geek guy I saw you with at the gaming convention. He had a ridiculous goatee and"—he waved around his head—"the stupidest green hair."

"That *loser guy* didn't last long, and… wait, are you jealous?" Max had no right to be. Why was he jealous?

"Damn straight I was , Sloan." He slammed his palm behind him, vibrating the mirrored wall, warping their reflections. The air between them thickened, and she had to suck in a breath from the force of his glare. "Seeing my woman, the one I wanted to marry, with some other fuckwit…"

The blood drained from her face.

Sure, they talked about starting a life together, even the whole kid business. Both of them had been a resounding, not yet, but maybe one day. He made it sound like it was a given.

"How come you went straight to dating some blond bimbo?" she pointed out.

"You know about Sammie?"

"Sammie." Yeah she knew about Sammie. She knew where Sammie worked. She knew where she went to the gym. She knew Sammie liked to drink Caramel Mochacinos after her workouts and then go back for seconds. Oh, the many times Sloan tried to figure out how to poison those drinks from oceans away.

"You were jealous, too," he murmured, confused.

She folded her arms and looked away.

"Bloody hell, Sloan. Sammie was a one hit wonder. If you know about her, you would have known that. If you needed more proof of your stubbornness"—he waved at her face—"Exhibit A."

"I'm protecting my heart."

"You're the only one hurting it right now, not me. I'm trying to sort things out."

She threw up her hands. "I want to get out of here."

He laughed callously, and it made her blood boil.

"You don't mean that." He crowded her against the wall, using his sheer size to intimidate her.

She wasn't afraid. Come at her. See what you get when you mess with the best. "Yes, I goddamn do."

"No. You. Don't." Eyes blazing like the morning sun, he stared at her, jaw working, breathing hard. Then his eyes darkened and dropped to her lips. A finger lifted to touch the vein at her neck. "Your pulse is racing."

His touch, so simple as it was, ignited something inside her. Heat spread from his fingertip like wildfire and warmed her entire body. She should say something. Say it was her anger that had her heart rabbiting, but it would be a lie. She was more attracted to him than she'd ever anticipated, and her pheromones knew it.

"I hate you, Maxi-Pad." Brave words for a cowardly heart.

"No, you don't." His touch trailed down her sensitized neck, dipped over her collarbone and kept going downward. "If you did, you wouldn't have made my office so hot that I had to strip half-naked."

"Don't know what you're talking about."

He only smiled. "Did you like what you saw?"

Yes.

"You've changed," she admitted.

His eyes flashed with pure masculine ego. "How?"

Bastard. He knew exactly how, yet, she couldn't keep her gaze from trailing down his stubbled jaw to his open shirt and the flash of golden skin at his neck. Hairless. Smooth. Sexy. Her gaze dropped to the flat stomach hiding beneath his shirt, remembering the cut abs she'd seen on the video, wondering how he looked in real life, how he felt to touch. God, she wanted to touch. To feel that satin skin, that fuzz of hair leading down. Lower. Her thighs clenched as her eyes tracked to his belt. Lower. The bulge in his pants. She gasped, eyes darting back to his.

"Yeah, I've missed you, Sloan," he rasped, finger still sliding up and down her strap. "It's time you admit you feel the same way about me too."

Frowning, he leaned in until their noses touched, until their hot breaths mingled. She arched forward, hating the whimpering sound that escaped her. Braless, she ached painfully against the friction of her dress, wanting his trail of sensation to land *there*... but he stopped. His hand hovered gently where the curve of her bare breast met her dress. Already panting with need, she lifted her gaze and found him looking down at her with so much pain in his eyes that she felt it in her heart.

It stabbed and twisted and beneath it all, she felt desire. *Raw, hot, powerful.* For her. Was this her power? Was she sensing his emotion? Was that why she felt the erotic echo in her core, tightening everything with anticipation? The fact he remained so stoic, so calm, while that turmoil of want tumbled inside him...

"Do you know how many nights I dreamed of you?" he rasped. "All those cold nights, sleeping in the dirt, hiding from the enemy, wondering if I was going to make it back alive... The memory of you kept me warm." He raised liquid eyes to hers. "The video didn't do you justice. You're beautiful, Sloan."

"It's just makeup," she murmured, throat tight.

"No." He grasped the back of her neck, angry. Lightning flashed in his eyes. "Don't do that."

"Do what?"

"Belittle yourself. It's not the makeup. It's always you, Sloan."

His lips crashed down onto hers. He was rough. Insistent. Demanding. Hot. And then his hands cupped her face, holding her in place, keeping her lips against his as if he feared she'd pull away.

For what seemed a long moment, Sloan did nothing. She froze.

It's always you, Sloan.

Then she melted against him and deepened the kiss. She was gone, lost in his passion. Soon, she didn't know where her emotion began, and his ended.

ten

MAX JOHNSON

MAX HAD NEVER WANTED anything more than he wanted Sloan. He kissed her as if she was his air, his water, his sustenance. He had to have her. Had to make her see how much he ached for her, explain how she felt like home. She was the sense of belonging his empty heart had lost. He desired her. Needed her. Had to know if she felt the same way, and she did. *She did.*

She might be too stubborn to admit it, but she kissed him like she missed him.

Hard up against her soft body, he devoured her mouth, tongue dueling with hers, teeth knocking. She smelled good. Soft, feminine, heady. His hand dropped to her neck, to her shoulder. He needed to touch more of her.

Touch her. Slide beneath her dress. Caress her bare skin.

God, *her ass.* Taut and plump at the same time. Curves built with muscle and a little extra on the side. She lifted a leg and dug her heel into the back of his thigh, drawing him closer, nudging their desperate bodies together.

She wants me.

He ground into her, cock painfully hard and needing relief. His mind, a starved beast, wanted everything she had to give. Wanted it all. He'd dreamed of her for so long.

The flat of his palm rubbed down her front, put pressure over the arch of her breast, felt the hard nub of her nipple pushing back at him.

"Tease," he accused and then squeezed. She groaned into his mouth, begging for more.

"More what?" he rasped.

"Everything," she moaned. "More everything."

Then his lips were on her neck, trailing kisses down her front, down to where he rolled her sensitized bud between his thumb and finger. Tweaked, tugged, plucked. He stopped. Fingers tucked into the edge of her dress, ready to pry the fabric down and set her free. His cock gave a jerk at the thought, at the image in his mind of beautiful bouncing breasts, the same image he'd built to perfection over the years. Ragged breaths plagued him as he waited, watched her flesh fill and rise each time she took a breath.

"What are you waiting for?" She stretched the fabric down, releasing herself.

"You're beautiful. Let me enjoy this." Holy fuck, he loved it when she got bossy, but damn him if he rushed this. Damn this elevator. He wanted to take his time, to know every perfect inch of her pale, teardrop-shaped mounds. Dusky rose nipples. More than a handful— her tits were his fantasy come to life. She whimpered, impatiently, and he grinned, heavy eyes lifting to hers. "So demanding."

"You don't know the half of it."

He drew her breast into his mouth and gave a guttural groan around her flesh. Bloody hell. This wasn't a fantasy. This was Sloan's wet, supple flesh in his mouth and it tasted so good. He gave in to his desire. He licked, laved, nipped, and sucked while he kneaded and molded the other with his hand. Sloan's fingers speared into his hair, gripped tight and pulled, crying out for more. More. *More.*

The floor jolted and moved beneath their feet. The room tilted, and...

Alert, Max drew back, his mouth popping off Sloan. "We're moving."

"We're what?" She blinked, dazed.

"Crap." Quickly, he lifted her dress to cover her, and then stepped in front of her in case the door opened. "The elevator is moving again."

"Now?"

Focus, Max. Breathe. He picked his jacket up. *When the doors open, just get out. Get Sloan to the room.* He shot her a look. Feverish eyes and flushed skin. Black strands haphazard over her face. A growl of sensual intent ripped from him. *Get her into his bed.*

The doors opened, he cleared his throat, preparing for an interaction, but no one stepped in. The hall was empty, and Sloan was taking his hand and tugging him out of the elevator so fast he had to jog to keep up. Somehow, they fumbled their way into their suite, checked no one was home, and ended on Sloan's bed.

She threw him down and straddled him, dress skirt hitched up around her smooth thighs. "Take it off."

"Yes, ma'am." He trailed his hands up her thighs, drinking her in, sliding under her dress. His thumb found the juncture between her legs and pressed, causing her to mewl and grind down on him. He pushed the dress up further, revealing her panties. Red lace. Holding her hips, he ground upward with his own. A long drawn-out moan fell out as the sensation speared through him, licking up his spine, dancing around his heart. Again, and again, he rubbed into her through their clothing.

"Max," she breathed, desperation lighting her eyes. "Off. *Now.*"

He lifted her dress higher, but she slapped him away. "Not my dress." She pawed at his shirt, popping buttons down the front. "Your clothes. Take them off."

Before he had a chance to correct, she'd ripped open his shirt, popping buttons off.

"All good," he murmured. "Didn't need it anyway."

As she took in the sight of him, heat burst in her eyes and he received a shock of satisfaction. She *so* wanted him. She missed him. He was a fool to think otherwise. No denying it now. He sat up, reaching for her mouth with his, letting her guide the shirt completely off. When her hands began a slow, mesmerizing quest around his torso, he felt his chest swell. From the way she savored, he knew she'd fantasized about their first time too.

She sighed appreciatively. "Okay, Max. I forgive you."

Every muscle in his body locked cold with rigidity. He swallowed. Forgive *him?* "What?"

She rocked against him, and it took every ounce of restraint to put his hands on her hips and halt her movement.

"What do you mean, forgive me?" he asked.

"For walking out on me."

His jaw tightened. Heat prickled his face. No. Absolutely not. He pushed her off him. "You're the one who walked out on me, Sloan. I've done nothing wrong."

Shock, then denial, then anger flashed in her eyes but he didn't care. The cold bucket of water had been thrown and his desire was thoroughly doused. With all the too-ing and fro-ing, his brain had turned to mush. He shuffled to the exit. She still had no idea. All these years, all this hurt banging around his chest. When he got to the door, he pivoted.

"For the record, Sloan. *You* didn't wait for *me.*" He paused. "And I needed you."

"I needed you! You came, and then you left! What the fuck was that, Max? Who does that after seeing their girlfriend get wrongly blamed for murdering a building full of innocents?"

He gaped. "I turned up, Sloan. I got called away."

"You said you'd quit."

"They needed me. A friend was in danger." *Gale.* He'd been taken. Missing in action. What the fuck was Max supposed to do? The mate who's family had basically adopted him after his parents died. The mate who'd saved his life countless times. The mate who'd taught him to surf and loaned him a stupid old seventies longboard when he couldn't afford his own. His stupid smiling squinty eyes and stupid beard that wouldn't grow. A band constricted around his chest, getting tighter by the minute.

Hands on hips, her brow puckered in the middle. "I didn't know that."

The deep breath he'd been holding expelled slowly. "Look. I'm tired. It's been a long day. I don't want to talk about this right now." It was the truth. He was tired. She might not be, but he had to get some rest for the big hike tomorrow. Besides, she would ask about Gale, and he just couldn't. It was too much. His raw heart barely pumped. *Fuck.* A few quick strides and he was in his room, closing the door behind him. ·

Sloan's fist pounded the door. "Max!"

"Go away, Sloan. I don't want to talk about it right now."

"But…" her voice trailed off. Maybe he heard her say she didn't know. Maybe he heard her say she was sorry, but by that stage, he was already stripping off his clothes and turning the private shower faucet on, setting the temperature to scolding hot. All he wanted to do right now was sleep and forget.

FIFTEEN HOURS LATER, Max trudged through the wilderness, strapped with his hiking pack and supplies. He followed three tireless Lazarus *inhumans* along limestone tipped mountainous slopes. A sprinkling of Aspen and Pine sheltered them from the view of possible roving drones. The trees thickened the closer they got to the encroaching mountain.

Since they'd left the hotel that morning, he'd not said a peep to Sloan, despite her silent attention. He'd kept his distance. Her confession still grated. She believed he'd left all those years ago without a word. But he'd left a message. It was all he had time for. Granted, when he'd found out about Wyatt's ex-fiancée being the cause of trouble in their lives, he should have suspected she'd never passed on his message, but he'd only learned about that a few months ago when Parker had hired him. Regardless, Sloan had the tech skills and resources to hack into military databases. She could have learned everything about his sudden mission, if only she'd looked. Instead, she'd taken the fact he'd not turned up as the end of their relationship. He'd been ready to marry her.

She knew about Sammie. The thought contradicted every prejudice he'd constructed since their separation. Sammie was nothing to him. A means to scratch an itch, but the fact Sloan knew about that brief moment of his life meant that she *had* looked him up... just at the wrong time. Could it be possible this was all a miscommunication?

"Stop here," Parker announced as the group made it to a patch of trees. He pulled out his canteen to take a swig. As with the rest of the men, Parker wore just his gray battle pants and a simple T-shirt for the hike. They had protective gear packed away for when they got closer to the site.

Max also took a swig from his canteen, letting the cool water run down his parched throat. When he was done, he surveyed the land-scape. More trees. Mores slopes.

"What does the GPS say, Sloan?" Parker asked.

With her hair tied at her nape, black boots, dirty beige singlet and gray battle pants, she was the epitome of one of her favored gamer characters. The cross bow slung over her shoulder also added to the tough, but feminine vibe. Sexy too. After their episode in the elevator, he'd had the most intense hard-on the entire night. Even after they'd fought, and he'd sorted himself out in the shower, it came back. Every time he'd thought of her, which was often, he couldn't get rid of it. He hated his body for already being *there* when his mind was not.

Sloan went to Parker and conferred over the data on her satellite connected iPad.

"Hey, dude," Tony said, coming up to him.

The man managed to look as though he'd sprung straight from one of his movie sets, despite coming in late, drunk, and with lipstick all over him. He somehow made the messy hair, puffy-eyed-bachelor-look like it was always meant to be that way.

Tony clapped Max on the shoulder. "No hard feelings about last night?"

Max frowned, trying to understand.

"The elevator."

"Oh. Yeah, nah. It's all good, mate. I get it, you were trying to help."

Tony inspected Max's face. "Thought it would get you two on the same page, but guess I was wrong."

"Me too."

Tony slid a gaze toward his sister. "Everything cool?"

Max also stared hard. He wasn't sure.

"How is it," Max said, avoiding the topic. "You look like you stepped off a movie set, while I'm in LeBron James Sweat-Mode."

"I don't do it on purpose."

It started as a joke, but Max detected a tone of resentment in his voice, and faint scowl on his face.

Tony added, "But you're used to this, right? The hiking, I mean. We're not pushing you too hard?"

"Yeah—" Max pulled his sweaty shirt from his chest and fanned the cool air in. "All good, mate. Piece of cake."

"So, look. Here's the thing. Remember that time we had to go into that forest overnight, and it was just us and no superiors?"

A smile tipped Max's lips. That year Tony had spent training with his SAS regiment had been one of the best in his life. Tom-Tom and Daymo were there. And of course, Gale. "That's when the boys started calling you Hollywood."

Tony gave an exasperated sigh. "Like I said, I can't help it if I'm beautiful. Where do you think I got the idea to act?"

A fly buzzed and Max waved it away. "Thought you got it from those b-grade pornos you used to watch."

For a moment, Tony stared back with wide eyes. Probably because back in Australia, the only way to deal with a tall poppy was to cut it down, and Tony had been the tallest of all. "Stay grounded" was their motto. Max and the crew had spent their training time teasing the shit out of Tony—and they expected Tony to do the same for them. They used to tell him the only person who'd ever watch him star in a movie was his mom, and then it would probably only ever be a porno. That spawned a crap-load of mom jokes.

For a minute, Max thought maybe the joke had worn off, but Tony smirked. "Good one, Johnson."

Max smirked, eyes crinkling. "I would add a mom-joke, but seriously, your mom scares me."

"Me too. Damn it's good to hang out with you again." The two of them chuckled and shared a quiet moment. Then Tony ditched a pebble at Max. "You know, if I'd been able to, I'd have gone back with you."

Max's throat tightened at the reference to Gale. "Yeah I know, but I get it. It wasn't your job. Not mine anymore either. You got important shit to do here."

Tony shrugged. "Sometimes it feels exactly like that—shit." Max didn't have time to query him because Tony continued, "Speaking of shit, I want to get back at Sloan for the stunt she pulled on me last night." Tony darted a glance at Sloan, then lowered his voice. "So, you remember that time you all pulled that falling animal prank on me during that squad training in the forest?"

Suspicion crept in. Why was he asking? "You mean the fake Drop Bear?"

"Yeah. Let's do the same to Sloan."

Max cast a wary eye to where Sloan stood, one boot on a rock, iPad balanced on a knee. Parker loomed over her as he re-tied his sweaty auburn hair into a masculine bun, biceps and pecs bouncing.

"It only works in Australia. You don't get killer koalas out here."

"What about some other animal, though?"

"You want to prank her out here?" While they were on a mission?

"Why not? She canceled my cards last night, dude. Picture this: two Victoria's Secret models on my arms, end of night, about to head up to their room. I'm ready to go. They're ready to go. I order at the bar for some late-night-action bubbles, and my black American Express card declines. That shit don't decline, you feel me? Right in front of the ladies. Sloan fucking cock-blocked me, man. After I spent all night dancing like a fucking monkey, she rewards me with that. She has to go down for this."

Max stifled his humor by pressing his lips together. Sloan must have done *that* after he'd retired to his bedroom. "I'm staying out of your family shenanigans. I get enough prank backlash from Sloan as it is."

"What are you two talking about?" Sloan asked, coming over with Parker.

"Nothing." Tony clammed up so fast it was obvious he'd been talking about her.

She snorted. "Probably about your lack of prank-game, bras."

"What's this?" Parker growled.

"She's calling me a lady's undergarment again." Tony pointed at her with his thumb.

"That's because you *are* a big girl's blouse," Sloan said wryly.

Max grinned. She'd taken that expression from him. He used to shout it at the screen when some loser pulled a soft move on him during a game.

"She deactivated my credit cards last night," Tony explained to Parker.

"He trapped me in the elevator!"

"You embarrassed me."

"Mess with the best, die like the rest!" Sloan got in Tony's face.

"Stop acting like juveniles!" Parker growled. His deep voice shook the surrounding Aspen. Birds took to the sky in protest.

But the siblings paid no attention.

Tony shoved her at the same time she stomped her foot. She lost her balance, slipped, landed palm first on a sharp crop of limestone and hissed in pain. "You asshole. You made me bleed my own blood!"

Pain stab through Max's palm and he hissed. Tony and Parker did the same thing. All four of them had their palms out, feeling the sting of a phantom injury, but it was only Sloan with the wound.

"What the hell was that, Sloan?" Parker rumbled, shaking his hand.

"He pushed me!" she snapped.

"I'm not talking about your bickering, I'm talking about my hand hurting in the same place yours is wounded."

She tried to cradle her hand, to hide the evidence, but Parker crouched low and pulled it out on display. Gently prodding around the wound, he looked on in awe at his own hand, sensing the same flash of pain respond, just as Max and Tony felt in the same place.

"You made us hurt," Parker murmured, deep in thought, then flipped Sloan's wrist to view her Yin-Yang tattoo. Max wasn't certain what he was checking for, but had heard the tattoo was made with a special biometric ink that measured the amount of sin in their system. If the tattoo looked too black, it meant their sin was getting a hold of them. If there wasn't enough ink showing, then it meant not enough sin was in their blood. Apparently, both extremes could be fatal—for others. She tried to snatch her arm away, but whatever passed between them had already been confirmed. Parker's jaw tightened. "You're perfectly balanced, Sloan. This is your power manifesting, isn't it?"

Max frowned, confused. Power? What power. As in, something like Evan's electricity, or Wyatt's invulnerability? How could her injury be a power?

He checked his aching palm, then shot another look at her, conclusions forming as the puzzle pieces came together. He stepped toward Sloan. "You stabbed your palm in the alley and that beast whined in agony."

Parker stood and folded his arms in a way that made his biceps bulge with intimidation. "Is this true, Sloan?"

She shot Max narrowed eyes of accusation.

Why would she want to keep this a secret? It was good. For any of the seven to gain supernatural powers was an advantage over their enemies. They all needed to know about this. Secrets got people killed. He wasn't keeping his mouth shut.

"It also happened when we sparred, Sloan," he added. "You kicked me in the face, but bled yourself. You can receive pain too."

Parker rubbed his stubble. "What else, Sloan?"

She bit her lip. "Maybe I made a few people in the salon cry when I was upset."

Max's lungs stopped. Why had she been crying?

At Parker's insistent stare, she rolled her eyes. "Okay. Maybe I made the entire salon cry."

"Interesting. Goes both ways." Parker scratched some more. "Could be linked to mirror neurons and theta waves."

Max offered Sloan a hand. She took it, and he levered her up.

"What's that?" she asked.

"Like the name suggests, mirror neurons work like a reflection of what they see, and fire when one animal witness another completing an act. They help us learn by imitating."

"I think I'm going to need a little more than that, bras?" She lifted her brows.

"A few years back, a study discovered monkey's brains fired like they were actually completing the task they watched another monkey do. I'm guessing our maker somehow enhanced that ability into some kind of psionic power for you."

"Oh great. I have monkey DNA."

Tony snorted. "Would explain a lot."

She shot him a glare. "You better be careful, or else I'll make you impotent."

Tony blanched and covered his groin with his hands. "You wouldn't dare. Can she do that?"

Parker ignored and continued, "Have you noticed anything else, Sloan?"

"It seems to be linked to sensations and emotions. Sometimes I feel them, sometimes others do."

"But you can't control it," Parker pointed out.

She shook her head, a sheepish flicker to Tony. "Not really."

Tony visibly relaxed and moved his hands away from his goods.

"Then you need training," Parker decreed. "We can't have you wounding yourself every time you use your power. We'll need to record limitations and—"

"Wait, wait, wait." Tony held up his hands. "I think we're all missing the big point. Who is it, Sloan? Who's your mate?"

After staring at the rocky floor in stubborn silence, Sloan lifted her reluctant gaze to lock with Max's. The rest of them fell silent.

What the hell was going on?

eleven

SLOAN LAZARUS

THE NEXT FEW hours were the most embarrassing of Sloan's life. While they continued to hike, she trailed after the three men discussing the ins and outs of the mating bond. To his credit, Max took it in his stride. Well, at least she thought he did. He walked alongside them, listening and asking reflective questions every so often. Hearing their murmured responses made her stomach roil. She wanted to be included in the conversation and equally wanted to run in the opposite direction. She settled for trudging behind them.

The sun dipped below the horizon, bringing a much-needed drop in temperature. They would have to camp soon. The Lazaruses could go all night without breaking a sweat, and Max would most likely keep up with them out of sheer stubbornness, but he wasn't built like them. Pulling her satellite connected device out, Sloan tracked their location as they walked, half listening to the conversation.

"So," Max said to Parker, "if you're out of balance, you black out and go berserk. You try to eliminate any sinner nearby, no matter what age or level of sin?"

"That's right," Parker replied. "It can't be helped, unless…"

"You've been in contact with your special paired mate."

"Yeah, bro. That's right." Tony nudged him with his shoulder. "Good to have you around."

Her brothers were now treating him like one of the family, whether or not he liked it. It was enough to drive her crazy. She wanted to say they were all being ridiculous, that he didn't have to do, or be, anything he didn't want... but she held her tongue.

A small part of her didn't want to scare him away.

A bigger part wished he'd accept the mating bond, and that they'd work out their problems. Discounting the fact she felt more energized than ever before, her mind was still in love with him. After last night in the elevator, her body was too. She couldn't relinquish the memory of his kiss, or the feel of his tongue on her skin. Hot, demanding, needy. God, the way his bare torso felt—hard as rock yet smooth as satin. She'd been so ready for him, and she still stood by her claim—she forgave him.

Except, maybe he'd been right, and it was she who needed forgiveness.

There was credence to his claim. She'd checked last night. He had been pulled away on an urgent mission—military flight records confirmed it. And it was entirely possible he'd left a message with Sara. She was exactly the type to not pass it on out of spite.

"Sloan?" Parker asked, snapping her out of her daze.

"I'm sorry?"

"What's the ETA?"

"About eight hours."

Parker scanned their surroundings. They were in a clearing, a few pine trees overhead. In the distance, Sloan could hear running water. She checked her GPS map. "There's a creek nearby."

"Perfect." Tony scrubbed his face. "I'm ready for a night cap."

"Let's stop here," Parker said, dumping his rucksack. "We'll get going a few hours before dawn."

Max dropped his pack. "I'll go set up a perimeter."

"No need," Parker added. "We can sense people coming a mile away."

Out of breath, Max put his hands on his hips. "Correct me if I'm wrong, but you'll only sense someone with pride, right? So what if they're not feeling very prideful?"

Parker arched a brow. "Between the three of us, we'll sense an intruder. Trust me."

"Well." Max retrieved a torch and pistol from his pack. "If it's all the same to you, I'm checking anyway."

"Suit yourself." Tony already tasted the contents of a new canteen, and from the way he winced, Sloan was sure it was alcohol. "Although, in my opinion, you need to learn how to relax."

While Parker and Tony made themselves comfortable with some refreshments, Max disappeared into the surrounding darkness. Nervous, Sloan stared in the direction he'd gone for long minutes, fighting the urge to go after him. Crickets chirped. After a while, she realized she couldn't sense him empathically. He became like a ghost. The man also held zero sloth. She'd bet he fell asleep and woke like the dead. No mooching or lazing about, just straight to sleep, then up the instant he woke. The man would be hard to live with. Did he even play video games anymore?

Flinching, she caught herself. Did she just imagine living with him? Had she made that leap already? Of course she had. She was in love with him. This revelation set her up for so much future pain.

Shaking her head, she set about creating a soft spot for herself to lie down, then propped up against her rucksack. She inspected the map while eating a protein bar. The site wasn't far off. Half a day's walk. They should get there by midday, but with the black-site drones her app picked up, arriving during daylight wasn't a good move. Using a jamming signal to shut down the machines would warn their enemy of her arrival. She could try hacking the control frequency, but it might take too long.

Sloan got up, dusted off her hands and walked over to her brothers, now sharing Tony's flask.

She gestured with her device. "We either have to keep walking through the night to get there before morning, or take a longer rest. We'll be spotted otherwise."

"Give me a look." Parker took her device, and she wanted to wring his neck. Her word was never good enough with Parker. He scrutinized the tablet. "You're right. Do you think Max can handle it?"

"He's special forces," Sloan pointed out. He'd once told her about a mission that had him hidden in a hole, unable to move or sleep, gunfire shooting overhead, for three days straight.

"We'll get going in a few then."

"I'll go find him." She stepped away, cheeks heating. She had no idea where to look. Hesitating, she turned back to her brothers for help. "Um…"

"North-East," Tony mumbled while snoozing languidly against his rucksack. "Must be gluttonizing something—probably eating a protein bar."

Right. Sloan packed away her device and headed off in the direction Tony suggested.

After floundering in the dark for a few minutes, her new ability sensed a gliding melancholy that could only come from him. She found him sitting on a log in a clearing, shrewd eyes watching the starry night sky beyond. The crickets chirped louder there, and the night birds called. The earth, still warm from the sun's rays, provided an aura of warmth against the cooler breeze wafting the scent of pine down the mountain.

Unlike Parker or Tony, Max wasn't relaxing. His muscles were taut as he leaned his elbows on his knees, tendons in jaw flexing as he ate something.

"Hey," she mumbled as she came up next to him.

"Hey."

After a stretched silence, she sat down next to him. He still wouldn't look at her. She didn't blame him. If their breaking up was a misunderstanding, then she had a lot to make up for. And she wanted to. Not because he was her mate, but because they were so much more.

"So... nice view," she started, then winced at her awkwardness.

He grunted in reply.

"You used to go camping a lot, right?" Camping and surfing. There was plenty of outback and wilderness where he'd lived in Australia. He used to tell her he would go every time he came off tour. Just him and his close buddy, Gale. Max had talked about his friend all the time. They'd grown up together. Joined the army together and always came home together. The camping was their way to acclimatize back to the real world after the ruin of war. Nothing but them and the bush and sky. "You should tell your friend Gale about this spot. He'd probably love it, right? Maybe he can come and visit one day."

Max's sharp intake of breath made her glance over. The moonlight cast his handsome face into soft relief. A devastating frown drew his brows together, echoed by a sadness she felt in her gut. It came from him.

"That would be difficult," he said, shuffling his feet.

"Why's that?"

"He's dead."

The insects stopped chirping. The wind stopped blowing. Everything stopped for a heartbeat. And then a rushing sound filled her ears, beating in time with her rapidly increasing pulse. Gale. Dead.

"I'm sorry." She breathed on a gasp. "How?" But the instant the word came out of her mouth, she knew. This was it. The missing link —it explained so much. Gale was the one who'd gone missing. "Oh, Max." Her heart squeezed. "He was the one you went to rescue?"

He nodded, making a small choking sound.

"I'm so sorry," she said.

"I needed you, Sloan. I needed you, and you weren't there." Eyes full of hurt and accusation and longing locked with hers.

"I didn't know."

"You should have known, Sloan. You know everything."

"I—" she cut herself off. Normally, he was right. She made it her business to know everything about everyone. So why had she given up on him? Could she really blame it on her sin?

"Why didn't you look me up?" Accusation. Anger. Hurt.

"I stopped checking on you. I'm sorry. I should have tried harder."

He wiped his nose. "Yeah, you should have."

"I was afraid."

"Of what?"

"That what they were saying was true. That we are evil."

"You're the furthest thing from evil. I've stared real evil in the face, and it's human."

Another silence stretched, and when he didn't speak again, she shuffled closer to him on the log. "Tell me what happened. I know I can't make up for it, but I'm listening. I'm here now."

A long shuddering breath racked his body, and she realized he was crying. This big, strong man who'd once been the high point of her day, the laughter of her life, was sad. It pulsed out of him, drawing her down. He'd been sad for years and she hadn't been there for him. She reached out, but he didn't reciprocate. Her hand wavered in the air, then dropped back down to fist at her side.

The lump in her throat grew. "Max…"

"I quit. Like I said I would. Gale didn't want me to go, but I had you. I wanted more than the military. I wanted my own family, not to be the tag-along to his. The instant my plane had touched down here, I got the message. He'd been taken hostage by the enemy during a ceasefire. They claimed to have no knowledge of it, but we knew he was with them, so the army called me back. They wanted me to hunt him down. I'd done a few tours already in the area and knew the terrain better than anyone." He stopped, scrubbed his face and took a deep breath. "I dropped my package at your place, but most of you were out on a mission. She was the only one left in the building."

"Package?" Sloan prompted. He'd left something for her?

"Doesn't matter now. Point is, I was there. I left a message, then I left. When I arrived on site with the crew, we tracked Gale down. The bastards still didn't admit to having him there, but we knew he was being tortured in this old run-down building. The reason the army was investigating the cell in the first place was they'd heard they'd received a shipment of armor-piercing shells. They tasked me with scouting the area. We found five trunks. The four I could get to held normal rounds. Instead of checking that last trunk, I assumed the all clear and gave the go ahead to move in. Gale wasn't the only one who died that day. Because of my negligence, they mowed down half the squad."

Sloan's heart broke for him. This was why he was so obsessed with remaining diligent and vigilant.

"They broke the terms of the ceasefire. We should have been allowed to respond with force, but they wouldn't let me go after Gale.

The thing is… Gale and I had always promised we'd have each other's back. And I didn't."

"You did," Sloan insisted. "You went back for him."

"Yeah but it was too little too late." He took a deep breath. "Anyway, that's when I went after the bastards myself. Daymo and Tom-Tom followed me. We found pieces of Gale… After that, it was all a blur. I can't remember how many of them we killed. Got dishonorably discharged for it, but we got the bastards. We got justice for Gale."

This time, she reached across and placed her palm at the back of his neck. When he didn't complain, she let her thumb rub in soothing circles.

"You were the first person I called when I got back, Sloan," he said, turning to meet her eyes. "And your phone was disconnected." He shrugged out of her touch and stood up. The deep canyon forming between his brows grew darker than the night sky behind him. "Then when I looked you up online, I found pictures of you with another man. Do you have any idea how much that hurt?"

She swallowed. "I'm an idiot."

"Yeah. You are." Then he strode back to camp, leaving Sloan speechless.

twelve

MAX JOHNSON

MAX TRUDGED OVER ROCK, twigs and stone. He felt
like he'd been hiking his entire life. His head was ready to explode,
and his heart was shredded. Running on reserves, they'd all stopped
talking hours ago and proceeded to the black site with dogged determination. Arriving under the cover of night was imperative. His body
ached, yet he pushed through. Had to keep up the with pace set by
the three genetically enhanced beings in front of him.

While he walked, his thoughts meandered. What would it have
been like if the Lazarus brood were in the army with him, not only
training, but going on tour? If he'd had their help during the conflict
that took Gale's life... Wyatt was bulletproof. Griffin could stop
metal projectiles with his mind. And Sloan... she could instill fear
into the enemy, making them quake with doubt, seize in pain, or
break down in tears. He wanted to be bitter about it, but the more he
walked, the more his emotional baggage eased. They were where they
were meant to be—stopping the fanatical Syndicate from making
more genetically modified soldiers, and turning them evil and then
loose on the world. They didn't ask to be born the way they were.

They weren't given the choice to enlist, not like he had, like Gale had.

Tony's reticence earlier came to mind and confirmed what Max had wondered, not all of them were happy about their lot in life, but they persisted.

Blood and viscera from the fashion store animal attack flashed before his eyes. It took him unaware, and so sharply that his steps faulted. Forcing the images out, he placed them in a locked box in the back of his brain. Mumbling the words to the school yard version of *Waltzing Matilda*, he cleared his mind. It was a technique he'd been taught to help cope with the sometimes unsettling results of war. When you just had to keep going, the song gave him something else to focus on.

Sloan hiked up ahead, darting a glance back to him now and then. Awareness of her attention trickled down his spine and soon his thoughts derailed to her, and only her. He marked the change in her since they'd activated her mating bond. She'd become more energetic, more vibrant, more focused. No more hiding out in her room, but diving head first into the conflict. The way she'd protected the patrons of that store was heroic. She could have exposed her secret, but that's what he was there for. Reluctantly, he admitted they made a good team. Knowing this, he forced himself to explore his anger with her.

It was clear she knew nothing about Gale's untimely death. He'd been dark about that at first, but after a few hours of physical activity, the distrust drained away. All that was left was a connection that tugged at his chest, keeping him tethered to the woman walking in front of him. He didn't know what it meant. He didn't know if he could go back to who they used to be, but he knew it was a start.

"Stop moping, Sloan." Parker's grumble reached Max with a gust of warm wind.

"I'm not."

"Yeah, yeah, you are." Tony stopped, turned and put his hands on his hips. "I can't take it anymore. And there's no more booze, so, suck it up and let us get on with it."

"What's all this?" Max strode up.

Sloan bit the corner of her bottom lip.

It was Parker who answered. "Sloan needs to train." He turned to his younger sister. "Try putting up an emotional shield."

"And how do I do that?" She shifted her weight to the other leg.

"Meditate, or some shit," Tony snapped.

"Like you know what you're talking about. The only time you meditate is in front of a camera."

"Harsh, Sloan." Tugging his bag from his shoulder, he inspected the contents. "I can't deal with this. I need a drink."

"Christ's sake, Tony. It's only been a few hours since your last one." Parker frowned at his brother. "There's none left."

"It's cool." Tony zipped his bag back up, eyes darting around, wild eyed. "I'm good."

"No, you're not." Parker dabbed the man on the forehead. "You're burning up."

Tony had a peaky sheen of perspiration not present on Sloan or Parker. He looked ill... or like he was going through some kind of advanced withdrawal. With their physiology, who knew how long toxins took to get out of his system.

"Maybe I've got some uppers," Tony murmured, reopening his sack and tipping it upside down. Supplies and contents spilled everywhere. "I'm sure I put something in there."

Drugs?

Shit.

Max caught Sloan's worried stare.

"You don't have any, because I emptied your bag before we left." Parker folded his arms.

"What?" Tony gasped. "You had no right to do that."

"Excuse me?" Parker replied. "I'm the leader of this Godforsaken group. It's my responsibility to ensure you're not wired off your nuts while we're on a mission. So, yeah. It is my right."

"Well, now look at me. If I don't stop to puke on the way there, it will be your lucky day. I hope you're happy."

"I'll be happy when you're checked into rehab." Parker crouched and began packing Tony's belongings back into his bag. "I swear to God, I'm the only one out of you lot who has their shit together."

Tony laughed at this. "Are you for real? You can't take a dump unless it's on a gold-plated rim, bro. That you're so uptight about not being the first of us to find their mate is laughable."

The dark scowl Parker shot his brother could have stripped leaves from the shrubs surrounding them. "Fuck you, Tony. Pick up your own goddamned mess." Then Parker straightened, smoothed his shirt and strode off. Tony threw his hands in the air and jogged after his brooding brother. "Aw, come on, Parks. Don't be like that."

Tony's rucksack was left upended on the ground.

"Um," Max said. "Should I?" Yeah, he should. He dropped his sack and collected the man's belongings, shaking sand from each item.

On a sigh, Sloan did the same. "Sorry, Max."

He paused, hand in the bag. "It's fine. Things like this happen with intense situations. If you all haven't been working as a unit, it's even more likely to happen."

"I meant, I'm sorry about everything. The way we ended. All this crap. The goddamned state of the world. Gale." She covered his hand with hers. "This probably isn't what you imagined when you accepted the job, huh?"

"No. It wasn't." He resumed packing, gathering fallen bottles. But, then again, he'd only accepted the job because he wanted to see her again. "Jesus. There're six hip flasks in here. All empty."

"Yeah, Tony's got a habit. I shouldn't have baited him."

Gluttony.

Max frowned. "And this is what can be eased when he finds a mate?"

She nodded, standing up with the last of the items. "Except, where he's concerned, I'm not sure if the addictions will switch off, just like that."

She paused, opened her mouth to speak more, but shut it again, then scratched the back of her neck.

"What is it?" Max took the last items from her and closed Tony's pack. "Spit it out."

"I just want you to know, that you don't have to do anything you don't want. You don't have to accept this mating business."

The wind whipped around them for a few seconds while they stared at each other. Stars glittered in her eyes, and he was struck, once again with how attracted he was to her. Even after all this time, across years, oceans and cyberspace, she was better in real life and he found his lungs struggling to draw breath.

He didn't have to accept the mating bond, so what did he want?

Someone else to be mated to her?

Hell, no. Shocked at the vehement response, he blinked. The very thought of Sloan with someone else made him sick to the stomach.

He took a deep breath, tasted her scent in the air and closed his eyes to savor the sensation. Despite everything, he couldn't deny how she made him feel.

"Maybe I'm okay with it," he murmured, tension in his shoulders releasing.

Her lashes lifted. "Really?"

"I mean, I'm just saying, I'll help you if you need it. I won't leave you struggling like Tony. You need physical contact, right?"

"Yeah. Any touch between us resets my internal equilibrium. Constant contact keeps it that way."

"Well, we can work out a schedule or something."

She exhaled in a rush, shoulders drooping. "Oh. Okay. Thanks."

Maybe he wanted more than a schedule too, but he wasn't ready to deal with that just yet. He locked that emotion away in another box and hoisted Tony's pack on his other shoulder. He staggered with the extra weight. The bag had protective gear and more weapons inside.

"Here," she said, taking the bag. "We can hold it together."

The bag dangled between them as they continued to walk. He'd seen Gale walk like this with his wife, except instead of the bag was a toddler. Max felt a simultaneous longing—both for his friend, and for a family of his own. The crew at Nightingale Securities were his family... but he wanted more. He yearned for more. Maybe it was all just a pipe dream. If a good man like Gale couldn't have the dream, then a man who got dishonorably discharged sure as hell couldn't have it.

Not long now.

After a while, he noticed the unsettled feeling in him remained. When he looked at Sloan, he could make out the line between her brows. Parker and Tony were right; Without her blocking out her feelings, the mission could be compromised.

"I think I have a way for you to select which emotions you project," he said.

She stopped, pulling him back by the rucksack between them. "You do?"

"Don't look so surprised."

"I'm not. I just didn't think you'd know much about this stuff."

He shrugged. "I was taught how to compartmentalize my emotions."

"Compartmentalize."

"Yeah." He tugged her onwards. "You visualize your emotions and painful memories, and then store them in a box. File them away for later use. It's not recommended to use this system for your whole life otherwise you'll end up an unfeeling robot, but for this situation, I think it can help."

"Okay. I'm listening."

"So… think of a box."

"Any box?"

"Make each box different and relevant to the emotion or sensation you're storing."

"Any color?"

"Whatever is easier to associate that feeling with, Sloan."

"Got it."

"Now, every time you feel an emotion you want to store for later use, put it in the box. Keep your process the same, envision yourself closing up the box, and keeping it contained. Then distance yourself and put a routine in place that will help cleanse your mind."

"What kind of routine?"

"It will have to be something you can do anywhere and do it quickly. Like, hum a song to yourself, or recite some words."

She gasped, face lighting up. "Like a magic spell."

He huffed a laugh. "Yeah, okay, like that."

"Hmm. I'm going to use one from the Elder Scrolls."

"I haven't played that game yet."

"You haven't? That's a travesty we must fix."

They continued walking together while Sloan worked on her process. He spouted random Latin words and, after a while, Max forgot about her efforts, but then a spear of lust shot through him and he stumbled, dropping his hold on Tony's pack. His heart rate sky-rocketed, and prickling heat engulfed him. What the hell?

"Sorry," Sloan murmured. "Guess it worked."

The erotic surge in his body dampened. Barely.

"It was the strongest feeling I could recall on the spot." She bit her lip. "All good now?"

"Yeah. Right." He plucked his sweaty shirt, forcing his ragged breath to ease.

"Stop doing that." Heavy-lidded eyes watched him avidly, and a trickle of heat zinged through him again.

"Bugger." He tugged at his pants, adjusting. He was hard. Just like that. "You just gave me a hit of Viagra, Sloan."

"My bad." But the smile on her face couldn't be contained.

Movement from up ahead drew their attention. The shadowed forms of Parker and Tony waved back at them.

"Do they want us?"

"Shh." Sloan waved him down, alertness replacing her mood. "I hear something."

A low, buzz came from overhead.

"Drone," Sloan spat. "Take cover."

They dropped to the ground, rolling near a tree. Max became like the dead, but Sloan ruffled around in her bag, cursing.

"I should have had this out instead of carrying Tony's damn pack." She pulled out a small black box and explained, "This is a signal jammer."

She flicked a switch on the box, and they waited. A few heartbeats later, and the sound of the drone cut off, followed by a crashing sound as the machine collided with nature.

Sloan scrambled up. "We need to hurry. They'll come and investigate soon."

When Max attempted to collect Tony's pack, she stopped him. "Leave it. It's his own fault if he misses it."

Then she took off, full pelt toward her brothers. Max cast a latent look at the pack. He could leave it. But that wasn't his style. *Never assume.* He hoisted it on his back, braced and adjusted his weight, then followed the direction Sloan took. Heavy boots thudded and crunched across the uneven ground. Catching up, panting heavily, he slipped off the pack and shoved it at Tony. The man took it on instinct. Even under the soft light of the stars, he could see the green tinge to Tony's complexion. That wasn't good.

"We're close," Sloan was saying, pointing North-East. "Somewhere just over there."

Max followed her direction, squinting at the shadows. He couldn't see a thing.

"Yeah, I got it," Parker noted. "Military compound. Fenced. Guarded."

Damn. How could he see from there? Max squinted again, wondering if now was the time to pull out his night vision goggles. He did, slipping them onto his head and tugging them down. Parker was right. A few hundred meters away sat the start of the compound. After the break in the trees, there was a fenced compound with a few buildings, but behind the buildings, dug into the mountain side was another big tunnel. The site could be enormous behind that, going deep underground.

Damn. Who were these Syndicate people?

It was a lot of ground to cover for a quick recon mission.

"Right. Where to first?" he asked.

"Max, you head with Sloan," Parker replied. "I'll go with Tony. Put your jackets on. Activate your mics and ear-comms."

"Affirmative." He did as told and caught Sloan doing the same. She'd retrieved her night goggles, too, but instead of a camera, held her rugged terrain iPad.

Parker pulled out four black balaclavas and threw one to each of the crew. They each donned a jacket made of some custom thin material from Parker's company. Stronger than Kevlar vests, but light and easy to wear. It took Max a moment, but then he realized the jackets were like their Deadly Seven combat uniform, but without the distinguishable D7 logo.

That knowledge gave him a sense of pride. They trusted him, completely.

Amused, Parker watched Max adjust the fitting on the jacket, and then he explained: "At first glance, this disguise could belong on any mercenary group. If they catch us on camera, we don't want their first conclusion to be the Deadly Seven."

If all went well, they'd see no action. This was a quiet, secret intelligence-gathering mission. But with these guys, Max was fast learning to expect the unexpected.

As he checked the rounds in his Glock, he wished for his crew. They worked well together, like another limb of the same body. He knew they'd have his back, and he would have theirs. But the less they knew about this side of the Lazaruses, the safer it was for them.

After dumping their rucksacks near a bush, the four of them trotted closer to the site. Adrenaline pumped in Max's veins and gave him a second wind.

Outside the mountain, there were five to ten warehouses, a few residential houses, and one admin type building.

"That's the one you want, Sloan," Parker said. "The admin."

"Got it."

"We'll take the rest. Ready, Tony?"

Tony rolled his balaclava down and lifted his hood. "Let's go sightseeing."

They paired off, and soon it was just Max and Sloan in the darkness. She had her device out, fingers tapping away as they approached the buildings.

"Almost done," she murmured as they came to a halt near a chain-link fence.

"What are you doing?" he asked.

"I just updated the code that recognized Barry's face and prints to recognize any of ours instead."

Max checked the guards standing at the closest door, a soft light flickering overhead from the eaves. The building was a large warehouse. The kind that usually housed weapons, or vehicles. Two men, military uniform, assault rifles. Whatever was in there needed to be protected.

Something Sloan said about Barry's biometrics tripped an alarm in his head. "All of us connected to the same ID? Isn't that dangerous?"

"Not if I get access to their mainframe as planned. I can erase our existence when we're home. Alright. Finished." She packed her iPad away. "I've also tapped the feed to the remaining drone in the sky. Doesn't look like they've noticed the other one we took down. They're either short staffed, or security is lax."

"*Good.*" Parker's voice rumbled over the comms. "*Keep that drone away from us. Rendezvous in thirty, back at the rucksack drop. Stay frosty.*"

Parker went quiet, and Max knew he and Tony were using Barry's fake credentials to access any areas they could. Max and Sloan slipped through a hole they created in the fence and trotted toward the admin building. No lights were on. No guards. Keeping to the shadows, they slipped up to the nearest door. An electronic keypad with biometric scanner locked the door tight.

Sloan held her palm to the scanner. They waited, breath hostage in their throats as the blue light scanned down her palm, then back up again. The light switched to her face. A green light on the proximity reader triggered. The distinct sound of the lock chambers releasing, snickered and clicked.

"Suckers," Sloan whispered.

In they went. After canvasing the interior, checking for late night workers, Max took up a position near the windowed door, and kept an eye out. There may be no one burning the midnight oil in the office, but out there, something was going on at the warehouse.

While he kept watch, Sloan darted around behind him, no doubt finding a computer to install her backdoor program. Once done, theoretically, they'd have access to the entire network of Syndicate secrets.

A few minutes later, Max was getting antsy. He checked over his shoulder to source Sloan's balaclava covered face and caught her bent over the glow of a screen, a look of pure concentration in her eyes.

A sound outside drew his attention, and he ducked further into the shadows, gun ready. Through the window he spotted a dark silhouette moving toward the warehouse. The closer the figure got to the door, the more light cast on his face. He cursed under his breath.

Sloan hissed, "What?"

"It's Barry." Max's grip on his weapon tightened. "We didn't expect him to be working so late. Will an alarm go off saying his credentials are being used twice?"

"I won't know until I've finished hacking their system and I'll need time to search…" She paused, staring in the direction Barry had gone. He was out of sight, but she probably felt his sin-signature. Max could virtually hear the thoughts ticking over in her head.

"Sloan," he urged, voice low. "Forget him. We get the job done. We get out."

"I can take care of the guards." She shifted from foot to foot, antsy. "I can get to Barry."

"Finish here."

She dipped her head and unplugged her device from the main computer before turning it off and jogged up to him. "Done."

"Alright." He gave a furtive look outside. "All clear. Let's get back to the rendezvous."

Opening the door, he stepped out cautiously. Before he could stop her, Sloan was gone, rushing quietly down the dirt path toward the warehouse. He froze, watching the distance grow between them. Alarm pricked his senses. Chase her. Stay? His finger hovered over the microphone, ready to alert Parker, but he eased off at the last minute. *Trust her.*

The closer Sloan got to the guards, the more their heads drooped until both slumped to the ground.

His heart leaped into his throat. She did it. Whatever *it* was.

Max trotted over, gun still held at the ready, checking his six. "What did you do?"

She turned toward him with humor in her eyes. "If there's one feeling I know well, it's sleep."

"What now?"

"Now we find Barry and the reason his sloth is off the charts."

thirteen

BARRY PINKERTON

RUBBING the sleep from his eyes, Barry Pinkerton continued down the elevator in the underground. In his opinion, it was unconscionable to get up so early in the morning, but when the lady of the house called, he answered. He had to. It wasn't only his life on the line if he failed to respond.

The terrible clunking metal grate elevator zoomed down levels, giving him a brief glance at each floor. So brief, that if he blinked, he'd have missed it. Weapons, biological experiments, soldiers, tanks. The lower he went, the louder the sound of feral animals. Growls, snarls, barks. It all grew to cacophony proportions until the elevator jerked to a halt. Usually this was the point he put earplugs in, but this time he couldn't. She waited for him. He yanked the grate door open and stepped out into the cold concrete hallway with nothing but flickering lights as his companions until he reached the lab shared with a botany geneticist.

When he entered, he found Despair staring at a wall of cages. Not the wall he expected. On one side of his overflowing lab, warped animals ran circles, chasing their tales in their small homes. On the other side, the cages held a range of flora. Relentless tendrils and leaves of all shapes and sizes spilled from any gap they could find, trying in vain to reach the heat of the hydroponic lights outside. If he didn't know any better, he'd feel calmed by the green beauty.

Dressed in a simple white tailored suit, Despair had her hands behind her back as she watched the plants with an impassive expression.

What's going on in her mind?

To find an answer, he studied her as she studied the plants. He couldn't see her face, but from the drop of her shoulders, and the tilt of her head, he believed she was intrigued with the plants. She almost appeared relaxed. Calm. Even happy.

But what did he know? The woman confounded him. And after he'd met her sister, who in all efforts appeared to be not only managing her sin, but thriving, he was even more confused. Maybe, deep down inside, she was redeemable. Maybe she could help him stop all this nonsense.

Movement near the plants snapped his attention there. A tendril unfurled its vine, coming for her. She reached out to meet it, finger to tendril. Horror formed in his mind as he watched the event unfold. She should know better.

Heart leaping into his throat, he searched for a weapon. Anything. On the lab table that separated the two sides, instruments, tools and equipment were scattered everywhere. Scalpel? Knife? Hammer?

He darted across the room, collecting a blowtorch as he ran. He aimed it at the plant, ready to release the fire, but as he approached, as the vine wrapped its deadly arm around her finger, Despair was on him in an instant. Her free hand snapped around his wrist, angling until he cried out and dropped the blowtorch.

"It's poisoned!" he shouted. "It will kill you."

Despair's violet eyes flicked down to her wrapped finger. "No, Mr. Pinkerton. It won't kill me, but you would have killed it, an innocent creature that had no say in its creation."

When she unwrapped the green length from her finger, a red puckered shadow remained. Sickness churned in Barry's gut. If she fell ill…

"You'll get sick," he said. "Is that what you want?"

"I want for nothing."

"I don't believe it. You shouldn't be without hope. Without—" he bit his words off before he betrayed his true desires.

Staring vacantly at the plant, now easing its vine back into the safety of the cage, Despair murmured: "My life is a perfect graveyard of buried hopes."

He gulped. Did she want to die? Did she feel anything at all? But then something about her unsettling words plucked at his memory. He'd heard them before. In a movie, a book… then it hit him. *Anne of Green Gables*. His daughter had an obsession with the red-headed heroine, and she had forced him to watch and read the series many times over. If Despair knew that line, then she too had read the books. Perhaps hope wasn't lost on her. He opened his mouth to plead, but she turned to him, hardness once again in her eyes.

"Where do you think I learned that quote, Mr. Pinkerton?"

"From the books."

"No. From your daughter's books."

Coldness grew from the pit in his stomach and they stared at each other while her intention soaked in.

"You bitch."

"I don't care what you call me."

"You care about nothing at all."

One of her shoulders lifted in a shrug.

"You could have been different," Barry snapped. "You could have been very different."

"But I'm not. And you have a job to do." She hurried to the animal cages. "After the success of our experiment, we have received the all clear to pervade the city. Julius wants you to double production. He wants that city to be the first to fall."

He frowned. Success? That animal had torn through the streets of Cardinal City with no purpose. To Barry, he couldn't make sense of the targeting. The animal was meant to be attracted to the sin of greed, but it had gone wild in the end.

"You hesitate."

He shook his head. Releasing so many into the city—no one would be safe. He didn't want to do it, but he knew not how to stop it. Not without putting his daughter's life in jeopardy.

"You have your instructions." Despair straightened and headed for the exit. "I expect you to comply."

"Don't you have a heart?" he asked.

"My heart died in a burning building over two decades ago." Then she left, lab door closing on soft hinges as her footsteps faded down the hall.

SLOAN LAZARUS

"HELP ME DRAG them out of the way." Sloan slipped her hands under the arms of a sleeping guard.

Half expecting Max to argue, it surprised her when he crouched low and asked, "Are you sure about this?"

When she gave a short, serious nod, he returned with his own. "Then I think we need to remove their uniforms and use them. Put them over our own. Take the balaclavas off and try to blend in. Looks like this base goes underground. Who knows how long we'll be down there."

"Good idea." She tugged her guard around the side of the building, stopping in a pitch black shadow and began removing his shirt.

Max did the same, and soon, both had put the military uniform over their existing clothes. They removed their balaclavas, hid their Deadly jacket hoods under their new jackets and donned the army hats. She tucked her hair underneath. They were roasting, but it was temporary. Sloan had to leave her crossbow and quiver hidden, but retrieved a rifle and slung it over her shoulder.

If you looked closely, you'd see the lumpy undergarments, but

Sloan wasn't willing to risk this extra mission without her bulletproof armor.

With Max at her back, Sloan traveled through the base door, stopping just inside. She closed her eyes and focused on the sin. Her stomach rolled, and when she concentrated, she noticed multiple points triggered the feeling. Sloth blinked into existence beneath her, a hundred fold. She almost lost her breath and ran back to safety, all the way back to her apartment.

"What is it?" Max whispered.

"There are a lot of signatures beneath us."

"And Barry?"

Sloan frowned. Like a beacon, his deadly sin tugged at her, pulling her from the core. An instinctual reaction sparked with purpose. *End the sin. Destroy the sinner.* But Mary had spent her life ensuring the Lazarus children didn't react instinctually, that they assessed the danger, and approached the sin with a level head.

She didn't have to destroy the person to destroy the sin. She could help him.

"He's down a few levels."

Max shifted, ready to move, but she stopped him with a hand to his shoulder. "There are many sinners down there, but I can only sense sloth."

"Meaning... there could be more?"

She nodded. "If Pride and Gluttony were here, we'd have a good understanding of what we're up against, but..." They would never let her move ahead with her plan.

Conflicted thoughts traveled behind Max's eyes. "We should alert Pride. I'm not saying change your plans, just be thorough. Tell him."

Taking a deep breath, Sloan gave a quick update of her position through her internal communication system. A few curse words came back, but Max was right, it was important to let Parker know what she intended. If shit went sideways, he could get out with Tony.

Finding an elevator with a metal grate door, they traveled deeper underground, passing floors with little time to investigate, catching glimpses of wide open spaces, weapons, aircraft, and more. Nerves tickled her neck. This operation was massive. It was breaking protocol to get to Barry, but a strong sense of duty had settled within. She had to do this.

She could do this.

Get Barry out without alerting the Syndicate. Save him from committing whatever sin he was about to. Wasn't that her reason for living?

They followed the sense of Barry's sloth until she exited at a dark level with dull flickering halogen lights above. Animal sounds came from further down and she knew they'd found the right place.

"He's down there." She pointed at the shadowed hallway.

"Let's go." Max adjusted his rifle, tugged his hat down to shield his eyes and with brisk efficiency, they continued.

As they got within a few feet of the noisiest door, it opened. A glimpse of white hair was all Sloan needed to duck her head, hiding her face. Despair, or Daisy as they'd renamed her. Sloan's sister. Heart leaping into her throat, Sloan froze.

"Act like you're on patrol," Max hissed, urging her onward. "Head down."

They adjusted their pace and kept walking.

Half expecting to be stopped, Sloan exhaled when Daisy walked by and disappeared into the elevator behind them. The moment the elevator left, Sloan lifted her cap and caught Max's eyes.

"Maybe we should back out now while we can," she said.

Brown eyes bored into her. "You still sense the deadly sin?"

She nodded, nerves tightening her throat.

"And we're talking deadly. Like massive scale."

Once again, she nodded. Something was coming. Dark, ominous and crouching, waiting to pounce. It was all tied to Barry.

Max's jaw clenched. "Then we follow through. We do what you came here to do. Be thorough. Believe in your instincts, Sloan. You will save lives."

Warmth encircled her chest and spread outward. Sloan looked at her mate, a sense of elation lifting her spirits. He had her back. After everything that had passed between them, in this moment, a moment that counted, he was on her side. He had faith in her in a way she'd never returned.

Keeping his alert gaze on the corridor, he didn't notice how she watched him. He had no clue about the intense emotion building inside her, bursting to get out. She couldn't put words to it. She only knew she was grateful, and so much more. It was too much for her to contain and slipped out of its box to reach for him, tendrils eager and full of longing.

Shocked brown eyes snapped back to hers. Heat flared. They held each other's gaze until she reined in her emotion and locked it up tight. Shoving all that need and want back in its box, she turned to the door Daisy had come out of. In there was Barry, and so much more.

"Let's do this." Shifting her rifle to one side, she opened the door.

Having Parker snap in her ear comms—telling her to hurry, didn't help.

I know he's down here. I know I can help.

Entering the loud room, Sloan's senses were overwhelmed, but Max entered behind her, all swift and brutal action. Animal sounds. Screeches. Roars. Barks. Growls. And the smell. A wave of nausea rolled over her from the blend of manure, hay, and urine. She gagged.

On one side of the poorly ventilated lab, animal cages lined the wall. But on the other side, reaching across the lab table filled with scattered instruments and documents, a wall of plants stretched the length of the forty foot long room. And the odd thing was, those plants were in cages too.

Max continued along the edge of the lab table, half in a crouch, gun trained and sighted. The pull of sloth tugged to the right, and lifting her own rifle, careful not to breathe too deeply, Sloan edged forward.

All these poor animals.

None of them resembled what they were born as, if they were born at all. For all Sloan knew, they could have been created in a petri dish and grown in a tank, just like the human replicate clones had been. A monkey-like beast with bulging eyes and fangs reached for her through a gap in the cage. Darting to the left, she narrowly escaped its claws. With her new skill, she sensed an insatiable need to attack, to survive.

"He's down there," she murmured, indicating to the end of the room where bags of food, hay, and other animal supplies were stacked against the concrete wall.

As she drew closer to the crouching form of Barry, dread deepened until it filled her chest with weight. He was busy with an animal and hadn't noticed them over the din. The animal was laying down, as though sedated.

Once sure they were alone, Sloan lowered her gun. She lifted her cap so her face was visible, and when Barry raised his head, he did a double take.

"What are you doing here?" he hissed, hand frozen on an open cage, the other mid air, paused with a syringe in his grip. "If they catch you, you're dead."

"I won't let you do it." Let him think she knew what his deadly plan was. Sometimes, bluffing was the only way to proceed.

He exhaled, slamming his cage shut. "There's nothing I can do to stop them."

Barry got up and straightened his white lab coat. His eyes went cold and he avoided Sloan's gaze as he strode beyond her, back to the table at the center of the room.

"Don't ignore this, Barry." Sloan strode after him. "Do you really want to be responsible for the death of so many innocents?"

He shook his head. "No. Only the sinners will go."

"You don't believe that," she said. "Otherwise I wouldn't feel deadly sin within you, Barry."

"I don't know what you're talking about."

"Sure you do. It's that niggling feeling you've been having. The one that's getting louder and louder, the closer you get to the end of your project. The one that's telling you to do the right thing. The one you keep ignoring."

Barry gathered a stack of papers and straightened them. His jaw clenched. He considered Sloan's words. Perhaps she could push him, nudge him with another emotion... but she knew not which. Fear might push him in the opposite direction. Trust... maybe, but she was still untrained with that. And she might open the wrong box. She needed more training.

"What's the plan, Barry?" Max asked, lifting his rifle back up.

Barry lifted his gaze. "It doesn't matter if you kill me. They'll go ahead with it. They don't need me."

"So why stay?"

"They have my daughter."

None of them spoke. Only the screeching, angry sounds of beasts clambered around them.

"Your daughter," Sloan repeated. "Where?"

"Does it matter?"

"Heck, yeah it matters. Barry, I want to help you. Let us help you."

"She's in town. At boarding school."

The town was on the other side of the mountain.

"We'll get to her before they know," she promised. "Come with us Barry. We can get you out without them knowing. There will be enough time to save her. We can set you both up with another identity."

Barry didn't answer.

Max shifted next to her. "They don't know we're here. Tell us the plan. At the very least, we can be prepared."

"The animals." Barry waved at the cages, avoiding their gazes. "They will be let loose in confined public spaces."

"Do you know which spaces?"

Barry shook his head. "Cardinal City. I don't know more. I'm sorry."

Sloan caught Max's hard stare. "We have to stop them here."

"Do that and your cover is blown. They'll know you've been here."

She bit her lip. "We have to do something."

"Let the animals loose," Barry offered. "Open the cages and the doors. Let them loose on the base and with no way of controlling them, the soldiers will have to put them down."

"It would create a distraction for us to get out unnoticed with Barry," Max noted.

"And it will buy us time to collect Barry's daughter. Good enough for me." Sloan activated her mic and spoke to her brother: "Pride. We're coming out with Pinkerton. Be ready in five."

When she met Barry's jittery gaze, she already noted his sin lessening. She smiled. "It's going to be fine, Barry. Stick with us."

fifteen

MAX JOHNSON

WITH LUNGS HEAVING and thighs pumping, Max ran through the underground base, refusing to look back. Minutes ago, they'd left the animal cages open. The distraction would only work if the animals breeched the lab. Hopefully, the outbreak would be contained to that level, attracting confusion and commotion, leaving them the freedom to escape with Barry unnoticed.

It wasn't until they reached the ground level that shit went sideways.

The guards Sloan had put to sleep were awake and standing before the exit door outside, barking orders into walkie-talkies. One of them held Sloan's crossbow and was attempting to draw back the rope to nock by hand. The action was difficult for any man without a rope-cocking device, and probably why Sloan liked using the weapon —she could do it effortlessly. Both guards, dressed in only their undergarments, turned their way. Expressions turned staunch, eyes widened in betrayal and then narrowed with intent. It all took a split second to comprehend, but long enough for Max to register the threat, lift his rifle, point and shoot.

Sloan took out the second guard.

The gunshots rang through the compound, echoing against the mountain next to the base.

Max forced his kill-reaction deep down in a box and used the adrenaline thrumming through his blood to grab onto the petrified Barry. He launched in the direction of the chain-link fence. Getting out with the man was his top priority.

He thought Sloan was right behind him, thought she was safe, but when a female screamed, his steps faltered. He turned back, heart leaping into his throat. Locked in hand-to-hand combat, Sloan clashed with her sister. In the poorly lit courtyard of dirt, he caught glimpses of white hair flashing along with the glint of metal. *Knife.*

Scanning the ground, Max zoned in on Sloan's firearm, close to where she fought. Oddly, she wasn't going for her crossbow only feet from her, and she wasn't using her power. He lifted his rifle, aimed, but couldn't get a clear shot. First things first. Turning to Barry, he pulled back the torn chain-link, allowing a gap for him to fit through.

"Go," he burst out and pointed. "Keep running due west. There are two more waiting for you, half a click that way."

Barry crouched and ducked through, then took off full pelt. The older man wasn't as fast as he should be. He needed a head start.

Steeling himself, Max raised his rifle and advanced on the women in battle, holding his aim, looking for an opening.

"Don't shoot!" Sloan shouted as she ducked, swung and kicked her sister's legs out.

Despair adjusted her footing, recovered, and stabbed at Sloan, sewing machine style. Panic gripped his heart. Sloan's stab-proof jacket took the force, stopping the knife from piercing deep, but the peppered holes in her guard's uniform proved how close she'd come.

This was the first time Max had seen Sloan's sister in action. Equally matched, the two were the same height. Despair was thinner,

Sloan curvier. Where empathy and longing poured from Sloan's determined gaze, Despair's held only cold hard calculation. The macabre dance became a symphony of violence as battle sounds grew. Bursts of breath, strikes, sharp feminine shouts, elbows crunching against bone. Max's breath caught. Fuck this. He steadied his aim and stepped forward, ready to decimate Sloan's attacker.

"Don't shoot!" Sloan gasped again, dodging the blade slashing across her hand, drawing blood.

"Use your gift," he demanded. "I'm not risking you, Sloan. Use it now."

Emotion flared in Sloan's eyes. She didn't want to hurt her sister, but she had to do something. In a maneuver Max never saw coming, Sloan used her body to circle around her sister, put her in a chokehold and drop to the ground, wrestling style. Despair's violet eyes flashed with fury, her face went red, her knife fell as she tried to release herself, and then she slumped, unconscious.

Easing her down, and heaving great lungfuls of air, Sloan's manic eyes met Max's. "My power didn't work on her."

He only let the panic engulf him for a moment before the alarm sounded. A great, whooping wail that almost shattered their eardrums.

"Let's go." He waved her forward.

She hesitated. "Should we take her?"

"No time."

Sloan retrieved her crossbow and quiver, and then together they dashed back to the hole in the fence, scampering through only seconds before guards shouted over the din of the siren. They ran until they hit their rendezvous point.

Under the cover of darkness, they retrieved their rucksacks from Parker's open arms and slung them on. Sloan ripped off the guard's outer shirt, leaving her Deadly Seven jacket free, and she synced her weapon to her back. The bow stuck there like it was glued. The hip-quiver, she attached to her pants.

Still looking green, Tony moved into the darkness, back the way they'd hiked. When the sound of a lone animal howling cut through the night, all five of them froze.

"What the fuck was that?" Tony murmured.

"The beasts," Barry gasped. "They're coming."

Max turned back toward the black site. "They won't get through the fence."

"They'll get through anything, even the small hole we went through. They'll climb if they have to," Barry said.

"How did they get up the elevator?" Parker asked.

"Daisy," Sloan swore. "Must have been her."

"You put her out," Max pointed out.

"We don't stay down for long," Parker replied and then stepped toward Barry. "Tell me what I need to know about these animals."

"Um. Oh God. Um. Okay. They're like you. They sense sin. Except, we have dulled their sense of self preservation."

"Which sin?" Sloan asked.

"All of them."

"Fuck!" Tony snapped.

"It's fine. It's fine. We can manage this." Sloan's gaze locked on the area they'd come, listening for warning signs the beasts were getting close.

Barry whimpered and, hell, seeing a grown man cry like that, petrified, was enough to unsettle any soldier.

"My daughter," Barry said. "I can't leave her. I'll go back."

Parker caught him by the shoulder, halting him. "You'll do no such thing."

"I have to save her! They'll kill her. Worse. They'll turn her into one of them."

"They still don't know we took you. We have time." Taking charge, Parker shoved Barry toward Tony, who took hold of him lest he run. "This is the plan: Sloan, Max—you head over the mountain toward Barry's daughter. You draw the beasts to you, buy us time to get Barry out. We'll take Barry back the way we came. Do whatever you can, Sloan. Use your gift to amplify sin. Lure the animals, then execute them. You think you can handle that?"

His snarky tone was not lost on Max and it ground on his patience.

Sloan scowled, but released her crossbow from her back, nocked a bolt and nodded. "Yeah, I got it."

"Once you're safe, continue on to find Barry's daughter. I'll have a car and supplies waiting for you when you arrive over the mountain. Check in when you get in range. We have to double back, and I dare say, you'll arrive before reinforcements—if we can get any. Go."

Without waiting another minute, Max and Sloan took off, racing through the darkness, circling back around the base and heading up into the mountain. The distant wail of an animal on the hunt followed them. He did his best to think sinful thoughts, wrath, envy, greed, whatever he could conjure.

"I have no fucking idea if I'm doing this sin thing right," he huffed as they dodged some trees, already half a mile up the mountain.

The only way to Barry's daughter was over and then hiking through the wilderness on the other side. His lungs were burning. His limbs were heavy and turning to jelly.

"Just keep watch," Sloan huffed. "I'll take care of the sin."

"Got it." He opened his hearing and strained for the sound of pursuit as he jogged, rucksack bouncing on his back.

Max pushed his body to the limit.

And then he heard it.

The panting, thudding, crashing of a creature, hot on their tails.

"I hear them," he barked. "On our six."

"Don't shoot yet. Get further away."

Shit.

They jogged up hill until a few minutes in, more animals crashed —pounding paws, wet snarls and intake of breath—possibly the entire caged population.

A ghostly howl followed the answering whooping screech of a monkey.

He jumped over a fallen log and almost tripped in the dark. The smell of pine wafted as their boots broke needles underfoot. The stars and moon only cast light on so much, but his adrenaline-fueled body and mind gave him what he needed. Readying his rifle, he mentally cataloged escape routes. Bush everywhere. Plants. Trees. Cliff.

Kill-zone.

"Cliff," he gasped. "We get stuck here, we're done."

Too late. They hit the rocky wall, turned their backs and aimed into the darkness. His heart pumped loudly in his ears and he tried to calm his steady breath. He strained his hearing to gauge impact.

"You ready?" Sloan breathed, aiming her bow.

He answered by lifting his rifle.

Impact.

Demon beasts breeched the darkness between the trees. At first, Max thought they got lucky and only a few animals approached, but the sounds of paws thundering through the bush kept coming. Yellow eyes glinted in the darkness. More were there... hunting them. He counted four more sets of eyes. The few that breached didn't stop. They didn't circle. They pounced.

Holding her bow but not shooting, Sloan gave a war cry. The three animals already mid air writhed and dropped in clear agony. Max fired at them. Sloan must have used her power, but it wasn't enough. With stubborn determination, the fallen animals struggled to re-correct.

Then Max's blood turned to ice. More animals arrived. One, two, four... he lost count.

Sloan released the string on her bow, bolt flying into the new beasts. She re-nocked, bolted, and sighted, firing again.

Max adjusted his aim. *Fired*. Shot after shot, they defended, but like the animal they'd faced in the city, these kept coming. Unfazed by flying projectiles, they were relentless. Soon, Max had run out of bullets and Sloan had depleted her quiver. All beasts were down but struggling to rise. He threw the rifle down, stripped his knife from his ankle holster and entered an attack stance.

"Put them to sleep instead," he barked.

"What do you think I've been trying to do? I can't focus. I'm too wired. Unpacking the boxes isn't working."

Out of nowhere, another black heavy shadow landed heavily on him. Max fell back, barely holding the beast's snapping fangs from his face. Something warm and wet rushed down his hand. Blood. From the animal's bowels. He'd stabbed it. The beast kept fighting. Teeth gnashing, claws scratching, all of it continued until, weakened by blood loss, it fell on top of him.

When he pushed it off, he found Sloan locked in battle with another. How many were there? More sounds crashing through the trees. *Jesus Christ*. More were coming! Hopelessness choked him. How did Parker think they'd be able to handle this many monsters?

He shoved his knife into the animal atop Sloan. Released. Black blood spurted. He turned for the next. "Come on!" he shouted. "Come get me!"

Soon, the clearing held a new shape. Pile after pile of black bodies mounted around them. The stench of fresh carcass swamped him until his body was covered in gore. Instinct rode his actions until

Sloan's voice pierced his battle haze. Dispatching the final beast, he found her at the rocky cliff.

"Climb." Sloan panted and pointed up. "There's a ledge up there."

Following her gaze, he noticed the flat space she indicated about thirty feet away. Too hard to tell if the ledge would fit them both, but it might. More beasts were coming. Good enough. Height gave them an advantage.

Sloan heaved in a breath, locked her fingers together and created a step for him.

"No," he said. "You first, Sloan. I'll boost you."

"Don't be a dick. I can leap higher. I'm stronger."

He bit back his pride—too late. A terrible howl came from somewhere nearby as it sensed his pride and he knew they weren't done.

"Hurry, Max!"

Damn it. She was right. He'd seen her strength first hand; his nose was still sore.

"Fine." He released his rucksack from his shoulders and swung it up with an almighty swing. The pack sailed through the air, and just landed on the ledge with a thump. He placed one boot into her hands.

"One. Two. *Three*." Sloan heaved. He launched, hands latching onto rocky protrusions. The top was still six feet away. Using the last of his reserves, he hauled his body heavenward, fingers scraping painfully, boots scrambling for purchase. But he made it. He climbed and breeched the ledge, rolled onto it, panting and heaving with breath.

Swiftly turning, he rolled to his stomach and reached down.

Sloan leaped toward him and landed a good three feet away, clutching outcrops with white-knuckled hands.

He froze, holding his breath.

A tsunami of animals breeched the forest and flowed into the clearing beneath her. Like a crashing wave, they hit the cliff wall, and soared upward, coming for Sloan.

"Hurry!" he bellowed.

She was too far for him to reach. Snarls, rips, snaps as the animals clawed up the rocky wall, caught her legs and tried to pull her down. Her face tilted toward him, eyes flashing desperately under the stars.

"I can't—" she burst. "Too many of them."

He had no rifle, only his knife. No, that was wrong. He had his Glock in his rucksack.

"Hold on, Sloan." He raced to his pack, ripped it open. Relief had never felt so sweet as his fingers locked around the cold grip.

Her scream curdled the air. He slid back to the ledge, arm dangling down. More relief as he registered she hadn't fallen, but in the torrid swarm of black beneath her, one animal had locked jaws around her ankle and tugged. Terrified, she'd slid down a few feet, enough distance to let other animals jump on her, latching onto her pack. They weighed her down. She wouldn't last.

Max fired.

One beast fell off. Not enough.

"Get rid of the pack, Sloan!" he shouted.

Her panic-stricken face turned up to him, her body jostling as it was tugged from behind. Her grip slipped. Then Max felt a wave of calm, of warm love, of horrifying concession.

It came from her... why?

"I'm so sorry, Max," she said, face twisted in sorrow. "Find Barry's daughter."

Then she let go of one hand, put two fingers to her lips and held them toward him. In slow motion, it came to him... This was their on-screen goodbye kiss.

She'd given up.

sixteen

SLOAN LAZARUS

MAX'S anguished face was the last thing Sloan saw as she released the rocky wall and let the animals tear her down. Jaws locked onto her rucksack, ripping and snarling. She shut her eyes and let the free fall enshroud her. The snapshot of his face stayed with her. At least this way, he'd be released from the pressure of the mating bond. At least this way, he could go forward and save Barry's daughter.

With a bone-jarring thud, she landed on her back. The wind knocked out of her, but the pack broke her fall.

"NO!" A roar of male fury thundered through the night as animals converged on her.

She lifted her arms, blocking her face with only one thought: *Max.*

One word. One name. One pain.

Her mind stuck on the echo of his roar, of his denial. He didn't want her gone, any more than she wanted to leave. Max wanted her to stay. She had to fight. *Keep fighting, Sloan.* The thought sent a surge of defiance through her. She kicked, twisted, reached for her ankle knife, missed. It wasn't enough. She tried to throw boxes of emotion at the animals, pain, sleep, sorrow—anything. But her mind was a mess, in shattered pieces. She could only focus on the sensations in her body, and right now, they were in chaos.

Shot after shot cracked loudly as Max tried to execute her attackers. Whelps, whines and hard breaths exploded as the monstrous beasts bit, clawed, and scratched. Pain knifed her limbs, stabbed her legs, flashed at her face, and cut into her heart.

She wasn't sure how long her stab-proof battle gear would hold. There was too much pain over her lower limbs to believe it had protected her.

Through the chaos, she heard Max shout, "I'm coming down."

"*No!*"

Panic speared through her. *Max.* If he came down, he'd die. She wouldn't let him die. No chance in hell. With all the resolve she could muster, she soaked up the blinding pain emanating through her body and relished it. She got to know it, studied it, and became one with it. Once she was sure the pain and she were friends, she fashioned the sensation into a psionic blade, adding the memory of herself bleeding from the palm. She hurtled her agony outward, amplifying it tenfold. Pain burst from her in a silent sonic boom. A gust of wind brushed outward, lifting sand and dust in its wake. Monsters screamed, screeched, and whimpered. They keeled from her body, rolling back as though punched—as though stabbed through the heart with a knife.

She didn't wait to see if they recovered.

Releasing herself from the shackles of her rucksack, she forced her heavy limbs to *move*. Every time she felt a stab of pain, she used it. She hurtled it outward, spearing anything within her radius. She *moved*.

"I'm coming," she rasped, jumping up to grasp a protrusion on the rocky wall. "Go back up."

"Sloan!" Max, already half down the wall, changed his trajectory. He scrambled back up, but then turned and shouted. "Wait. We should kill them while they're out."

Dammit. He was right.

"Stay there!" she ordered.

For a heart-wrenching moment, she couldn't move. Her limbs locked. Panic knocked on a door to her brain.

"You can do this, Sloan. I know you can."

She nodded, breathed deep and believed her mate. She could. She would.

Pushing down her fear, she let go. She dropped and landed on her feet then, using her knife, she systematically put each beastly nightmare out of its misery. One. Two. Three... she lost count and her heart ached with each kill. Some were just little bodies when sleeping. Some were enormous. All were monsters. *Damn the Syndicate. Damn them to hell!*

By the time she was done, her energy began to wane, but she pulled every bolt out of the dead animals and returned the quiver to her thigh. She synced her crossbow to her back and then threw her rucksack to Max, and then she climbed. Up the wall. Up to safety.

Up. Up. Up, she shouted in her mind. Fingers gripped any outcrop she could find, any protrusion, anything. She climbed with haste nipping at her heels.

Just in case.

In case there were more, she had to get to safety.

When a warm, steady grip latched around her wrist, she almost wept and let go. Lifting her other aching arm, Max caught her second wrist. He pulled, growling with effort, face reddening, veins bulging. Helping him with her feet, she scrambled over the ledge until she fell into his arms and they rolled across the limestone, locked in a punishing embrace.

Whimpering and panting, they held each other, faces buried in the other's neck. Max's big palm cupped the back of her head, arms like trembling rocks.

I'm alive.

Max is alive. The adrenaline that held her together, rapidly rushed down. Dizzying shudders gripped her body while Max refused to let go. Both laid there with their eyes closed, breathing in the comforting scent of the other. Musk, sweat, salt. Home. Safe.

Max's hold relaxed and Sloan almost protested, but he only looked into her eyes as he freed her pack from her arm. He made her un-sync her bow and quiver. When the weight dropped, he rolled them until he was on top, thighs caging her hips. Eyes glistening with fury pinned her. He cupped her face and growled, "Don't you ever do that again, you hear me?"

She nodded, tears still brimming in her eyes.

"Don't ever say goodbye." Punishing lips slammed onto hers, and everything they couldn't speak came through with a kiss. He claimed her in a euphoric haze of dueling tongues. Sloan clutched his head between her hands, just as he held her. Emotion swirled between them. Longing, want, and need. Need so strong she wanted to tear his clothes from his body and press her naked skin against his, to have nothing between them but a heartbeat.

And then her blood began to flow again. Pain flashed in every cell. Reality slammed home. She winced, drawing apart, gasping in the tepid night air.

"Shit," she burst. "I think it got my leg."

"You're hurt." A self-deprecating statement. A desire to come down to earth. "Of course you're bloody hurt. I'm such a dickhead," he muttered, and then his weight lifted. He ran his hands down her body, testing. "Where?"

She sat up, groaning. "Everywhere."

"Come on." Max helped her further away from the ledge.

Under the light of the full moon, they could see their surroundings. Their platform was halfway between the cliff bottom and top. A cave-like alcove dug deep into the recess of the wall. That would do fine.

"I just need to rest for a bit, then I'll be okay," she said, exhausted. "Give me an hour and I'll be good. Got good genes." It was an attempt at a joke, but neither laughed. "I think they got my rucksack more than me, and the uniform helped."

Max didn't look convinced and deposited her on a lump of rock good enough to use as a stool. She perched down, wincing as she stretched her sore leg out. Her pants were in tatters and she was afraid to lift the flaps to see what damage had been done. Her arms weren't bad; they'd missed the brunt of the onslaught when she'd been climbing, and the stab-proof jacket protected the rest. The few bites that got through were superficial. But her legs... that's where they hit her the most.

She squeezed her eyes shut. It's fine. She'll heal. Whatever it is, she'll heal.

"Here." Max's soft, deep voice near her face. A gentle touch on her knee.

The man kneeled at her feet. He lifted the fabric at her ankle, tacky and wet with blood. The fabric resisted, sticking. He retrieved a canteen from his pack and opened it. Dripping water onto her leg, he peeled the fabric and squinted down.

"Do I have a leg left?" she joked.

"Actually, it's not so bad."

"Really?"

"I think most of this blood is theirs." Max continued to check Sloan, running water over any wound he could find. "You could grow back a limb, right?"

"Don't really want to test it."

"Don't blame you."

The worst was on her right calf. Bite lacerations had dug deep, but no flesh was torn from her body. Just piercing stab wounds. Parker's wonder fabric had saved her.

Knowing she would survive, that she wouldn't lose a limb, she relaxed.

Max grinned at her, dimple in his cheek deepening. "Bloody hell, Sloan. If you wanted to prove you're tough as shit, that was one way of going about it."

A small smile tipped her lips. She *was* tough. She was a woman, and damn it, she was just as mighty as her brothers. She didn't know why she had to keep proving it to herself.

His humor dropped. "But don't do it again. I can't lose you, too."

The heavy statement hung in the air and her heart tugged at her failure. She hadn't been there for him when he needed her most.

In the starlit night, warm wind rushed up the cliff and brushed their faces, lifting her hair from her sweaty neck. Birds squawked in the trees. Crickets chirped. The world passed in that moment and all Sloan could think was that she needed Max. All of him.

She didn't want to lose him either.

Max cocked his head, gaze turning distant. "You hear that?"

Oh God, no. "What?" she whispered.

Please let the beasts be done. No more. Please.

"Dripping."

She perked up. "Water?"

With a nod, he straightened. "Stay here. I'll be back."

Panic squeezed her throat. "Max."

Don't leave, she wanted to say. But he gave her a warm smile, tipped down and left a lingering kiss on her lips. "I won't be long."

He found a small torch in his rucksack, collected his firearm and checked the chamber. Muttering about one bullet being left, he ducked into the dark alcove which turned out to be a cave entrance. Heaving a sigh of relief, Sloan's heavy head fell backward to rest on the rocky wall. Despite everything, she smiled. Max had kissed her. He didn't want to lose her.

Over the ledge, she could see the tops of trees swaying, the starry night beginning to lighten with pre-dawn, and somewhere in the distance, further down the mountain the soft glow of lights from the black site.

No howls. No beasties following them.

She hoped Parker got away with Tony and Barry. Limping over to her shredded rucksack, she rifled around for her device. She found it next to her toiletry bag, and pulled it out, but the glass surface was cracked, despite the rugged protection sleeve.

"Bummer." She tried to turn it on. No go. Dead.

Crunching down the cave tunnel alerted her to Max's reemergence. The grin on his face eased her worry.

"You'll never guess what I found," he said.

"From the dripping cuffs of your pants—water?"

"Damn straight." He picked up her pack and heaved it on his shoulder along with his. "Let's go get you washed up, then we can rest for a few before continuing. Can you walk?"

Nodding, she hopped up and followed him, wincing with every step as they traveled down the tunnel, following the echo of dripping water. The further they walked, the temperature cooled. Down they went, on a decline until they emerged at the base. Max's torch beam glowed, revealing a large cavern. Rocky and crystal clusters had formed on the ceiling and a breeze wafted through, keeping the air fresh. Must be an opening somewhere else. When Max shone his torch across the expanse of turquoise water, it reflected shimmering patterns on chalky walls.

"This will do." He dumped the bags, propped the torch and then held out a hand to Sloan. "Come on. Smells fresh in here. Water will be good enough to bathe in."

He supported her weight as they went down to the soft muddy shore where he helped remove her shredded boots. He took off his own and stepped into the water first, testing it to make sure the surface was safe, then he held out his hand. She frowned at him. Did he think she couldn't get into the water on her own? He rolled his eyes and stepped back into the water. She followed, breathing a sigh of relief at the cold water on her aching flesh. They stepped further, feeling the squishy silt between her toes, descending until the water reached her thighs.

"So good," she muttered, shoulders dropping.

"Yeah. It is." Max's voice had turned deep, and he tugged her to him.

A sparkle of light reflected from the torch on the shore. It was enough to see the yearning in his eyes. Enough for her to connect to his innermost emotion. A desire so deep and raw called out to her. It was more than lust. He wanted to belong. He wanted to love her.

She did.

Still holding each other captive, Max lowered, his face inching towards hers. She lifted her lips— but he bypassed her face and splashed water up her side, cleaning the filth. She gasped, shocked.

"*Psyche.*" He splashed her again. "You thought I would kiss you."

Heat flushed her cheeks. "You're such a tease."

"Gotta pay you back for your pranks somehow."

Yeah, real hilarious, buddy. She smiled and continued to splash water on herself. He tried to help her, but she shrugged him off.

"It's cool. I've got this."

"Let me help."

Awkwardly, he tried to clean her as she cleaned herself.

The mood darkened when he got to her front and he couldn't see her skin to check her wounds. Her shirt was in the way. Tugging rudely, he huffed and made a gesture for her to remove it, but she playfully jumped away. When she refused to move, he straightened, all business. "Stop being immature. You're covered in blood. You need to submerge yourself."

Fine, grump. He'd started it with his psyche business. *Jeez.* She turned her back and peeled her shirt off, wincing as she lifted her arms over her head, trying to put her finger on what she'd said to make his mood swiftly change. Stop being immature?

A deep sigh came from behind her. The weight of a warm hand landed between her shoulder blades. Then he took his hand away, and it left her cold and alone. His emotions were in turmoil. One minute, she sensed longing and love from him… the next he went cold, shut off and distant. Having enough, she held her scrunched up shirt in front of her sports bra.

"You're being a jackass. Pick a feeling and stick with it."

"Screw you, Sloan." He frowned. "After everything you put me through, you don't get to call me names."

She gaped. "After everything I put you through? Me? What— trying to save your life down there? Sacrificing myself so you can live? Well, I got news for you, Maxi-Pad. I never asked for you to come here. I never asked for you to come to this city, start a security team and be in my face every day. I never asked for you to be my mate!"

"That's exactly my point. You never asked."

"I just wanted to wash myself. Jeez."

"It's more than that and you know it."

And there it was. "If this is about how we left it years ago, then screw you. You hurt me too. I may not have lost a friend, but I suffered. My feelings matter too."

"And what feelings are those?"

167

"I fucking love you, dumbass!" Her shout echoed through the rocky chamber, repeating. When it died off, tears burned her eyes.

"If you loved me, you would have tried harder to find me," he murmured, voice scratchy. "You never called."

He was right. She lost all will and fell to her knees in the water, submerged to her shoulders. She gave up. "I'm supposed to be this big, badass woman who can handle shit on her own. I know I should have called, but I didn't."

"But you never had to be like that with me."

"I was lost, okay? I'm sorry. You have no idea what it's like to live with this sin plucking at my conscience, telling me to ignore every-thing, telling me to forget. I can't fight it on my own. I'm not good enough to do this on my own."

He pressed his lips. "So now the truth finally comes out."

That she wasn't good enough? Bastard. She looked away. "I hate you."

A harsh exhale, and Max splashed down into the water, kneeling before her.

"Look at me, Sloan."

"What?" she snapped, but refused to meet his eyes. She felt humiliated. Weak. Unable to fight anymore.

He fixed her with hard eyes. "I love you, too. Always have. Never stopped. And it cut deep that you ever doubted that. That you couldn't trust me enough to ask for help, to goddamn pick up a phone and communicate! All you had to do was ask. That you didn't…"

It hit her. He didn't think she believed he could, that he wasn't good enough to help her. Not when he'd failed the closest friend he'd ever had.

"Max," she whispered. "That's not why I hid. It was my sin. One hundred percent my sin. Me, not you."

"It's my fault too." His eyes softened. "I should have called. Stupidly, I'd hoped the engagement ring I left was proof of my intention to come back but, I guess, you never received it."

She sniffed. "No, I didn't."

"Too bad. It was perfect for you."

Perfect for her…

She sat there, letting the words sink in. Wasn't sure why, except they triggered a reaction. Some deep memory tugged loose from the corner of her mind. Bit by bit, the puzzle came together. The ring Wyatt had delivered to her room the other day flashed before her eyes. Perfect for her, not Wyatt's ex, Sara. *Holy mother of…* Max was right. He'd turned up all those years ago, never intending to leave on an emergency mission, always intending to come back… and ask her to marry him.

Gingerly, she lifted her fingers to his rough jaw. "Sara had a ring. It was silver with a pink diamond heart at the center. Was that meant for me?"

Confusion, then fury flashed in his dark eyes. "Hell, yes. It was meant for you!"

He'd wanted to marry her. He'd left a ring. She was the first person he'd called after Gale died… and she'd moved on. That was enough to make him doubt her feelings.

There was only one way to make him believe.

Let him feel it.

She let the bindings holding her emotions go free. The flood gates opened and poured into him. The aching love, the fiery passion, the need.

His lips parted. "What—?"

"That's how I feel, Max. It's how I've always felt."

When vulnerability splashed over his face, she took his head in her hands and kissed him.

seventeen

MAX JOHNSON

SLOAN WAS KISSING HIM.

At first, Max didn't respond. He was too overwhelmed with her emotions still smashing into him, but slowly, surely, he deepened the kiss until their tongues danced, their hands explored, and they gasped and panted with need. He pulled back, breathless. *Was this real?* Then they clashed again, kissing and falling backward into the water.

Engulfed, all sound disappeared.

Time stopped.

Weightless ambience cocooned them as they held onto each other. It was as if they were floating through a dream.

Not a dream.

Real.

He ached for her with a madness that consumed him. Years of fantasy, eons of lust, all flooded to the surface and tore out of him with single-minded tenacity. Forgetting where they were, or what they should do, he only knew one thing. He needed her. No more messing about. He had to make her his, once and for all. *No doubts.*

Slipping his arms under her legs and arms, he planted his feet and carried her out of the lake, never taking his mouth from her skin. Water dripped from their bodies in a mad rush as they stepped onto a shore of fine muddy silt. He wanted to give her diamonds, silk sheets and more. He wanted to give her time. None of it mattered now. The silt was soft enough. It would do. What was important was she understood his feelings, that she learned his heart.

He couldn't release every feeling inside. He had to show her.

He laid her down, pushed her gently onto her back and stripped the pants from her legs, careful not to drag against her bite marks. Satisfaction bloomed when he noticed they'd already scabbed over. Nothing would stop him now. Shoving the pants under her ass for protection, he bent and trailed a long, salty lick up her front, from navel to bra. She shivered and arched into him. He unclipped her bra and covered her nipple with his mouth, suckling until she moaned, begging for more.

He looked up, caught her heated gaze and grinned. Rightness spread through him, warming his blood. "You will look at me like that every morning for the rest of your life."

She arched a brow. "Only mornings?"

Chuckling, he went back to tasting her, running his tongue all over her sweet, gorgeous body. When he hit the hem of her panties, she rolled her hips into him, challenging him. Over the cloth, he buried his face between her legs. He nibbled, bit, licked and rubbed. Made love to her mound with his mouth. When he'd had enough, he bit the fabric with a growl and pulled her panties aside. Holding them with a finger, he licked between her folds, groaning at her satin smooth skin. She'd waxed everything. His Sloan.

Watching her face under the torchlight, he dipped a finger inside her and held firm with a growl. Her cry of pleasure hit every button on his lust, and he went back to lick with his tongue, smiling as she likened him to a god. Only when she tensed up, panting and whimpering for more, did he move his finger inside her, adding a second and increasing the pace until she froze, tense.

"Max!" she shouted, fingers ripping his hair as her pleasure climaxed. Uninhibited, she couldn't hold back her emotion. He felt it in his soul. It was the warm sun beating down on him as he surfed in the ocean. It was the call of the birds as he relaxed by the campfire. It was home.

He lifted to see her face. He wanted to remember how she looked before he—

Shit.

She scowled at him from over her chest. "What's wrong?"

"I didn't bring protection. Did you?"

She snorted. "On a mission?"

Of course not. What was he thinking? He sat back on his haunches and scrubbed his face. "We shouldn't be doing this."

"What?" She sat up, panic widening her eyes.

"I don't mean, this-this. But, here, now." He glanced around the dark cavern then back at her. "I mean, I want children, but—" Not now. Not like this.

She bit her lip. "You're right. I didn't even think about that."

He glanced over at her. Naked from the waist up, and only in her panties, she was a vision. He couldn't look away. Dark hair plastered her face. Lips so rosy they bloomed in the shadowed cavern. Big eyes sparkled heavy with want. Breasts bared and rock-hard with desire —*his*. The sudden thought moved him. His forever. This was the defining moment. Everything he'd wanted. Everything he'd dreamed impossible but hoped for from the bottom of his heart, prayed from the depths of his despair.

A ring. A family. Together.

But not like this.

Later. He gathered his fly and went to zip up.

She stopped him with a hand to his wrist, furious. "What are you doing?"

"What does it look like?"

"My turn." She reached for his pants.

He jerked back. "No."

"No?" She blinked, shocked. "Why not?"

Always so demanding. "I can't be gentle right now. Next time."

A sound caught between a purr and a growl came out of her throat. "Who said I need gentle?"

He pushed her away. "I say you do. I want to give you gentle. You deserve diamonds and satin sheets."

"Max," she protested.

"Please. Let me do this."

She stared defiantly, but in the end, she nodded.

It was the hardest thing he'd had to do in months, but it was right. When he got his time with Sloan, he wanted it to be special. It would be how she deserved, and not when she was still recovering from being bitten by genetically modified beasts.

"I'm tired," he said. His finger hooked her under the chin and pressed his lips gently to hers. "I'm going to set up a place to rest."

He knew she was disappointed, but in the long run, she'd thank him. And it wasn't a complete lie, exhaustion filtered in as his lust seeped out. He really needed to rest, and so did she.

SOMETIME LATER, they'd cleaned off and set up a makeshift bed using a combination of clothes and a bedroll at the opening of the cave. In only his boxer shorts, Max collapsed beside Sloan on their bedroll, hands possessively around her despite her reacting stiffly. Tugging her body to his side, he hoped she was listening with her heart and her sixth sense, because then she'd know the truth. Unable to keep his eyes open any longer, he blacked out, falling into a deep dreamless sleep.

When he woke, stiff and sore, the sun shone brightly into the cave. Disorientated, he struggled to get his bearings. A glance around told him they were now deeper into the cave, avoiding the direct sun. Sloan must have moved him in his sleep. Considering he'd not noticed, he must have been out cold. Cursing at his sore ribs, he searched and found her close to the entrance, keeping watch.

"Did you sleep?" he asked.

She gave him a sweet smile. "I don't need as much as you. Well, not anymore."

"Oh?"

"Before you, I slept all the time. Now… not so much."

"How long was I out?"

"About four hours. You needed it."

Dressed back in her clothes, she used a tiny screwdriver to poke at the insides of her device. She was trying to fix the damaged thing. Incredible. Clever, beautiful, and funny. He was a lucky man.

But she wasn't feeling the same love. A frown marred her face and she looked out at the scenery with concern.

Finding his clothes, he put them on, watching her intently, wishing he had an ounce of her ability so he could understand where that frown came from.

"What is it, Sloan?" he asked.

"Do you think I'm a whiny bitch?"

He blinked. Didn't expect that. Then a surge of dissent flowed through him. "Is this about last night?"

"What?"

"Because, I know I stopped things early, but…" He strode over and took her nape. Squeezing her neck, he locked eyes with purpose, and planted his lips on hers. The kiss was only meant to be a brief reminder of his passion, but once he tasted her, he was all in. Her flavor was something more than feminine. It was heavenly. Her tiny whimpers of approval aroused him, and it took all his resolve to draw away.

Diamonds and satin sheets, he reminded himself.

"Wow," she muttered. "Every morning starts now, huh?"

"Damn straight." His voice came out rough. "Whatever it takes to make you believe what I feel for you is real."

"Oh, I know that."

"You do?"

"Yeah, I can feel it. Literally."

"So what's with the frown and the question?"

She chewed her lip. "Nothing. Just something Parker said to me."

"Parker's got a carrot stuck up his arse, so I'd take whatever he says with a grain of salt."

She snorted. "You speak weird."

"You're weird." He flicked her nose playfully.

"You love it."

"Yeah. I do." Lifting her from her perch, he pulled her into his arms. The sun had baked heat into her skin, and it infused his own. Sky reflected in her eyes as tenderness washed over him. He rubbed his nose against hers. "Sloan."

"Yeah, Max."

"You're not a whiny bitch." She didn't respond, so he elaborated. "I think he's jealous."

She scoffed in disbelief.

"I'm serious," he added. "Maybe it's because you've got better hair than him."

The laughter squealed out of her until it ended in a snort. Fucking adorable.

"I know, right?" she laughed.

"Sloan. Someone like Parker has a hard time seeing beyond his own reflection. I like him, but he's not immune to saying things he shouldn't out of frustration. For the record, I think you're smart, beautiful, and talented."

"You're just saying that because you're you."

"I'm saying it because it's true. What brought this on?"

"Things didn't go according to plan. I messed up last night."

"No, you didn't. You rescued a blackmailed man. You put a serious dent in their operation. All we need to do now is rescue his daughter."

She lifted the broken device, still in her hand. "I can't get it to work. We're screwed."

"Why?"

"Well, I have no idea how to get where we need to go."

"You know you're dating the Bear Grylls of Australia, right?" He smirked and to his surprise a ruddy blush crept up her cheeks.

"Dating?" She arched an eyebrow.

"Yeah. That's what we're doing, right? Unless. Um. I mean… there's the mating thing, and—" he dropped his gaze. Wasn't that what she wanted?

"I'm teasing you." She touched his cheek softly. Fondness flashed in her eyes as she studied him. It went on for such a long time that he imagined her committing his face to memory.

A sheepish smile and then he disengaged and stepped out onto the ledge. He checked the position of the sun. "We need to head east, right?"

"In that general direction, but I don't know exactly. I usually use my tech."

"That's a good start. I have my cell in my pack. Once we get within range, we can check our coordinates from there."

"You have your cell in your pack. Why didn't you lead with that?"

He grinned. "I enjoy watching you squirm."

eighteen
SLOAN LAZARUS

IF SLOAN COULD RATE how much she'd been sweating on a scale of one to stuffed, one being dry as a desert, and stuffed being wet as the ocean, she'd be... she couldn't even finish the comparison. The heat had fried her brain. She could see mirages in the dirt and ghosts in the trees. They'd spent the first half of the day clearing the mountain, and now Sloan and Max were drained and tired. Both were approaching heat exhaustion. Water supplies were half gone, and with Max impressing more compartmentalization sessions on her, she became irritated.

But the good news was, they'd hit a spot within range of a cell tower. Max had triangulated their GPS coordinates on a map, and they headed in the right direction. If they continued through the bushland, they'd hit civilization in an hour or so. The trek down the mountain had been decidedly quicker than the trek up.

After attempting to phone Parker, they'd come up with nothing. He was still out of range. But Flint wasn't. Sloan called home base and had a quick conversation outlining the new mission, only to discover Parker had called home at some point. He was still trekking, but like them, must have received some spotty cell reception. Sloan's iPad was the only team device connected to a satellite. She made a mental note to upgrade all their cells when she got back.

Communicator watches. Satellite cells. Polymorphic visual algorithms. Phew, her workload was expanding exponentially. So this was what it was like to be productive. She liked it. She'd like it even more after getting to a nice cool shower and washing the thin layer of silt off.

"Okay," Max said to Sloan as they trudged through a clearing. "Tell me everything you know about this Barry bloke and his daughter. What are we up against?"

She swatted a fly out of her face and grimaced. "I don't know much. She's sixteen. Goes to boarding school."

"What's her name?"

"Beatrix."

"Beatrix Pinkerton."

"Uh-huh."

"What does she look like? Tell me everything."

"Everything?"

"Yep."

"Strap yourself in. You ready?"

"Hit me."

She took a deep breath and then let it all out. "Beatrix is the captain of the debate team. She's in the swim squad. Practices on Tuesdays and Fridays at five in the school pool. She's got brown skin and black hair like her father, but silver eyes like her Caucasian mother. Parents are divorced and the mother now lives in France with her new husband—Pierre. Beatrix has a lot of friends, but none of them truly like her—probably because she's super bossy."

"How do you know that?"

"Facebook."

He arched a brow. "Care to elaborate?"

"I hacked her account. And I hacked her friends' accounts. Her friends are a total bunch of mean girls. She can do better. Anyway, I'm not done."

"There's more?"

"Absolutely."

"Anything we can actually use?"

She gasped. "I'm offended."

"No you're not."

"You're right. I'm not. But you don't know what we can use, so I learned whatever I could."

"You snooped."

She shrugged. "Maybe I call it being thorough."

"Good work. Just stop here for a minute." Max squinted up at the sun and pulled out his cell to check for reception. "Battery's almost dead, but we're heading in the right direction. Not long and we'll hit our target. I've let them know where we'll end up for Parker's contact to deliver the car. We'll need the supplies."

"Thank God. I can't wait to have a proper shower. I've still got mud in weird places." She continued after him, catching up to walk side by side.

"Yeah, well, get used to it if you want to come camping with me."

She feigned excitement. "I get to have mud in weird places all the time?"

A pink tinge flushed his cheeks. "You know what I mean."

"Oh my God, Max. Are you embarrassed?"

He averted his gaze. "I didn't mean for you to get so filthy. You were still hurt, and... I should have controlled myself."

Sloan sidled up to him, wrapped her arms around him and held his gaze. "Are you telling me you have regrets?"

"Hell, no. Except… maybe next time I buy you dinner first. At least pizza."

"No pineapple."

He smirked, brown eyes sparkling. "Loads of pineapple."

She made a gagging action, but he kissed her, swallowing her protests. The kiss turned deep and heavy, and he squeezed her on the ass, lifting her a moment before placing her back down. Brushing her fingers through his hair, she felt all together happy. "I shouldn't feel so happy when we're on our way to rescue a teenager from the clutches of a fanatical organization hell bent on ruining the world."

"Just another day in paradise, right?"

"You don't think they know Barry is missing yet, do you?"

"It's hard to say. Perhaps if they've gone over their camera footage, but that could have taken a few hours, depending on their system. Barry could come and go as he pleased, so unless they have tagged him as missing, they shouldn't notice his absence until he was next due to work."

Sloan let those words sink in. Hopefully, since they'd seen Barry in the early hours of the morning, he was due to go home and not return to the base until the afternoon. They wouldn't know unless they could get through to Parker and ask.

They walked onward for another hour or so, and then Sloan noticed something strange. "Are you sure we're in the right place? That tree looks very familiar."

He squinted at it. "They all look familiar."

"No, I'm serious. That cropping of rock with the dried moss on it. We've come this way. I know, because the moss looks like the baby Moses in a basket."

"Baby Mosses," he joked with a goofy snort.

They chuckled, but then Sloan's brows drew together. "We'd better check. How's the reception on the cell?"

Max took his cell out again, but groaned. "Dead."

"We're lost, aren't we?"

"We're not lost. Just time to do some good old-fashioned Alby Mangels shit."

"Who's that?"

"Australia's Bear Grylls of the Seventies. Except he traveled with hot babes." Max waggled his eyebrows. "Kinda like a traveling James Bond."

"Yeah, okay, you old perv."

"You weren't calling me that last night. In fact, I think you shouted something about me being God." He dodged the pebble she ditched at his head with a smirk. Then he dropped his pack and rifled through it. "Be prepared to be amazed."

Sloan couldn't fight the smile on her face. This was the old Max. The one she'd fallen in love with all those years ago. Effortless and enjoyable banter. She could chat about anything and everything with him for hours. Just wait until they sat down at a console together. Which game would they play?

All of them. She laughed evilly in her head. All of them.

He pulled out a little metal box, opened it and stood.

"A compass?" She folded her arms. "That's your amazing Alby Mango shit?"

"Mangels," he corrected. The cheeky, dimpled smile he shot her made her stomach flutter. The compass was old, beat up and rickety, but it worked. They said nothing as he adjusted himself to point North. When he found it, his silence stretched and a slow trickle of emotion wriggled into Sloan's gut.

Sadness.

Confused, she puzzled over his emotion and then noticed an engraved G on the side of the metal compass casing.

She ran her hand down his forearm and covered his hand. "The compass was Gale's wasn't it?"

He nodded.

With her other hand, she embraced him and laid her head on his shoulder.

"He gave this to me on our first solo camping trip before we enlisted. His dad had given it to him for good luck, but… he gave it to me instead."

Sloan turned him until they faced each other. "I wish I could have met him."

"Me too." Then his gaze hardened. "We need to keep walking."

He picked up his rucksack and put it back on. "Keep telling me about Beatrix. Will she be at school? What's the school like? Is there easy access?"

"Whoa, dude. Hold your horses. We can figure all that out when we get there."

"No. We keep planning, and you need to keep working on your emotions. The more prepared we are, the more likely we'll have a positive outcome."

"You don't think we can do this?"

"Look. I just…" His voice trailed off.

"Okay." Sloan stopped. "Now, it's your turn to spit it out. What's going on?"

"It's just—I think maybe I agree with Parker about last night."

"What?" She blinked. "I thought you were on my side. I thought you said I wasn't a whiny bitch."

"That's not what I'm talking about. This is coming out wrong."

She folded her arms and raised a brow. "Uh-huh."

"I meant… with Barry. You kinda just jumped in. And at the time I thought I should just go with it. I trust your instincts, I really do."

"So what is it?"

"Not planning makes me nervous." His eyes flashed with some unnamed emotion, but she felt his doubt prickle at her.

"I thought you said 'no doubts'."

"It's not you I'm doubting."

Her breath hitched. "Are you doubting us?"

"No! I'm... look, it's me. I'm doubting me. I'm not okay with leaving a stone unturned. I need to know everything before going in. So, can you please just continue briefing me with everything you know?"

"I thought I was."

"You haven't told me about your other sister."

"Oh."

He moved ahead with quick strides and Sloan jogged to keep up. A rush of compassion washed through her.

"Max, Gale's death wasn't your fault."

He kept walking doggedly. "It was, and you know it."

"You can't blame yourself for the actions of crazy people."

"Can we not talk about this now?"

She took him by the shoulder. "Stop."

His dark scowling eyes met hers. "We don't have time for this."

"There's always time for me to tell you how incredible you are." He tried to look away, but Sloan dragged his face back to hers. "I mean it, Max. Just look at what you're doing. You're not only helping us fight the Syndicate, but you're helping a complete stranger find his daughter. You've set up a security company purely to employ your friends—"

"Because it was my fault they lost their jobs. I'm lucky we weren't sent to prison."

"—and you were ready to help me, even though you hated me. You offered to create some sort of touching schedule to ease my sin."

She shook his head between her palms. "Don't you dare say you don't deserve to be happy."

He frowned. "I didn't say that."

"No, but I can feel it in your heart, Max. Every time you get a flash of happiness, you immediately stomp on it."

Eyes spearing each other, they stared for long moments. Then Max's face softened. "I'll never be able to hide anything from you again."

She grinned. "There goes poker night with the boys."

"Oh, I'll still go. But you'll know it." He leaned down and pressed his lips against hers and then he pressed his forehead against hers.

Both inhaled and exhaled, letting the air take the tension that had crept into their bodies. Or maybe it was Max's touch. Misha had been right. Just touching him made every irritation seep out like an ebbing tide.

"Thank you, Sloan," he murmured.

"You won't be thanking me when I kick your butt at poker. Oh, yeah. I'll be coming. Don't you worry."

"I'm not worried. You can be my secret weapon." He kissed her again, then stepped away. "Right. I want to know everything about your sister. Not Liza, obviously. The one you called Daisy."

"Information overload!"

He only shot her a "don't-mess-with-me" glare.

"Okay, okay. Whatever you say, Maxi-Pad."

"That's Mr. Maxi-Pad to you."

For the next hour, Sloan followed Max's relentless pace, spitting out anything and everything she'd learned about her eldest sister, and the place they were about to visit. Max was thorough. It was like talking with a questioning toddler. *What's this? Who's that? Elaborate.*

Sloan went into great detail about her long-lost sister. Mary and Flint had escaped the Syndicate around thirty years ago. Sloan was a toddler at the time, but Daisy had been nine—the eldest. She was the caregiver of the brood, always helping the nuns with the younger children. When Daisy sensed despair, she would do anything in her power to help that person feel hope again. Sloan confessed that her family had believed Daisy died in the fire that provided cover for their escape. Only months ago did the family realize she'd been alive all this time. Alive, and working for the enemy.

"You can't imagine how it feels to know we've left one of us behind," Sloan said as they came upon a long, deserted road.

"I think I have a pretty good idea."

"You're right. I'm sorry. You do." She sighed. "Of course you do. That was stupid of me to say."

Max gave her a small smile and took his compass out.

While he was orientating, Sloan said, "I set Daisy a place at our table at the last family dinner. I think we will keep doing it at the family dinner until she's sitting with us. Do you think that's silly?"

When he met her eyes, they were full of determination. "No. It's one thing I love about you Sloan. You don't give up."

Max went back to his compass and scratched his head. "I guess we head east still. This should be the road they've left the car on."

They continued to walk until a car pulled up and stopped to ask if they were lost. Max replied that they'd detoured a little too much on their hike but were looking for their car. Between the two of them, they worked out that, yes, this was the correct road and, yes, the driver had seen a white sedan parked not far back. He offered the two of them a lift and deposited them five minutes further down the road.

They waved to the driver as he drove off. When he was gone, Sloan frowned at the car. No people in it. So far so good.

"Do you think that's it?" she asked. "Are we in the right place?"

"Only one way to find out."

Max went to one side of the vehicle, and Sloan the other. She inspected the tires.

"No key," she said.

"I got it." He caught her eye over the car roof with a grin.

Relief melted through her. Thank God. They needed the ammunition. By the time they sat in the car, exhaustion battered her defenses, but resting would have to wait. They had a girl to save.

nineteen

MAX JOHNSON

MAX HAD HEARD a lot from Sloan on the hike and stayed silent most of the drive while he processed. They were in a bind with Sloan's sister. The woman was a psychopath. She didn't blink or think twice about doing the Syndicate's bidding, even if that meant kidnapping and torturing a scientist's innocent daughter. The old Max would have discarded Daisy as being a lost cause. But the new Max, the one who failed to have his friend's back, that Max knew dire consequences were the result. That part of him understood the Lazarus family shouldn't give up on Daisy. It would be hard. It might be impossible. But he had to support Sloan.

After stopping at a rest stop to eat, drink and change into some fresh civilian clothes that had been left in the car, Max and Sloan were on their way to the St. Peter's Academy boarding school. It was late afternoon on Sunday, and they were confident they'd find Beatrix in her dormitory studying. Sloan told Max the girl was an over-achiever and rarely commented on her Facebook about attending social events. Knowing her father was a brainy scientist, it wasn't a far stretch to believe his daughter was smart and diligent.

The school was set on a sprawling green estate, complete with tennis courts and other sports fields. The residential buildings were part of a big red brick converted abbey. Other buildings on the campus took the same old-style architecture. They parked the car in the visitor lot out the front.

"Not many around," he noted as they got out of the vehicle. As he stood by the open door, surveying the lot, he tucked his reloaded Glock into the back of his waistband, being sure to cover it with his jacket. Tension creeped into his shoulders. "With this many cars in the lot, I would have thought I'd see more people on the property."

"Probably all just inside," Sloan replied. "You're being paranoid. Relax."

Still with his eyes on the lot, he counted cars. Maybe twelve. How many were expected for a school like this during summer? Perhaps a few teachers were still there, despite school hours finished for the day. Maybe a few students had vehicles. He hesitated. Maybe he was being paranoid. But paranoia could save your life.

They checked around to see if anyone watched, and then Sloan leaned into the car and retrieved a new gun from the pack of supplies. Whoever Parker had as an assistant must be trusted, paid well, or terrified of them, to run these kinds of errands. Max wasn't sure if he was comfortable with this kind of extracurricular help. It was a potential leak and threat to all of them.

"You ready?" Sloan asked. "The girl's dormitory is that one."

His sense of wrongness followed them the entire walk toward the building nestled between lush trees and white flowered shrubs. An old Victorian style manor, it must have been made at the turn of the previous century. As they climbed the steps, the front double doors opened. His hand twitched for his firearm, but stopped as a gaggle of girls in summer shorts came bursting out. There were four of them, all holding an oar and some swimming supplies. Must be a lake around there. Sloan jumped behind him to avoid being knocked by the cluster, squashing herself behind the door and the wall of the building.

"Excuse me, ladies," he said, holding the door wide.

The girls stopped, lips parting as they took him in. He supposed he was a bit intimidating, towering over them. He went for a smile.

"I'm looking for Beatrix Pinkerton. Could you point us in her direction?"

A taller blond girl bumped the closest girl out of the way with her hips. "Ooh. Are you British too?" she cooed, stepping toward him. "I love your accent. Can you say something else?"

"I'm Australian."

Her girlfriends began chattering excitedly amongst themselves.

A loud sigh expelled behind him and Sloan pushed him out of the way. "Girls, focus. Beatrix."

"Room one-oh-two. Jeez, lady." The blond pouted at her then pointed inside. "But you'll need a visitor pass. That's at the main admin building back that way."

Sloan gave her a tight-lipped smile and nudged Max inside, mumbling under her breath. "Yeah, I got your visitor pass right here."

Max chuckled as he followed, also ignoring the visitor pass instruction. Thankfully, they'd avoided running into any teachers by the time they located Beatrix's room. When they knocked on the door, it opened.

A teenage girl with long straight black hair and big square glasses greeted them with an open book in her hand. She slammed it closed and packed it into a bag. With a posh tone, she snapped, "About time."

Both Max and Sloan were taken aback.

Sloan pushed into the room. "Who do you think we are?"

"You're the people my father sent. Obviously." She spun on her heel and gathered a packed duffel bag from her bed. She handed it to Max. "There's more."

He arched a brow at Sloan and she gave him eyes that seemed to say "I told you she was bossy."

"What else did your father say?" Max asked.

"He said it's not safe for me here, and a man and a woman we can trust are coming to take me to him." Beatrix gathered a small suitcase on wheels, and pointed at a final backpack sitting on the floor next to an empty shelf. "Seeing as you're the only man and woman I've seen all morning, I'm assuming it's you."

"Never assume," Sloan said. "It makes an ass out of you and me."

"Uh. You sound like my father."

"Yeah, well, your father and my father knew each other. They must speak the same dad language." Sloan went to lift the bag, but it weighed down, slamming back on the ground. "What have you got in here?"

Beatrix blinked back at her. "Books."

Sloan shook her head. "We don't have time for books. This isn't a vacation."

Beatrix folded her arms. "If we're not coming back here, I need those. They're very important research books."

Before Beatrix could stop her, Sloan unzipped the bag and took one out. *Anne of Green Gables.* Max thought maybe Sloan would make some offhand offensive comment, but she returned the book carefully and zipped the bag up before hoisting it over her shoulder.

"Okay. Let's go," Sloan said and headed for the door.

Avoiding Max's gaze, Beatrix rushed after Sloan.

It was sheer luck that had them down to the car and half loaded before a woman came running toward them from the small administration building on the other side of the parking lot. Max was hoping they'd be able to leave quickly and quietly, unseen, no fuss.

The woman's long brown dress fluttered behind her. The yellow ribbon in her long brown hair left a trail. When she arrived, huffing and puffing, Max noted the wrinkles around her eyes and age spots. She was older than she dressed. No makeup. Flat shoes. A face ready to do battle.

Max's internal alarm went off.

"I'm sorry," the woman said as she arrived. "I can't let you leave."

"It's okay, Dean Hartly, my father called and approved." Beatrix came around from the other side of the car.

"I know that, sugar, but you haven't been signed out and we have procedures to adhere to. Sir," she said to Max. "If you could follow me to the administration building, we'll get Beatrix all signed out."

"I'll do it," Sloan offered.

"No." Alarm pricked in the dean's eyes. "I asked the gentleman to do it."

Had his unsettled stomach not still been there, Max might have laughed at the poor dean. Telling Sloan to *not* do something was the easiest way to get her to actually do it.

Seeing Sloan's lip twitch in irritation, the dean added, "I apologize if that came out rash. It's just, the girl's father mentioned a man would pick her up. A Maximilian Johnson? I need the signature of that person."

Neither of them wanted to cause a scene, and the quicker they got out of there, the safer Beatrix would be, but Sloan was the one with the supernatural radar. He met her gaze and waited for permission. It took her a moment to realize what he was doing, and then she huffed.

"Fine. You go, I'll wait here." She opened the car door and ushered Beatrix inside. "Don't be long."

Max opened the trunk of the car and hoisted the luggage in. Once he was done, he bent low toward Sloan as she strapped herself into the driver side. He tucked his finger under her chin and titled her lips to meet his in a slow kiss. When he drew back, and her eyes glazed and softened, he was glad he took the moment. "Don't go anywhere. Keep the doors locked."

Still smiling to himself, Max followed the dean halfway back to the admin building, and then stopped. His smile dropped. The hairs on his neck stood to attention. Wind caressed his face, bringing with it air laced with something unnatural. A chemical. What made him stop? What was that smell? Kerosene? He craned his neck back, but noticed nothing in his periphery except the school buildings and empty grounds. Standing there, frozen solid, he listened.

The girls who went to the lake weren't chattering anymore. Were they out of earshot, or...

"Please, sir," the dean's voice wavered. "This way."

His sight landed on the sweat beading across her forehead. It was a hot day, but not *that* hot. It had cooled considerably since the morning, yet she had a green tinge to her skin. The yellow ribbon in her hair was loose. When she darted her eyes back to the school's entrance, Max received a jolt of adrenaline.

Get out! his instincts screamed. *Run!*

He reached for his gun and pivoted. Pushing off on strong legs, he ran back to the car. But when he arrived and tried to open the door, it wouldn't budge. He slammed his palm on the window. "Open up."

Inside, Sloan tried in vain to open her door. She pumped the handle.

Locked.

How could it be locked?

Max tried another door. Locked.

He ran to the opposite side. Still locked. It was then he caught the view over the car. Walking at an unhurried pace, coming down the steps of the dormitory, were two Faithful, and Sloan's sister Daisy.

193

Must be her. She wore the bird mask to cover half her face, white leather outfit—neck to toe. Red spatters marred the sleeves and a bullwhip hung at her hip. The Faithful, dressed in their white robes and white faceless masks flanked Daisy down from the dormitory.

The dean looked like she was about to pee herself. Clasping her hands together, she prayed to the white woman. "I tried to get him to come, he wouldn't…"

Daisy didn't answer, just had eyes for Max. Violet eyes full of rage, yet her face was slack.

"Will you let the children go?" the dean asked, voice shaking.

Daisy refused to reply. The way she walked with purpose toward Max, not Sloan or Beatrix, had his heart hammering.

He aimed his weapon. "Stop right there, or I shoot."

A banging in the car told Max that Sloan still couldn't get out. They'd done something to the locks and windows.

A few feet from where he stood, Daisy stopped. Her foot soldiers kept walking toward the car. They had a container in their hands. A metal can… similar to the type that held kerosene. He swung the gun their way.

"Stop. I swear to God, I'll shoot."

"You won't shoot." Daisy's low and monotone voice was devoid of life. Her long white hair swayed on a phantom breeze. "You won't shoot because, unlike me, you feel something for the people in the car."

"I don't see what that has to do with these men and their intent."

"My soldiers are doused with fuel. You shoot them, you'll set them aflame. They'll run straight to the car and… well, I think you can use your imagination."

The world closed in. Max forced himself to not panic. Breathe. Think about this calmly. He was not back on tour. These men were not insurgents with a bomb strapped to their chests.

Calm.

Max trained the weapon back on Daisy. "Then I'll just shoot you."

One shoulder lifted in a shrug. "You could, but I think you know as well as I that a bullet won't kill me. I'll just regenerate."

Fuck! Panic screamed in his brain. "What do you want?"

"You know, Mr. Johnson. I must admit that I did have my doubts. But after seeing the way you kissed her... my suspicions have been confirmed."

"What are you talking about?"

"You, Mr. Johnson. We want you."

twenty

SLOAN LAZARUS

TRAPPED.

She was trapped.

"Max!" Sloan shouted and slammed her palm on the car window to get his attention, but he refused to look. He was right there! Why wasn't he looking? Pushing out with her new power, she tried to project, but nothing connected with the people outside. *Sleep*, she urged. *Sleep*. The Faithful standing stoically on either side of her car, stumbled. That was it.

When Beatrix yawned behind Sloan, she realized her aim was off. *Dammit*. Reining in her power, her mind went to dark and terrible places. Why was her precision so off? Maybe it was just like with the animals and she was too confused, too wired? Too panicked? Or was the glass and car between them creating some sort of block? Was her power bouncing back inside as though reflected by the metal and glass?

All these thoughts and more, rushed about Sloan's head. None made sense.

She pounded against the glass again. *Turn around Max!*

He shifted slightly, profile coming into view. The man's jaw popped as he clenched. Eyes like two beams of hate pointed at her sister. He braced his weapon with two steady hands—aimed and locked.

What the hell were they talking about?

Damned door. She tried again, knowing it wouldn't open. She couldn't understand why. She tried the window, but the electrics wouldn't respond. The car was dead. She tried the key fob, also dead.

"What the fuck!" she shouted in an angry burst.

Beatrix shrank in the back seat, hugging herself. "What's happening? Who are those people?"

"Get down," Sloan ordered. She took off her jacket, ready to wrap around her fist. "I said, get down, Beatrix. Get down and stay down until I say so."

The girl squealed and dropped, lowering herself into the gap between the back and front seats.

"Cover your head." With the jacket wrapped around her fist, Sloan pulled back, ready to strike the glass, but Max held out his palm toward her. She paused, frowning.

Stop?

Max dipped his head so he could catch her eyes. The brown in them sparked gold with the sun. He held a finger to Daisy, indicating for her to wait, and then strode quickly to Sloan's window.

Panting with panic, she forced herself to check his senses, to feel out his emotions. A trickle of emotional energy came through, but she couldn't grasp the meaning. The sensation was still too weak through the glass and metal insulation of the car.

Then he kissed two fingers and pressed them on the window. His brows joined in the middle in a pained expression. She touched the window and their fingers met, strengthening the surge of his emotion.

What echoed at her was... Love.

Why now? Why…

Her throat closed up. Her eyes burned. "Max?" she whispered.

Movement behind him drew her attention. Her sister took hold of Max and dragged him away, and the worst thing was, he let her.

"Max!" Louder this time.

No response, only his back turning on her. Only the sight of his broad shoulders hunched as he walked away.

Sloan struck the glass. Pain engulfed her fist, but she soaked it up and stored the memory of the knifelike sensations for later use. Her skin was protected, just bruised. She punched again, this time, shattering the window, but with all modern vehicles, the glass was tinted. A film held the window together, only letting her wrapped fist through. It was enough for her voice to carry. "MAX!"

His shoulders lifted and tensed. A whispered word from her sister, a warning perhaps. He kept walking and got into an awaiting car. Range Rover. Black. Dark tint. License plate… *no plates.*

The stench of kerosene wafted into the car, snapping Sloan's attention back to her immediate surroundings. A new sense of panic rose. White robes flashed in her periphery. Two Faithful, one on each side of her car. The moment the Range Rover drove off with Max inside, they sloshed kerosene on Sloan's car. The horror of what they were about to do dawned on her.

Max must have made a deal for their safety.

That damned dumbass sacrificed himself and, despite this, whatever deal he had made, they weren't going to keep it.

If she couldn't get out, they would burn alive.

Resolve hardened in her gut. Leaning back, Sloan kicked out with her boots. The entire window flipped out of the car.

Snarling and full of rage, Sloan dove through the gap. Tucking and rolling, she somersaulted onto the concrete lot. She landed awkwardly on her shoulder and pushed the pain outward in a reckless arc, hoping Beatrix would be safe inside the vehicle. She didn't wait to find out. In one swift movement, she whipped her gun out and aimed at the two sniveling Faithful, moaning on the floor in a puddle of spilled kerosene. Flammable. The puddle connected with the car. She couldn't shoot. Too dangerous. Instead, she hit the closest Faithful with the butt of the gun. He passed out.

She tugged the white mask off the second Faithful. Beneath was a scarred and puckered face. He'd already been burned alive. He knew the pain it caused, and he was about to do it to an innocent girl. Anger bubbled in Sloan's blood and she grasped him by the scruff at the neck.

"Where did she take Max?" Her voice cut like a knife.

The man ignored her, just peered vacantly to the right of her face.

"You wanna do this, asshole? I can make you hurt."

He brought his gaze to hers. "Pain is a construct."

"Yeah it's a fucking construct, and I'll construct it right up your ass if you don't answer me."

"Nothing you can say will make me betray my makers. Nothing you do to me will be carried to my next life."

She let loose. Her fist smashed his nose, spurting blood everywhere. She did it again. And again. He laughed through it all, which made her even more furious. "Where did they take him!" she shouted, shifting her hold on his robe to hold him up.

He craned his neck to lean closer and peer into her soul. "You can't hurt me."

"You're insane!" Sloan shoved him to the ground. He laughed and laughed, giving her a perfect view of blood covered teeth.

She roared in outrage and paced up and down next to him.

She needed him to talk. Gritting her teeth, she pointed her firearm at his head, but he just smiled calmly.

He wanted to die.

The knowledge hit her like a sledgehammer.

A few months ago, Evan had encountered the Faithful in the streets of Cardinal City, and he'd discovered they'd all made an agreement with the Syndicate. These sick, injured, scarred, deformed and disabled people made deals to become virtual suicide terrorists, all so their DNA would be used to bring them back as healed, and genetically enhanced new beings. Clones of themselves, but better. Replicates, was the name they'd been called.

Wyatt's psycho ex Sara was a replicate. She'd killed herself in a bomb. Her DNA had been salvaged from her dead body, and used to create another version of herself, except that version had an expiration date. The replicate project hadn't gone according to the Syndicate's plan.

Evan had destroyed the replicate lab.

They thought the clones were done... but from the sound of this fanatical man, he still believed he would come back as a demigod among men. Then, the only thing that would get him to talk, wasn't to threaten his life, but to keep him alive.

A slow grin formed on her face. "Oh, you'll talk all right."

His smile dropped.

"You'll only be reborn if you're dead, right?" Sloan asked. "So... if I keep you alive for years and years... what will happen then?"

He shook his head. Sloan tapped the barrel of her gun against his temple. "I'll make it clear for you, asshole. You tell me what I need to know, I shoot you. Kill you dead right now. You refuse, I'll make sure you die a long, slow and painful death curtesy of our penal system. How much fun do you think it will be in there for a man who looks like you?"

Doubt flickered in his eyes.

"Where did they take Max?"

"I don't know."

She held her chin high, refusing to let him see her disappointment. "Why did they take him?"

"He's linked to you and your powers, that's all I know."

Dammit. They knew about the mating bond. They knew about Max being the only thing on this green earth keeping her sane. A dark insidious feeling churned in her belly.

"How did you lock me out of the car?"

"We hacked the fob frequency."

"Can you reverse it?"

He set his jaw and shook his head. "I don't have the equipment. She took it with her. I don't even know how to do it, I'm just a—"

"Idiot. You're just an idiot." She sent him to sleep.

She didn't need that car, anyway. There were plenty in the lot she could borrow. She tapped on the window, getting Beatrix's attention.

"You got a laptop in there?"

Beatrix nodded, eyes wide.

"Good. Get your shit out. We're commandeering another car to meet your dad."

While Beatrix scrambled out, Sloan stalked to the admin building. Bursting through the doors, she expected to find the dean and others, but found no one. Hiding. Probably a good thing. Behind the receptionist's oak desk was a key rack. Dangling right there was a set with a fob. Perfect.

Back outside, she pointed the fob at the lot, pressing the lock button until she heard a beep. There it was, a red Honda Civic in the dean's reserved parking spot. It was Sloan's now.

Hurrying Beatrix inside the car with her luggage, Sloan got into the driver side and urged her passenger to get her laptop out.

"You got a phone?" Sloan asked, turning the engine on.

Beatrix nodded and pulled out a girly red glitter covered phone.

"Seatbelt on. Good. Open the Wifi settings on the laptop. I will give you a password that will give you access to the Lazarus Satellite."

"Got it," Beatrix replied.

"And then I want you to do exactly as I say."

twenty-one

SLOAN LAZARUS

SIX HOURS LATER, Sloan pulled the Civic into the basement garage of the Lazarus building. In her haste, the wheels clipped a curb, sending a screech of protest from the tires echoing into the dark cavernous space. In the passenger seat, Beatrix also squealed, her knuckles white as she gripped her closed laptop. Yanking on the wheel, foot on the breaks, Sloan slammed the car to a stop right before the elevator door. No time to park.

Max was out there somewhere. Alone, possibly hurt… worse.

Swallowing the lump of fear in her throat, she pushed out of the car. The door stayed open. She strode toward the big metal locked door next to the elevator. Beatrix scrambled to keep up. Sloan had spent the drive placating her, telling her it was going to be fine, but it wouldn't be. Max was missing.

A fire had been lit back at that school, but it wasn't the kerosene that caught ablaze, it was her blood. Full of adrenaline, Sloan had relentlessly used the girl and her computer on the long drive home. The poor girl was probably frightened out of her wits, but she took it in her stride. She hit every keystroke Sloan had ordered, completed every task. They'd traced Max's cell and discovered it in a ditch not far from the school. If Sloan wasn't completely wired, scattered and on edge, she might have respect for the girl. She took Sloan's barked orders like a boss. As it was, all Sloan could think of was the growing list of things to do.

Leave no stone unturned.

After AIMI had checked her credentials, Sloan pushed open the heavy metal door. A few quick strides down a dark hallway, and she emerged in the underground Operations Room of their headquarters. Most of her family had gathered around the central strategy table. Evan. Flint. Mary. Parker. Tony…

And Barry.

She zeroed in on the man with predatory focus. The sin of sloth wiggled in her gut… and it still came from *him*. Shouldn't he feel free from sin now? After all that? Confusion whirled in her mind with anguish. Her wired, scattered thoughts clashed as though on steroids. She thought she had herself under control, but her irrational fury and fears rushed to the surface.

It was his fault.

That man.

Stifling agony wrapped around her throat and squeezed. It lowered to her chest—to her heart. *Max.* Her Max. Her mate.

Missing.

A flash of their fingers touching through the car's window hit her mind's eye.

If he was dead—pain suffocated her chest, solidified in her bones. She froze, rooted to the spot, in silent torment, unable to voice her fears.

Instead, her eyes glued to the man before her. She was stupid to think she could save him. So stupid. Because of him, Max was gone. Her sweet Max who sacrificed his own happiness to go back into the field and hunt for his missing friend. Her beautiful man who deserved more than this creator of monsters ever did.

She should never have deviated from Parker's plan to save him. Instead, she'd listened to her gut, and fucked up again.

Sloan blinked, and Barry was at the center table, chatting quietly to a smiling Flint. Her father's happiness was a betrayal to everything Sloan felt inside. And that monster-creator was in the center of it all, looking innocent as he adjusted his spectacles on the bridge of his nose.

End his sin.

She blinked, and then her hands wrapped around the man's throat, shoving him backward, rushing him toward the wall housing flat screens broadcasting local news reports, shaking the foundations.

She didn't know how she'd closed the gap, or how she'd even moved, but it happened too fast and the older man responded with heavy limbs. He did nothing to protect himself. Nothing. A lamb to the slaughter... just like he'd led Max. It was Barry's idea to rescue his daughter. For all they knew it was a trap. A well-played trap, and here he was, sitting in their secret headquarters, no doubt coaxing any precious information he could out of Parker. And then what? *Who's next?*

In her periphery, Sloan vaguely heard protests from her family, but they were just obstacles in her path. Barry deserved to sleep. Sleep forever.

A feminine scream snapped Sloan's attention to alert.

Reality slapped her in the face. In horror, she realized she'd been choking the man so hard that he couldn't breathe. Why had no one stopped her? Why?

She let go, stumbled back, and slowly turned around. Everyone in the room was on the floor, moaning, rubbing their head or... still asleep.

Fuck.

She did that. She'd caused a room of warriors to drop with a single reckless thought. If it wasn't for the daughterly love of the teenage girl, now crawling to her heaving and rasping father… if it wasn't for her, Sloan would be a murderer.

"I DIDN'T MEAN TO," Sloan stuttered. Coldness crept into her body. It all had happened so fast. So goddamned fast.

One minute, she was walking into the room, intending to have a strong word with the scientist. The next minute, her hands had been wrapped around his throat, choking the life out of him, and sending every person in the room to sleep.

Get rid of the obstacles.

That's what she had done. She got rid of anything blocking the path to end the sin she still felt sizzling in the gut of the man who was at the center of it all—Barry.

Groans came from the floor. The first to come to was Evan, dragging himself to a standing position.

"What the fuck was that, Sloan?" Evan rubbed his head. "I feel like I've been hit by a truck."

Sloan covered her mouth and backed up. What had she done?

Then Evan's green gaze caught on the still rasping figure of Barry, leaning against the wall, holding his daughter. It wasn't clear who was trying to protect who, but both stared wide-eyed at Sloan, as if she were the enemy.

Evan's eyes narrowed on his sister. "You did this?"

Although it pained her to admit, she nodded.

Menacing electricity arced up his tattooed arms, crackling and sparking with light. "Move away from Barry and his daughter, Sloan."

"I didn't mean to."

Another masculine groan sounded as Parker came to. His fist slammed on the table, shaking the contents as he pulled himself up. Tony was next. Flint and Mary were last. When all eyes comprehended what Sloan had done, they stared at her.

Just stared.

She could almost hear their thoughts ticking over. What to do with her? Was she family, or foe?

"I said, move away from Barry, Sloan." A divot formed between Evan's brows.

She held up her hands in surrender. "I'm sorry. I lost control. It won't happen again."

It was Mary who made the first move. Sloan's deadly mother smoothed her hair back, but couldn't hide the tremble in her hands as her eyes locked on her daughter. She was afraid.

The notion almost floored Sloan.

Afraid of me. Me, the whiny bitch. The one no one took seriously. The one who slept and gamed away entire days. *Me.*

Fear... not respect. She gasped. It wasn't meant to be like this.

Mary sidestepped the bench and approached. Her movement was the switch that sent everyone into action. Flint rushed to his old friend.

"Evan, see if you can get Grace down," Flint ordered before crouching down and seeing to Barry's injury.

"No," Barry rasped. "I'm fine. She stopped in time, mate. I'm fine."

"*Mija,*" Mary said softly to Sloan. "What happened?"

Sloan blinked. "I called you on the drive. You all know. Max was taken. It was a trap. Why aren't you all looking for him?"

"I meant, what happened now? Focus on one thing at a time."

"Max is the priority." Sloan shook off her mother's hand and went to the center strategy table. A laptop was open. Perfect. She needed to start searching. First, she'd source a picture of Max—there must be one of him somewhere in AIMI's feed—then feed it into the facial recognition databases. She'd have AIMI searching for Max on every camera feed in the country.

"*Mija*, you can't ignore what happened."

"I'm not ignoring it. I'm very sorry for what I've done, but I'm putting it in a box. Compartmentalizing. If I don't, you'll all be drowning in my regret and self-pity. I'll unpack the box later."

Mary's big sigh brushed the back of Sloan's neck. "*Mija*, please relax."

"No time to relax." Her fingers tapped the keyboard at a manic speed.

"Sloan!" Mary's curt voice cut through Sloan's purpose. It was the *mother* tone.

"What?"

"Check your tattoo."

Sloan tilted her wrist and frowned. Since she'd met her mate, the Yin-Yang tattoo was meant to be a circle equally balanced, half black, half white. Not this time. "It's almost all white. I've never seen it like that. Why is it like that?"

Parker moved in and inspected it. "How do you feel?"

"I feel fine. Ready to find Max. We got things to do."

"You look like you've snorted a rail of coke through the nose, Sloan." Tony arched an eyebrow at her. When he took in her confusion, he added, "You look wired."

She shrugged. "Sure, I feel a little more energized. Maybe my adrenaline's still kicking. Wait. Are you saying that I've got too much of the opposite of my sin, whatever it is?"

Parker's voice lowered as he checked Barry and Beatrix over his shoulder. "You flipped, Sloan. Flipped the switch."

"I'm still confused."

With the help of Flint, Barry got to his feet. He held his daughter's hand and stepped bravely toward Sloan. "I think I can explain."

All eyes rounded on the man.

"Let me preface this by saying I had no idea about your mate being taken—that's what he was, right? Your mate?"

Sloan nodded, eyes narrowing. "We didn't think you all knew about the mating bond."

"We only recently found out." He nodded toward the upturned chair. "Do you mind if I—?"

No one moved.

With a jolt, Sloan realized they waited for her permission. Everyone in the room was walking on eggshells—because of her.

Her mind whirled at the shift in dynamic. What was happening?

She gave a curt nod, and the man picked up the chair. Flint found another for Beatrix to sit on. Seeing her clutch her father's arm did something to Sloan's heart, especially since the girl had worked so hard to help Sloan on the drive over.

Sloan blurted, "I'm sorry. I wasn't in control of myself. You have to believe I would never willingly hurt either of you. It's just… in my head at the time, something snapped. I felt your sin, Barry. It's still there… I thought it would be gone after we stopped you from unleashing those beasts on the city."

"It's okay, love," Barry fixed the spectacles on his nose. "I don't blame you. What you went through is something called the *Godiver Reflex.*"

Gloria Godiver was the geneticist who created them, and their biological mother. Unease spread through Sloan's gut.

"What's that?" Parker folded his arms.

"Initially, Gloria was instructed to modify your genome sequence so you were instinctively motivated to end deadly sin. A search and destroy urge, if you will. Gloria did this because she was manipulated into believing she was making the world a utopia, however, as you all know, this was not the case. Julius Allcott wanted—sorry, still wants —to unleash you seven upon the world in order to eliminate all sinners indiscriminately. The Godiver Reflex occurs when the body registers too much sin, or too much of its opposing virtue. You become out of balance and will snap. Lucky for you, when Gloria discovered Julius's true intentions, she secretly changed your DNA with a solution to the reflex by programming a balancing mate. Unlucky, I guess, that the Syndicate have now discovered that if they remove your mate, then this reflex is triggered again."

"How do you know this?" Parker asked, then shifted to Flint for confirmation. "I thought you said he wasn't in the main lab with Gloria."

"He wasn't." Mary's eyes narrowed on the man. "How do you know so much, Barry?"

The scientist sighed, looking much older than his late fifties. "Obviously, you've discovered by now that Despair survived the fire. Gloria may have died, but some of her research was also saved. The rest, we surmised from reverse engineering Despair's modified genetics, and... well, from the recent samples we've gathered from your family."

"Daisy. We call her Daisy here," Sloan insisted. "Why didn't my power work on her?"

Barry scratched his head. "I'm not sure what you mean?"

"My new ability just allowed me to send almost everyone in here to sleep. I tried to do that on her, but it didn't work."

"Without running some tests, I couldn't—"

"Just take a guess."

Parker jumped in. "I think it's related to mirror neurons and theta waves."

"Okay. Right, then. My guess is your power seems related to feelings and emotions. Being linked to mirror neurons would mean that you can make someone believe they're experiencing the sensations for real. Since this power is stemmed in some sort of empathetic connection, I'm afraid to say that your sister probably has none left."

A cloud of dread descended in the room, making it seem like an ice box.

Sloan shivered. "Are you saying she's a psychopath?"

"That moment you had with me, the moment your switch flipped, is not like her. She's different. She never snaps. It seems as though she's fully aware of her functions, but somehow emotion stands apart from it. It's like she's left her body and watches from a distance. Some sort of dissociative response to her trauma." Barry's gaze turned distant. "I watched her play with a killer plant as though it were Catnip."

"Hold up—" Tony put his palm in the air. "Did you say killer plant?"

"Dad?" Beatrix's voice wavered. "Is this what you've been working on?"

Barry's head dipped. A frown creased between his brows. He looked ashamed. "Yes and no, love."

"Can we get back to what you were saying about Sloan's blackout?" Parker prompted.

"Right. Sorry. In order to do that, I need to speak about your eldest sister. I believe she is almost completely inhuman. I'd be grateful she hasn't developed powers."

"Almost." Tony pointed his finger at Barry. "You said almost."

Barry's eyes lifted heavenward. "I don't know if this is the truth, or wishful thinking, but Despair—"

"Daisy!" more than one of them said.

"—sorry, Daisy. Well, that plant she was playing with is created to seek out the sense of sin, and try to eliminate it. Either by poison, or from strangulation."

"*Santa mierda.*" Mary sat down hard on a stool.

"The point is, she got too close to one. I tried to help her, but she stopped me. She didn't want me to hurt the plant at her expense. Someone completely devoid of emotion wouldn't care if the plant lived or died. For some reason, she did."

Parker rubbed the scruff on his jaw, thinking. "She used to love that little potted plant we had in the observation room of the lab we grew up in. Do you remember, Mary?"

"Yes. I seem to remember her going back for it when we tried to escape." Mary sighed. "She was the most caring child. This is my fault. I left her behind."

"It's not your fault, Mary," Flint consoled her. "It was a tough decision to make."

"How can we trust you?" Parker asked Barry, coming to stand next to Sloan. He gave her shoulder a squeeze.

The simple gesture sent warmth spiraling through her. She'd come close to committing a heinous act, but her family understood. They had her back. Just like Max had—*did*. Just like he did. She'd find him and she'd rescue him. Jaw set with determination, she locked eyes with Barry.

"You feel that sin in me still, Sloan, because I'll never stop feeling guilty for my part in all this." Barry's arm went around his daughter. "I'll never be sorry for protecting Beatrix, but I should have known any children of Flint's and Mary's would be trustworthy. A part of me knew that the instant I saw you at that gala."

Flint gave his wife a tender look.

"There are still things I should be doing." He shook his head. "So many things I need to make up for."

"Well, you can start right now. Tell us what you know," Parker ordered.

"Where do you want me to start?"

"Everything. Start with Max. Where would they take him?"

Mary quickly stepped forward. "Beatrix, would you like to clean up and have something to eat? I'll take you upstairs."

"I'm not leaving my father."

"It's all right, poppet." Barry kissed her on the cheek. "We know why Sloan reacted the way she did. Now that we know, we can monitor her. It's safe."

Beatrix cast Sloan a worried glance. "Are you sure?"

It took some convincing, but eventually Mary got Beatrix to leave with her. Flint got Barry a drink of water. Not willing to wait until everyone was ready to chat, Sloan continued her onslaught on the man-hunting databases of the country. She found a few pictures of Max's face from different angles and uploaded them to the search parameters.

The minute Beatrix left the room, Sloan asked again, "Where's Max, Barry?"

"I don't know."

She exhaled. It was fine. She was going to find him. She ground her teeth and kept working.

"But I can tell you why he was taken."

Sloan's fingers paused, clenched. She lifted her gaze to the man. "Elaborate."

Don't throttle him. Don't throttle him. Put that anger in a box.

Goddammit. She was going to have so many boxes that when she worked out how to unpack them, it would be like the Grinch's Christmas stash.

Barry took a deep breath. "From what we gathered, this mating bond was a failsafe. It was Gloria's way of putting a Band-Aid on the mess she'd made."

"Hey!" Tony waved his hand. "We're standing right here."

"Sorry. Didn't mean it like that. I mean, the modified beings—you all—couldn't be controlled once matured. The mating bond would not only give you all the tools to survive and live rationally, but to flourish. Take that away… and Allcott gets his monsters back." Barry shifted his tie, gentling his fingers around his neck. "As we've already witnessed."

"Shi-*yet*." Tony scrubbed his hand over his face. "You're telling us… that those who've had their powers unlocked are ticking time-bombs?"

Realization dawned on Evan's face. "You mean they might try to separate Grace from me? Just like they've done to Sloan?"

"Exactly!" Sloan said, voice raised and tight. "They've taken Max. Can we please get to the business of finding him?"

She rubbed her temples.

"Whatever we can do, Sloanie, you know that." Evan's chin jutted. "As soon as we've got actionable intel, it's all hands on deck. In the meantime, I'm finding Grace. We need to alert Wyatt and Griff. And God knows what we're going to tell Max's team."

Sloan jumped to her feet. "Max is a priority. Max!"

With a calm, patient tone, Evan spoke. "I know that, Sloan, but what's worse than one of us unhinged?" He arched a brow. "All of us."

Evan left the room.

Energy bubbled within Sloan, and she couldn't contain it. Her jaw clenched so tight, she almost cracked her teeth. She had to do something. Holding her emotions in check took every ounce of control. Sounds warbled in her ears, and she fell forward to brace herself on the table. Deep breaths punctuated the conversation going on around her.

"I can't deal with this." Her eyes burned. "I need to find Max."

It was an urge tugging deeper within her body, underneath the sin sense... it was Max, but where the sin-sensing gave her a direction to follow, the pain from losing Max was just a gaping hole spreading. It terrified her.

Seeing her struggle, Tony came over and placed a steady palm on her back. "You're slipping Sloan. Rein it in."

"Can't."

"You can."

"No."

"What would Max tell you right now? Think of him."

She shut her eyes and pictured Max. His sunshine face and coconut musk. His winking smirk and his serious stare. His smooth breezy voice.

You got this.

Sloan calmed. Blood flowed in her body again and she sent Tony a small smile. "Thanks for talking me off the ledge."

His lips curved slightly, eyes softening. "If there's one thing I'm good at, it's coming down from a high."

"That's not true. You're—"

"Doesn't matter. Forget it." Tony shook his head.

Parker's voice floated back into her void. "Barry, are you telling me you have absolutely no idea where they might have taken Max?" Parker moved in on him, and bent to meet his eyes. The intimidation factor worked well for Parker. Anyone would be afraid of a giant grizzly getting in their face. "What about the black site, would they go back?"

"They won't take Max there." Barry shook his head. "Not since you've seen it. They'll most likely keep the projects running at the site, though. They think they're untouchable."

A spark ignited in Sloan's memory and she jolted upright. "I can't believe I forgot. The backdoor program I installed. I need to access it now. There might be something on it. Wait." She bit her lip, turning to Parker. "You don't think they know, do you?"

"Unlikely," he responded. "They probably think we were there to rescue Barry but, just in case, be quick and start accessing now."

"On it." Sloan shuffled back onto her stool and accessed the terminal on her laptop. After a few directives, she plugged in the IP address of her target. "I got this."

twenty-two

MAX JOHNSON

IN THE CAR that had spirited him away, they'd put a hessian bag over Max's head and tied his wrists together with a cable tie. The ride from Beatrix's dormitory took hours, and the sounds of traffic, horns blaring and people talking had eventually filtered through. He guessed he was back in Cardinal City.

Sloan and the rest would be looking for him. Would they think to look in their own backyard?

Daisy had deposited him in a small, windowless, empty room. She'd attached chain manacles to his ankles and wrists and then left.

That was hours ago.

Running escape scenarios occupied his thoughts for a while. He then moved to basic training practices, drills, and techniques for handling capture by the enemy. He refused to lose control of his thoughts, afraid that if he did, he'd be haunted by memories.

When he ran out of mental training sessions, he shifted his thoughts to Sloan. She'd always been his security blanket while he was on a mission. Thinking of her was a comforting routine. If he ever felt lonely, or desperate, he'd conjure the sight of her pretty face, rosy lips and lusty, larger-than-life laugh. Usually they were playing a game—that's all they seemed to do when they'd first met. Her rusty voice in his ear. Her face on the screen in a small box, next to the bigger screen displaying the game play. He'd never admit this to her, but sometimes she'd beat him, or he'd screw up the game because he'd be looking at her face instead of the game. He'd loved watching how her eyes turned narrow and dark, and how a little pink flash of tongue would sit at the corner of her lips when she concentrated. The complete opposite of the face she made when he brought her to climax in the cave. A dark stain to her cheeks. Lips, all plump from being ravished. That sense of urgency, of need, in her expression.

A flood of warmth filled his body. That face was a new memory to add to his arsenal, and if he got out of this, he'd make it his mission to see that face in the light of day.

Sighing, Max leaned his head back on the cold wall and looked at the ceiling. It, too, was plain.

This waiting was a tactic. He'd used it himself against the enemy. Leave them with nothing but their own thoughts and doubts. Make them fragile.

But he wouldn't reveal secrets, no matter what they did. He was special forces. Like Gale, he'd been trained hard and his resilience was implacable. The only way they'd get secrets from him would be to pry them from his cold, dead body... just like they'd done with his best friend. He squeezed his eyes shut against the onslaught of vile images —bloody pieces of his friend, still recognizable.

Clenching his jaw, he knew that was a possible outcome for his current situation, but he wouldn't compromise Sloan's safety. She was more precious than his own life.

She was all he had. Always had been.

His thoughts shifted to Gale. He'd been a good man. A father of two. A husband. Brother. Son. People missed him.

He should really call Gale's parents. His avoidance was unconscionable. That was another thing to add to his list when he got out of here.

Seeing those people in agony at Gale's funeral had broken something inside Max, made it all too real. It churned and twisted in his mind. Why Gale, who had everything to lose? Why not Max?

Max was the one who'd left the army, and when he went back, he was the one who'd messed up. That was a lot to accept. He scrubbed his hand down his face and groaned.

This was the kind of self-doubt the enemy wanted.

Instead of continuing down that path, he built a wall of Sloan-shaped memories around his heart. Conjured her smell—another tool for his arsenal—and immersed himself in love.

twenty-three

SLOAN LAZARUS

"I *DON'T* GOT THIS!" Sloan shouted into the echoing void of her apartment. She slammed her laptop lid closed and rolled on her bed, letting loose a scream of frustration into her pillow.

It had been weeks since Max was taken. Thirteen days to be exact.

Still no sign of him but plenty of Daisy's insufferably perfect face. Not even bothering to hide under her half-face bird mask, she'd been popping up on the camera feeds around the city, taunting Sloan, going as far as to stare into the lens with her disturbing violet eyes. At first Sloan had rushed to the location only to find no trace of the woman, or Max. The only thing she succeeded in was inadvertently sending a school bus of children to sleep. They had their windows down in the heat and in her haste to cut through traffic, she'd not contained her power as tightly as she'd hoped. Traffic had literally stopped, causing accidents all round as people nodded off behind the steering wheel. Only cars with their windows up were safe. All she remembered thinking was an offhand comment that everyone should slow down so she could pass. Somehow her brain subconsciously projected sleep.

Miraculously, no one had been injured.

Sloan knew she needed training, and not the physical kind. She'd had plenty of that at the gym in the past two weeks. Her powers were unpredictable when she was stressed. She'd barely slept, instead, putting her feelings in a box and locking them up tight. Problem was, she'd not unpacked any boxes—she was too busy trying to find Max.

If sleep slipped out and affected people around her, it wasn't good. What next? What if her heartbreak broke loose? What about her pain? Her despair?

What if she snapped?

She flinched as the image of her fingers choking the life out of Barry came to her.

Parker was right to confine Sloan to Lazarus House until her internal equilibrium returned to normal. She understood his point, but not heading out every time Daisy's face popped up on the alert was counterintuitive. Being the only one manning the surveillance almost twenty-four-seven, she was the first line of attack, and her family wasn't fast enough acting on the intel. How could they catch Daisy if they didn't chase?

It was a game. A game Sloan would win, or go mad trying.

That was exactly the point, Parker had pointed out. Daisy wanted Sloan insane with her power, ending sinners all over town.

Sloan wanted to hate her sister. A dark cruel twisted feeling inside wanted to smother the woman, but it wasn't all Daisy's fault. She was a product of their evil twisted makers. It could have just as easily been Sloan causing the trouble. Sliding doors, and all that.

The closest they'd come to catching a lead was Daisy's game of peekaboo, and it frustrated the living daylights out of Sloan. The woman wanted Sloan out in public. She wanted Sloan causing havoc with her unbalanced powers. Daisy was back in the city, though, and that's why on the second computer down at her desk in the living room, she searched the city's feeds—CCTV footage, local news networks and so on. Lilo, Griffin's mate, worked at the Cardinal Copy, and was doing her best to use her contacts to chase down any information, but Sloan had better access than anyone. If Sloan couldn't find Max, then maybe he couldn't be found.

Rolling to her back, she stared at the ceiling for precisely the count of three, then pushed out of bed to find something to do. The longer she stayed still, the more her thoughts derailed toward dreadful outcomes and she kept hearing Max's voice in her head, *Leave no stone unturned.* Without him, they'd never have broken the lead that brought them to Barry. Also, Max would have never been kidnapped. Liza said kidnapping victims rarely remained alive beyond a few days from their capture.

Shut up.

She wasn't going there. Not today.

Moving from the bedroom to the kitchen, Sloan went to the box Wyatt had delivered weeks ago. The box still sat on her kitchen bench. It still had his ex's belongings in there, including the little velvet red box. Unopened.

The box glared bright in her dimmed room.

Red. Angry red. Blood red. Love red.

Her chest constricted. Max had said he'd bought her a ring, and she knew the ring was inside. She'd seen it, but she didn't have the heart to open the box. It would be a glaring symbol of her failure.

With trembling fingers, she picked up the red velvet box and opened it. It creaked and resisted. Old, unused and discarded, she had to use force.

There it was.

The ring.

The polish seemed to have lost a little shine. The diamonds were lackluster. A lump in her throat formed. She snapped the lid shut, the sound of it echoing darkly in her mind. It was the sound of a door slamming closed, for the second time.

A bird warbled through the open window at her fire-escape. Placing the box down on the kitchen bench, she jogged back into her bedroom and growled the Bluebird away from the pizza box sitting on the sill. She lifted the lid to search for a slice, not caring the box had been delivered the previous night. Nothing but picked off pineapple pieces were left. It was probably what the bird was trying to get, but Sloan didn't want anyone touching those pineapple pieces.

No one.

Tears welled in her eyes, burning. That lump in her throat wouldn't move and her throat closed up over it. She sniffed, wiping her nose with the bottom of her ratty pajama sleeve, but the sleeve couldn't hold back the hot tears that spilled, the snot that clogged her nose, and the puffy eyes.

The cat meowed beneath her bed.

Sniffing, Sloan wiped her nose again. "I'm sorry Luna. I'll—" she fanned her face with her hand and gulped in a breath "—I'll manage my emotion. *I will.*"

While she took deep breaths, her gaze darted around her apartment, looking for a distraction. Weeks ago, it was a filthy mess. Now, apart from the pizza boxes, everything was spotless. She'd exhausted all her cleaning efforts, and she'd spent any other available moment in the gym or searching for Max. There was nothing left for her to do. She supposed she could clean herself. She was a mess, after all.

Luna meowed and crawled out from beneath the bed. She blinked up at Sloan with her yellow eyes and then made a weird mewling sound as she reclined and rolled, using her claws to pluck at the fallen blanket draped half off the bed, half on the floor. If Sloan didn't know any better, she'd say Luna was moping. Just like her.

Sloan also supposed she could use this time to get better at controlling her ability.

Get more lethal. Get invincible.

She wanted to be on her A-game when that computer pinged Max's location. And it *would* find him. She'd already honed her body, now it was time to work on her power. She went to stand at her computer station to watch the three monitors as they searched the city for her mate.

Tony answered after two rings.

"Ye-es?" he drawled, voice smooth and deep.

"Are you home?"

He paused, then responded again with another suspicion-laced drawl. "Ye-es."

"I need your help."

"You're not going to retaliate, prank wise, are you? Because I'm not in the mood."

"No. I'm done with that. I need your help to control my emotions." She thought about it, then added, "Please."

"Oh." Another long drawn out pause. "You want *my* help?"

"Yes."

"Oh."

"Pretty please?"

"I mean, sure. I don't know how I can help, but sure."

"You're an actor, Tony. A good one. If there's anyone who knows the ins and outs of emotion, it's you."

"Oh."

"You keep saying that. Are you all right?"

"I'm good," he mumbled. "When do you want to do this?"

She walked over to her computer and checked the time. It was still early. Nine a.m. "I need to clean myself up. How about in ten minutes?"

"I can give you a few hours. See you in the training room."

They disconnected, and while she was at her computer station, Sloan checked the screen that displayed the keystroke program she'd installed on the Syndicate's black site servers. A search of the server database had turned out to be frustratingly fruitless. When mentioned to Barry, he had pointed out that none of the research was stored on the administration computers. Julius was extremely secretive, and he kept research cells isolated.

That was good information.

Sloan should be happy that she'd followed her instincts to rescue Barry, but without Max, she was fast becoming lost in nothing. No, that was wrong; she wasn't lost in nothing. She had Tony, her family, and she had hope—something Daisy sorely lacked. It was something.

twenty-four

SLOAN LAZARUS

SLOAN SHOWERED and dressed in workout attire. Puma joggers, black leggings and a sports bra that strapped around her shoulders and stomach. She tied her hair into a ponytail and gave Luna a kiss. Just before she left her room, she spotted the red jewelry box sitting innocently on the kitchen counter.

A beat.

Another.

Then she rushed over, opened it, and stuck the ring on her finger. Not on the wedding ring finger, but on her right hand. The diamond winked at her as though happy to get out of the box, to be free. Smiling, she replaced the red velvet box back in the container of other belongings and noticed the cell phone that belonged to Wyatt's ex. Reaching in, she pulled it out. It was dead as wood, but if she went down to the workshop after her training session, she might find a way to restore it. If Flint was down there, even better.

With a renewed sense of purpose, she left her apartment. She was ready.

She arrived in the basement and found the entire floor empty.

Her mother and father, who were usually in the workshop, were also absent. The rest of her family were most likely at their day jobs or homes. She couldn't help feeling a little peeved at that.

Max was missing.

Logically she knew there was only so much to do without a lead to move on and they had exhausted their options. Their investigation into Max's whereabouts had stalled. Life went on in the meantime. Parker and Evan had a business to run, Griffin and Liza had day jobs, Wyatt was with Misha, Tony…

Oh shit.

Tony had not been well during their mission to the black site. He'd been erratic, irritated, sick. His dependency on alcohol and substances had taken a hold of him. She knew as well as anyone that if not kept in check, their sin had a way of sneaking up on them and her heart went out to her brother. With so much going on in their lives, she wondered if he'd had time to talk to anyone about his situation—besides Parker and his bossiness.

She'd been so intent on finding Max that she'd failed to think about Tony's plight. Only a few short months ago, she'd admonished Wyatt for selfishly abandoning their family, for abandoning her, when he knew she needed him.

She owed Tony more. He didn't have a mate to balance his sin out. Like Parker and Liza, he was fighting a silent battle—alone. That was fucking hard.

Sloan searched the large training room for Tony. Gym equipment, mirrors, and a central rubber mat for sparring. No windows. A bench on one side. Boxing bags on another. Parker had recently installed a huge flat screen on one wall that was connected to AIMI so they could monitor anything they wanted while keeping themselves fit and fighting ready.

No Tony.

Unconsciously, she tugged on her ponytail with the intent of stuffing the end into her mouth. She was still frowning at her hair in her fingers when Tony entered the room. Honed to perfection, his movie star body was the epitome of buff and a lot of hard work. She knew he kept regular personal training sessions, separate to his time here at Lazarus House. His appearance was picked apart by the tabloids. He had a stylist, a nutritionist, an agent, a publicist, and personal shopper. But he had no entourage, no assistant, no friends. Only brief hook-ups. Their life prohibited close connections and Parker was the first to remind everyone of that commitment.

The Deadly Seven were often vilified in the media. Nobody liked vigilantes taking the law into their own hands, but the lowering crime rates spoke enough. It was just coming to Sloan's attention that the media also crapped on Tony in his personal life. If gluttony was knocking on his door, he couldn't eat—he would put on weight and the media would have a field day. She felt bad enough about letting herself go without the paparazzi watching her every move. So if he couldn't satisfy the urges of his sin with food, he was left with sex and substances, and since being in a relationship where the partner was not his mate seemed counterintuitive, he had to get his sexual kicks from different sources, often.

"Sloan," Tony greeted as he dumped a water bottle on the side bench. He wore a pair of loose shorts, and a navy blue singlet that hugged his ripped torso. He swept his short, brown hair off his forehead as he flicked his gaze her way. "How's the search going?"

"Same as before. No leads."

"That sucks."

"Yeah, but I have Sara's old cell. I'm going to try to bring it back to life after this, so hopefully I'll find something on it."

"You don't sound convinced."

"If I was, I wouldn't be standing here." She sighed. "The truth is, it's a Hail Mary, but I have to keep trying."

Tony strode to a wall that housed gym supplies. Towels, weights, and a water station. He pulled a towel from a folded pile and returned. "And what about the Nightingale Securities team?"

She frowned. Keeping Nightingale Securities cool about Max's disappearance had been tough. As professionals, they knew Max would notify them before going anywhere. Parker had told them he'd been tasked with a top-secret assignment and will explain when they get back. They'd retrieved Max's cell from the side of the road it was discarded and faked a message to his team. It was enough to keep them satisfied. Just. But if Max never—

Don't go there.

"Sloan?"

"Sorry, was thinking about our excuse with the Nightingale team running into an expiration date. We'll have to think of something else to tell them soon."

"What if we bring them into the fold? Can they provide assistance?"

"What can they do that I can't?" she scoffed.

"I heard one of them was CIA in a past life."

"She's not now. Besides, we're not supposed to know that and I don't want to go over there. I'm not a good liar and they're getting antsy."

He rubbed his chin. "Yeah, Tom-Tom and Daymo served with Max for many years. They won't last much longer."

"It's the woman. She's the one who's been hounding us."

Tony perked up. "A woman?"

Sloan rolled her eyes. "That's the one who was in the CIA."

"I didn't know that." He frowned. "Is she old?"

"God, you're hopeless."

That earned Sloan a sly smirk. "I volunteer as tribute to go over and update them on our fake story. I can say Max has been reassigned somewhere else."

"Keep your pants on. I just want to get better at containing my powers so I can go out and physically search for Max."

"Fair enough. Where do you want to start?"

Sloan blinked and realized she'd been completely rude. The moment Tony had mentioned something he was interested in—who cares if it was a woman—Sloan had changed the subject. Damn her.

"I'll start with an apology."

"Sorry?"

"I've not been fair on you. The pranking, and… well… you're going through something and I've not even asked how you're handling it."

"I'm not going through anything."

"Tony," she admonished. "You almost puked during the mission to the black site from lack of alcohol. Maybe you did. I never asked."

"Can we drop it?"

She couldn't force him to speak about it. "If you want, I'm sure I can get you introduced to the woman on Max's team. Her name is Bailey."

"I was kidding." He narrowed his eyes as if he suspected her words were another prank.

"I'm serious."

"And I said drop it. So… where are we starting? What do you want, acting lessons?"

She sighed. Okay, she supposed she deserved his hesitance. Onward and upward, she guessed. "So, I'm having trouble conjuring the memory of the right emotion during periods of elevated stress."

He nodded, eyes glued to her.

She continued, "As you know, I can recall the feeling of sleep the best, but sometimes, like with those wild beastie-animals, I couldn't call forth a feeling on purpose in a rush. The only time I could was when I actually got hurt or if I had time to concentrate. I want to be able to do it on command, during stressful moments, and I want to be able to pull up a variety of helpful emotions."

"Okay."

"Okay?"

"Yeah, I think I know how to help." He gestured for her to come closer. "First, come stand next to me and face the mirror."

Feeling awkward, she shuffled next to him and stared at their reflections, side by side. Immediately, she felt inadequate next to the perfect specimen standing next to her, but then she looked harder. She hadn't looked much since she'd resumed her training, and now that she was, it was easy to see how much she'd changed. Her crop top only covered her chest, but left her midriff free. She had abs. There was not a layer of fat on her body. Her curved hips fit snuggly into her leggings. Her legs were toned—not the cracking nuts kind of toned like Tony's—but still, toned. Seeing that for the first time sent her eyes roaming over the rest of her body. Flexing her fists, the small muscles in her arms bulged. Nice.

Tony caught her self admiration and smirked. "And they call me conceited."

"Shut up," she laughed. "It's just that… I've not noticed my body in a while."

"I've seen you down here for hours every day. You worked hard and now you look good, sis."

She smiled at him. "Thanks."

They shared a moment of mutual connection, then a shadow flickered over his gaze and he turned back to the mirror. "Okay, so this method is called the Chekhov Acting Technique. Basically, to recall an emotional memory, we act it out. Then the idea is that through repeating physical actions, your recollection will come stronger, and with little effort."

"Not to point out the obvious, but how will I find time to act out an emotion if I'm in the heat of battle?"

"We start with acting out the gestures here, then we internalize them. With enough training, you'll be able to recall that earlier physicalized emotion. So, act, internalize, act, internalize. We do it until you can recall that emotion without effort."

"That makes a lot of sense, bras. I should have come to you for help a long time ago."

His lip twitched. "What have I told you about calling me a ladies undergarment?" Then he folded his arms and held his chin between his forefinger and thumb, watching her. "Okay. Start."

"Just like that?"

"Once you got this down, we'll spar at the same time. Go."

So she had to act out an emotive memory... then learn to internalize it, then learn to do that while getting beat up by this big burly real life action hero.

Sloan caught her reflection's eyes. Okay. She's got this. Think of a feeling. What feeling? Pain, was her obvious first choice. Making an opponent crippled with that feeling would come in handy. She was tempted to use her nails to bite into her palms, but shook her head. What if she was incapacitated and couldn't hurt herself? She wanted to do this properly. No more cutting corners.

That thought promptly brought up feelings of Max and she had to shut her eyes.

Soon, baby. Soon.

Seeing her hesitance, Tony suggested, "What about a strong feeling you can recall from a recent event. What about how you felt when you knew Max was leaving you in that car with Beatrix."

Her brows snapped together and she glared at him.

But he wasn't fazed. He turned to his reflection, took a deep breath and... simply became *someone else*. His face crumpled his eyes glazed, and he collapsed, hands covering his head as it shook in denial. He acted distraught for another moment, and she believed it! Then he straightened, reset, and said, "Or maybe it was like this." Then his eyes darted about the room, struggling to find purchase. He muttered "no" multiple times and paced listlessly.

Damn he was good. "You're pretty good at this acting thing, hey, bras."

He grimaced, ignoring her compliment. "You try."

Sloan's heart clenched. She didn't think she was ready for this. "Can we try something else? Another emotion?"

His gaze softened. "Okay, what about pain? Can you picture yourself having a headache?"

That, she could do.

For the next hour, they acted out a variety of feelings. Pain, sleep, and fear. They'd decided to focus on three main sensations. The following hour, Sloan practiced conjuring that physicality internally. Then the hour after that, she was sweating it out on the rubber mat, taking a beating from her brother.

"Arms up." He jabbed at her head.

She blocked, breathing hard. A dart back on her feet, and he jabbed again but she surged back again. Twisting, she sidestepped and ducked under his swinging arm to come in and put a fist in his side. He grunted, but used her low position to grapple and throw her down.

The air knocked out of her, but Tony took no quarter. He used the full force of his strength to wrestle her into a choke hold, legs and arms both trapping her inside the cage of his body. Panic flared and her training froze in her mind.

"Any day now, Sloan," he taunted. "I'm still waiting to feel —ungh!"

Slam! She'd conjured her headache and shoved it outward. That pain knocked into Tony and had him releasing her to clutch his head.

He rolled away and entered the fetal position. "You can stop now," he burst.

She swapped the internalized headache with sleep and watched his eyelids get heavy until his long lashes swept his cheekbones. Only when she saw his body go lax did she let go completely and unlock a compartment of calm. Over the course of the day, she'd found a combination of Max's compartmentalization techniques, and Tony's internalization techniques worked best.

Crouching down, she placed a hand on Tony's shoulder, giving him a shake to wake him. "You okay, Tony?"

He groaned. She'd projected those horrible feelings at him for three hours and he didn't complain once. With another groan, he uncurled and lay on his back, long arms and legs splayed like a star, and he stared at the ceiling.

"And the grasshopper has become the master," he joked, then rubbed his head. "Jesus Christ, that last one still hurt. I'm so glad you didn't make me bleed." Something occurred to him and he snapped his eyes at her. "You'd better not make me bruise. Makeup will hate you."

She laughed. "I'm pretty sure the bleeding thing was only while my powers were settling in. I haven't had another repeat occurrence since. Sorry about the pain, but I think I'm getting the hang of it. I owe you one."

"How about a beer?"

"Done." She could do with one too.

"And then we'll do it again tomorrow."

twenty-five

SLOAN LAZARUS

OVER THE NEXT TWO DAYS, when Sloan wasn't training with Tony, she was working on Sara's cell. It was late in the afternoon when she sat in the basement headquarters workshop, sitting next to her father. The smell of oil, metal shavings, and something chemical filled her senses until she rubbed her nose to rid it.

Flint's spectacles rested halfway down the bridge of his nose. He handed her a small Philips-Head screwdriver and then went back to collecting a pile of errant bolts and nuts that had spilled when she'd first arrived and knocked them over with her laptop.

After working diligently with him for the following two hours, she'd felt herself calm and submerge in the task at hand. So far, they'd pulled it apart, and tried hacking the sim. What finally worked was sourcing a new charger to fit the old battery. Such a simple thing to do, but neither of them had thought of it for hours, and then it took a few minutes for the battery to retain enough power for the cell screen to come alight and make a ping sound.

Her breath caught in her throat.

She thumbed through the contents.

"Just as we suspected," Flint rumbled, clapping Sloan on the back. "The cell wasn't backed up to the sim, but there's history in there. Good thinking, squirt."

"It's basic," Sloan replied. "Not much inside. A few numbers in the call history." Simple social media accounts set up to act as a cover for Sara's false identity—but Sloan knew about those. Messages between her and Wyatt—but she knew about those as well.

"Here." Flint offered her a USB cable. "Let's try the file recovery software again."

She plugged it into the port on the cell, with little hope. She was out of ideas. She'd tried everything.

Evan waltzed in at that moment and came over to their bench. He flicked a stray screw out of the way so he could lean on his elbow to watch her. Flint scowled at him, made a point of picking up the rolling screw and put it back in the collection container.

"Sorry," Evan mumbled, noticing his mistake.

Flint grumbled in response and took his container to a supply shelf on the wall.

Evan turned to Sloan. "Shouldn't you be in your room keeping an eye on the monitors?"

Giving him the side-eye, she continued running the program on her attached laptop. "Shouldn't you be covering some poor soul in permanent ink?"

"Nah. Shop's closed."

"It's that late?"

He nodded. "Only just gone five."

"Wow. I've been immersed in this, then training with Tony, then this. We shared a beer at Heaven, then I left him to come here. Some fan recognized him and he decided to hang."

It was funny when Sloan thought about Tony and his acting success. When Tony had announced Gluttony's alter-ego would be a movie star, no one really thought he'd be successful. A forever auditioning actor was a decent cover for being a vigilante. But then Sara came along and ruined their team. All the Deadly Seven had scattered to the wind and become immersed in their day lives to get away from the fact that they may have been responsible for the death of over forty innocents—or at least the public thought they were. When Tony got cast in a starring role, it took him by surprise. It took them all by surprise.

Parker had been on his case to find a new career for months. His rigid hours weren't easy to work around and fighting the Syndicate came first. She knew that better than anyone.

"So what you doing?" Evan asked again.

"I'm searching the cell Sara left at Wyatt's."

"Why?"

"Are you kidding me?" She turned to him. Had his electric power fried his brain?

"What?" He looked offended.

"Well, bras, maybe if you'd actually had a psychic vision or something about Max, we'd be able to find him and I wouldn't need to do this."

"No need to get snippy. I can't control them, you know that. I've only had weird random dreams about Daisy and gardening."

She slumped. Flint, who was closing up a drawer on his shelf, glanced over with a look that told her to settle down.

"Sorry," she said. "I'm still on edge."

"S'cool. Besides," Evan said as he poked at the cell. "It looks different."

"What do you mean?"

"That time I followed her up to Wyatt's apartment and found her making a call, the cell she was on looked different. Maybe like..." He reached into his back jeans pocket and pulled his own cell out. It was the same brand the entire family shared. "Maybe like this."

Silence shattered the room.

A heartbeat passed. Then another.

Almost too afraid to speak, she asked, "Did you overhear the conversation? Did it sound like—"

His eyes unfocused as his mind turned inward. "She was giving them an update on her plan. It was how I knew she'd been lying to us. That's when I confronted her."

Maybe Sloan didn't hear right because it sounded like he inferred Sara used another phone to call the Syndicate—a phone that looked like his, and like the rest of their family's—like Wyatt's. Or was her mind reaching, and it was just a coincidence?

Flint cleared his throat. "Evan. Did you just say Sara may have used Wyatt's cell to call the Syndicate?"

"I guess. We all have the same phone model, right?"

Sloan shouted at AIMI. "AIMI. Pull up Wyatt's cell phone records from—" she looked at Evan and whispered. "What date?"

Looking flustered, he shrugged. "I don't know. What date? Shit! Why are you so excited?"

"You idiot." She poked him. "If Wyatt's cell has a record of the number belonging to the Syndicate, it could lead us to their location."

"If that number is still active," Flint reminded her. It was his way of saying, don't get your hopes up.

She bit her lip. "We could still find something."

"Okay, let me look." Evan activated his cell and opened up his calendar application. "What was the date?" He murmured to himself. "Got it. November thirtieth."

Sloan relayed the information to AIMI and directed her to bring up Wyatt's cell phone records on her laptop. While that was happening, she pulled up the GPS history from Sara's phone. On its own, the information from Sara's cell was a needle in a haystack, but coupled with the location of the caller from Wyatt's cell on the day she'd called the Syndicate… they'd have a location. It might not be the place Max was being held. But it was a start.

After five minutes of searching, she looked up and met Evan's eyes. "Found something."

twenty-six

MAX JOHNSON

"WAKE UP."

Pain burst in Max's cheek and he jolted awake, wincing. The crusty dried blood on his face cracked and itched.

After the cloud dissipated from his vision, he saw the woman who'd kidnapped him crouching, watching his reaction with curiosity. He could see how she was related to Sloan—same beautiful features, wide mouth, plump lips. Except… Sloan's glossy black hair stood out, framing her face while this woman's hair blended with her white leather collar. Sloan's eyes always smiled with mischief, but this woman… when she stared back at Max, he saw a dark chasm yawning with the depths of despair. Soulless, and lonely. She reminded Max of how he'd felt at his lowest—when he believed Sloan had left him after Gale had died.

He'd lost track of time in this place. No windows. No hope of discovering if it were day or night. Having only eaten soggy bread and water, his stomach cramped, revolting at the smell from the bucket in the corner he'd done his business in, and he desperately wanted to raise his hand to test the spot on his cheek where she'd hit, but he couldn't. His hands were tied.

Daisy moved suddenly and Max flinched. He couldn't help it. She'd beaten him often, but so far, he'd never been hurt beyond superficial wounds and it was the anticipation of something worse that played on his mind. His eyes went to the blood spray on her white collar and then his mind moved to a conflicting idea. Could it be possible she avoided permanently maiming him for another reason? Was she thinking about her family, about Sloan? Maybe she didn't go too far on purpose… because she had hoped one day they'd forgive her.

She cocked her head to the side allowing her white mane of hair to swish over her shoulder.

"You are a curious person, Maximillian Johnson," she stated.

"So are you, Daisy," he replied.

She blinked. A flicker of something passed in that violet chasm and then her delicate brows puckered. "My name is Despair."

"That's not your name. That's your duty."

Keep her talking.

It's all he'd been doing for days on end, and the more they talked, the more likely it was she let slip something important.

"What do you know about duty, Maximillian Johnson?"

Grinding his teeth, he stared back, gaze never wavering.

"I know that duty is what you make of it," he said. "I know that it's hard, and sometimes you think you're doing the right thing, but you're not. You make mistakes. I also know that there is no mistake you can't come back from." Her eyes narrowed, but she said nothing, so he added softly, "Your family misses you."

She backhanded him. He breathed through the numbing pain on his other cheek. This was good. It meant he was getting to her. He spat blood on the floor.

"You're a filthy liar," she declared, and Max actually heard emotion in her voice. "You speak of duty, but I know what you did for your friend. I know that you went on a killing rampage all in the name of so-called justice. How are you different to me?"

"I'm not proud of what I did," he replied as a suffocating feeling sat on his chest. He frowned, fighting back the memories of his time exacting revenge on the insurgents that murdered his friend. His mind went completely dark and filled with utter chaos. It hurt him to talk about, but if it kept her attention away from Sloan, then so be it. He snarled at her. "Those assholes killed my friend. It was war. But I should have listened to my leaders. It's a regret and a stain on my heart that will follow me to my grave."

This made her blink and her toneless voice was back. "You are stained. You embody everything she fights against. You murdered in cold blood. You are a sinner. You are unwanted."

No. He shook his head. That wasn't true. He'd *felt* Sloan's emotions. He knew the truth. She loved him as much as he loved her. She and her family would find him. He just had to hold out. He trusted her. But, even as he repeated the mantra in his head, the doubt Daisy had planted began to grow.

What if their brief reunion wasn't solid? What if Sloan oscillated back to whatever motivation kept her from coming after him the first time? What if she got to thinking about their relationship, truly thinking, and decided that someone like her—a warrior for justice—couldn't love someone like him… a flat out murderer.

Max took a deep, shuddering breath.

He pushed out the doubt and replaced it with hope. If he couldn't trust their relationship, then they were back in the same place they'd been two years ago, and he wouldn't do that. Not on his end this time. He could only hope Sloan felt the same on her end.

"I can feel your despair knocking at the edges of your soul,

Maximillian Johnson." She leaned closer and whispered. *"Let me in, little piggy. Let me in."*

"I won't let it in. You shouldn't either."

One of his escape scenarios involved turning Daisy to his side. She was a Lazarus; the eldest of eight. Sloan had told him they thought Daisy perished in a fire. Looking at her now, Max could barely see the faint pale sliver of scar tissue down the side of her face. Being burned alive as a child would be a horrific memory, perhaps one the Syndicate used against her. That fire started when their biological mother decided to destroy all the evidence of the project. What if the Syndicate told Daisy she was part of that evidence and that her mother wanted her dead? There were many gaps in the reasoning and knowledge of what really went down that day, and Daisy only went by what the Syndicate had told her. Perhaps these gaps could be exploited to bring her back to the right side of the battle.

He knew one thing for sure: whatever they'd told her to make her believe she was worth being left behind, it had eaten away at her psyche. She *was* despair.

"How did you meet Sloth?" Daisy asked. Again.

They'd been at this for an eternity.

He gave her the same answer he gave every single time. "You mean Sloan?"

She pursed her lips and stood to tower over him. "You know who I'm talking about. Enough of this nonsense."

There was that tremor of emotion again.

He smiled. "Can't remember."

A boot to his ribs was her response. He coughed, doubled over.

"When did you know you were her mate?"

Now he laughed. "In Australia, we're all mates."

Another eye-watering kick to his gut. This time he rolled, curled to protect himself. His head lolled and pressed against the cool floor, taking a small comfort in the temperature. The specks in the stone aggregate were green.

Daisy dragged him back to sitting and shoved his back against the wall. He winced at the pull from the cable ties around his raw wrists and ankles.

"When did she discover her powers were linked to you? Was it the first time you copulated?"

He arched an amused brow. Copulated? That was new. She'd never asked about intimate details before. "Now, I've been told my dick is magic, but that's taking it a bit far, don't you think?"

Besides… they'd never gotten that far. Not yet. Thoughts of that event kept him warm at night. He knew exactly how their first time would go. Already, his mind took him there, sliding into fantasy, and away from reality. Silk sheets. Diamonds.

Daisy let go and stood back, nostrils flaring as she glared down at him.

He was getting to her. Why? The crude language? Unlikely.

He stared at her while he unpacked his thoughts. She'd been on a roll until the talk of sex. It made her awkward. Daisy's fingers twitched at her side.

"You've never been with a man, have you?" he asked, curious.

The flicker in her eyes told him, perhaps no. Perhaps she'd been too busy, doing her master's bidding. Perhaps she was too deep in the pits of despair to want love, or maybe, she couldn't feel desire at all.

But that twitch, that hesitation, that tremble of emotion and pink tinge to her cheeks. She longed for that human connection as much as anyone.

Stained. Unwanted.

His heart went out to her, and it must have shown on his face because her expression morphed into disgust, then anger. "You answer *my* questions, not the other way around. Tell me exactly what Sloth can do."

"She talks about you all the time," he replied, resting his head back on the wall behind him. "I don't see why. They should just give up on you. That's what I would do. But that entire family is determined to bring you back into their fold." He paused. "Do you know they set a place for you at their table every time they have a family meal?"

This time, her attack sent white stars and black dots clashing behind his eyelids. She hit his face, kicked his body. She was relentless, unforgiving. He had to lift his arms as well as he could to protect himself, but with the cable-tie around his wrists, he left his sides open.

"That's enough, my darling." A deep masculine voice rumbled from somewhere.

"God?" Max said, laughing and spluttering through his bloody mouth. "Is that you?"

"You jest, but as far as you're concerned, I *am* God." The man who stepped into view was tall, pale-haired, and square jawed. You could tell he was used to having orders obeyed from the set of his physique and lift of his chin. His luxury tailored suit complimented his broad shoulders. He was sickeningly handsome.

And he looked like... *holy shit.* Max could see Tony Lazarus in this man. And the moment he saw that connection, he saw the familiarity with the woman standing next to him. Then Sloan. The rest of her siblings...

This man was their biological father. This was the man behind the Syndicate machine.

"Let's get this straight, Mr. Johnson." The man put his hands behind his back. "You're only alive because we say so. When we decide you've outlived your purpose, you're gone."

"Exactly," Max said. "Why would I give you anything, when you'll just kill me afterward?"

"As long as you keep feeding us information, we will keep you alive."

"Nah. Think I'm good."

"We have ways of making people talk."

"Yeah? How's that working for you?"

The man leaned forward. It was enough to make Max want to shrink back, but he had nowhere else to go.

"We've barely begun to use our ways."

A coldness seeped into Max at the sight of him pulling out a syringe filled with liquid. "Truth serum?" he scorned. "Hate to break it to you, mate, but that shit don't work."

"It's not truth serum."

Max's jaw clicked shut.

The man stared at Max for a long time, but Max refused to say anything else. Eventually, the man sighed and held out the syringe in Daisy's direction.

To Max's surprise, she hesitated.

When the man turned to her with a questioning eyebrow lifted, she frowned. "You didn't discuss this with me."

Both the men's eyebrows lifted, incredulously.

Daisy shifted her boots. "I thought we would keep trying to flush her out, test the effect of her missing mate on the public."

"We tried that. You know this. Sloth came out once and hasn't returned. She's not taking the bait."

"But when she did, she sent a busload of people to sleep. Isn't that worth exploring?"

"That wasn't enough for our investors." The boss's jaw chewed from side to side. He didn't like being argued with.

Max held his breath, trying not to move. Funny what information people gave away in front of a dead man.

The man waved his syringe. "This will expedite results."

"I thought you wanted him to talk." Daisy flicked her gaze to Max. "You will ruin him."

Okay, now Max was sitting up. Ruin him? Ruin him how?

"If I needed your opinion, my darling, I'd ask it. Now be a good girl and do your job."

Daisy stared at the man for what seemed a long moment. She blinked once. Max had the sense he was witnessing a rare thing—her dissent. He wanted to feel triumphant; he wanted to believe that he'd gotten through to her, but when she took the syringe from the man's hand and turned on him, he could only feel despair… and with that, her lips curved in a cruel smile.

"Don't do this, Daisy," he urged.

She flicked her finger against the cylinder of the syringe, then depressed the handle to make fluid squirt out. "I told you, my name is Despair."

And then she stabbed him in the arm.

twenty-seven

DESPAIR

AT THE LOWER END OF the Cardinal City Quadrant, bordering the highway separating the haves from the have-nots stood the tallest southern building filled with shared office space and business corporations.

Workers had begun to file in for the day, and Despair was among them.

Dressed in a simple white pantsuit, she held a small potted plant in her hands. Pink Freesias, a perennial flowering plant from South Africa. Family: *Iridaceae*.

Acknowledging the security guard at the turnstile simply by looking at him, she pushed through and made her way to the group of three elevators. As she approached, the waiting office workers parted like the red sea to make way for her. There were so many of them that they stretched across the lobby, crowding the entrance to the lifts.

Their proximity irritated her. She rarely left the building during rush hour, especially morning. Most people hated going to work. She felt it.

She stared at the closed metal doors of her private elevator, saved only for access to the secret Syndicate floors. Even though none of them knew her true identity, they were still afraid of her. She could see it in their minute twitches and bodily shifts away. She wanted to laugh. To scoff. They all tried so hard to not let their fear show. It mattered not. She wasn't there to make friends.

The elevator pinged, and the doors opened. She stepped inside the empty car, heels muffling on the carpet, and hit the button for the top level. She turned to face the front. The doors were still open. The group of workers goggled. Instinctually, she dipped her head until her long hair covered the scarred side of her face. Mouths gaped until the doors closed, hiding her from view.

Craning her neck to the side, she glimpsed her reflection. Long white hair. An uneventful face. Deep blue irises that faded to purple around the pupil in a way that reminded her of the ever expanding expanse of space, the nothing inside her soul. The only other ounce of color came from the Freesias in her hands.

This was when she looked most human, and still they feared her.

She watched the indicator light flash up the levels, going beyond the empty office space insulating their top floors and past the level where her living quarters resided, along with Julius's.

On a whim she rarely felt, she'd only left the building to purchase the plant, otherwise she may have dressed in her work leathers and traveled straight to the basement in preparation to administer the second dose of the serum on their captive. But she had all day to action their plan.

The doors opened, and she stepped out onto the maroon carpeted hall, continuing until she reached her father's office door.

When she pushed through, she found it empty. Good. The meeting hadn't started yet. The elevator and hall were in the center of the building. The office covered the entire floor. Floor-to-ceiling windows gave them an unrestricted view of the city, from the decrepit slums of the south-side, to the prestigious districts of the Quadrant and further north. She strode to the solitary mahogany desk facing the south-side and put the plant down. There were too many monitors there today for the meeting, and she had to squeeze the plant behind the narrow space before the edge of the desk dropped off. Not ideal, but it would do. The only other item occupying the space was a picture frame of Julius's first family. The one that came before her.

With nothing else to do, she switched on the monitors and computer, readying the station for the video conference. Within moments, Julius arrived.

Mary, her nanny from the lab in her youth, had once described Julius as a tall, sophisticated nightmare on legs. At the time, Despair had only been eight or nine, but she remembered thinking he was just misunderstood. Despair rode the man more than anyone she'd ever sensed. She'd felt sorry for him. Still did.

Nothing he seemed to do eased his sorrow, and he hid it behind his work.

Without a word, he sat down at his enormous leather high-back chair and dialed into his meeting.

While they waited for the connections to click, Despair wondered if she should say something. Whether to greet him, or announce the plant, but decided against it. Idle conversation wasn't in their repertoire. Instead, she stood behind him, same as usual, and joined her hands at the front.

One by one, little squares on the screens winked into existence. Two for each monitor. Six in total. Seven people, if you included Julius.

An Asian business man named Akiko Ito, a brown-skinned military man named Amare, the blond Brigit Johansen from Norway, and

Mr. Andrews—a white middle-aged man from Australia. Roger Kelly from Ireland and José Garcia from Columbia were last to sign in.

With all seven present, there was a representative from each continent in the world. Seven who made up the Syndicate, with Julius at the head of research and development here in the States.

"I trust you have some good news for us, Mr. Allcott?" Brigit fidgeted with the bow-necktie on her white blouse. "As you can see, we are not getting any younger."

"Yes," the Australian said, arching an eyebrow. "We're all waiting for an official report on the fallout of the base being compromised."

"That wasn't our only base. It matters not if we send a cleaner in." The African waved his hands, dismissing the Australian. "I'm more interested in your latest development."

"Agreed." The Irish man leaned forward, eyes flicking to where Despair stood. "I'd like to have an actionable weapon before I die of old age."

All six of them bickered amongst themselves.

Beneath his tailored suit, Julius's shoulders tensed, but he didn't take the bait. This had been going on for the decades since Despair's birth. He was well versed in how to handle the pressure from his investors.

"First," Julius said, taking control of the conversation. "Let me address your concerns about the integrity of our base." He needn't have raised his voice. It commanded respect simply by being. Conversation hushed. "We haven't had any indication they've successfully penetrated the classified information, and the invasion allowed us to gain another blood sample of an activated soldier. That gives us four. Four complete DNA structures to help us unlock the puzzle to replicate the project once and for all. Even if we are behind in unlocking this puzzle, we now have four soldiers we can control by manipulating the proximity of their mate."

251

"Four is not seven, señor," José pointed out. "You promised us one soldier for each continent."

"Four is over half-way there. We have time."

"Time is precisely what we're running out of." The Australian shifted in his seat.

Akiko raised his voice. "Not to mention funds. These latest drawbacks have been costly."

"I'm well aware of this. I'm not the one who so readily suggested cleaning our base. We can salvage what is there. But all this aside, as you can see, they're doing half our job for us."

"How's that?"

"Have you not read the reports I've sent through? Of course you haven't. You leave everything for me to do, and then you whine about results."

"You are not funding the operation. We are," replied Amare.

Julius ground his teeth. "They have created their own virtually impenetrable armor, and one of them is basically invulnerable without it."

"Your point?"

"Once we have them under our control, we can study them further and replicate. We will save money in our defense department. We can use their intellectual property for our own gain."

"And when will that be, Allcott? When will they be in our control?"

"That day is coming. If you've read my report"—he pushed derision into his tone—"then you'd have seen that we've captured one of their mates, and the separation is garnering optimum results. One trip into the city, and she sent an entire bus load of people to sleep, simply by riding past."

"One bus load?" Roger's face grew red. "I can rid the world of more than that with a bomb. You're failing to marvel us, Allcott."

"You want to be marveled?" Julius's voice rose an octave. "Imagine the destruction one of these soldiers will cause, simply by walking through a neighborhood. They can get in and out of airports undetected. They are a person, no trace elements to set off bomb detectors, no physical weapons to alert authorities, just a simple human being with the power to destroy inbuilt. And that is only one. As soon as we gain all activated blood samples, we will have the power to replicate an army of these soldiers. You will have your destruction, and then once the dust settles, you can rebuild your continent to your liking and your control."

Silence. Then the woman said, "Yet, we are still waiting."

"Well, if you wait just a few hours, you will see first-hand the destruction one of these unbalanced soldiers can create in a city. You will witness a taste of your future."

With that final word, Julius cut the conference call. He stood, straightened his tie and jacket, then turned to Despair.

"I trust everything is in order for the demonstration?"

She nodded, but something had been bothering her. It niggled at her mind. "You said only seven were needed, but there are eight of us."

He leaned toward his reflection on the black monitor and shifted a strand of pale hair from his temple. "You're not included in the deal."

Because she was his most cherished? His most loved?

Seeing her silence, he straightened. "You're the first, my darling. The practice run. Gloria trialed and tested her theories on you, then she replicated them in the rest."

For some reason, a tightness in her chest constricted. "I thought I was perfection. That was what you've always told me."

"I would never sell you to the wolves, my darling. It's you and me against the world." He frowned, noting her stiff posture. His voice softened. "They left you for dead. They knew you ran back into that fire to save your mother, but instead of saving you, they left. They could have come back, but they didn't. Never forget that. I came back. They didn't. It's you and me against the world, my darling."

He'd said that already. He always said it. She wasn't up to scratch —she was the display model—except, she was beginning to wonder… perhaps that was only his thinking.

They set a plate for her at their table.

When he gripped her shoulder in his version of affection, she stiffened more.

"We have a demonstration to prepare, one that needs to marvel our investors. You have work to do. Put away the monitors and, while you're at it, throw out that plant. You know I like an uncluttered desk. Then meet me down in the basement."

He walked out without another word.

Throw out that plant.

You have work to do.

She blinked, hands trembling as she lifted the small, fragile pot of Freesias.

If it was the two of them against the world, then why was she the only one getting her hands dirty?

twenty-eight
SLOAN LAZARUS

IT WAS GO TIME.

Having just slipped on her Deadly Seven combat uniform, Sloan hit the form-fitting button with trembling fingers. She hadn't worn the suit for a while, and her body shape had changed from all the extra training sessions. Air whooshed out and the special fabric sucked in, molding to her body. She tried to swallow and produce moisture in her mouth. Nope. Dry as dirt.

She collected her crossbow and synced it between her shoulder blades. Testing the grip, she tugged until she was sure the weapon was secured. Then she attached her quiver to her thigh. For good measure, she also included a few daggers, throwing stars and grappling hooks around her midsection belt. Nothing was going to stop her from getting to Max.

The inauspicious mood stifled the air in the room—and most of that came from her looming two brothers, Parker and Evan. Griffin and Wyatt were on their way. Tony had been notified, but hadn't responded and, to be honest, she didn't expect him to. After they'd trained earlier, she'd left him at Heaven, well on his way to being inebriated. It was better he didn't come. Liza, as usual, preferred to contribute officially from the precinct.

"Are you sure this is the location?" Parker stood near the central strategy table, frowning down at Sloan's iPad and the digital map she had displayed. He hit the form-fitting button on his own suit, triggering the whoosh. Fabric sucked tight against his musculature, showing Sloan his massive strength. She used to be intimated, but not anymore.

She walked up to stand next to him. "As sure as I can be."

"It's the best lead we have, right?" Evan strode in from the weapon's room, the handles of twin katanas peeking out from over his shoulders. He picked up the broken cell Sloan had recently salvaged and looked at it with a frown. "Can't believe it took me this long to remember Sara had made a call from Wyatt's cell."

She sighed. "Well, we've all kinda been busy."

Evan looked sheepish. "But if I'd remembered earlier, perhaps we'd have been able to track the location of the call recipient sooner. If it's a Syndicate base of operations, then we could have destroyed it, and maybe none of this would have happened."

Maybe Max would be safe.

"The road to insanity is paved with what-ifs, Evan," Parker muttered, still inspecting the iPad like he owned it. Stabbing the screen with his big brute fingers.

Sloan took her device from him, shooting him a chagrinned frown. "It's not a piece of meat in need of pulverizing. Be gentle with her." *Jeez.*

Parker grunted, pushed Sloan to the side and cleared the strategy table. Made from glossy mirrored glass, it also doubled as a flat computer screen.

"AIMI," Parker said. "Bring up the blueprints for the building mapped on Sloan's iPad."

She steadied her temper, and ignored the fact he wanted to run point. She knew more about this mission but, whatever, the dude had control issues and Max's safety was the important thing here.

Half-way through discussing the best plan of approach—roof or ground—Griffin walked in, already dressed in his Deadly outfit. His blue face scarf gathered around the base of his neck, leaving his face free. Mussed up dark hair indicated his hood had recently been up. Without his spectacles, he looked completely different, and sometimes Sloan did a double take before she recognized him. It was stupid, really. They were only frames around his eyes.

"Apologies, I'm late." He strode to the strategy table. "Wyatt's just finished up with an antenatal appointment, he'll be here any minute." He folded his arms and inspected the glass screen. "This is where you think Max is being held?"

Sloan's stomach fluttered. "It's where Daisy was phoning Sara from."

"And you found the data buried in Sara's phone."

"Together with Wyatt's cell," she corrected.

He arched an eyebrow but said no more. "That was months ago."

"We know." Don't remind her.

"Okay. What's the plan?"

Sloan opened her mouth, but Griffin held up a finger for her to wait. He lifted his hood to cover his head and tapped the microphone activator on his breast pocket emblem. The micro-speaker was inbuilt into his hood. "Yes?"

Griffin's gaze turned dark.

"What is it?" Sloan asked.

"Lilo," was all he said, and then he walked out of the operations room and into the hallway, no doubt wanting to focus his attention on the call.

Sloan shared a worried look with her two brothers. Lilo, Griffin's mate, rarely called and asked to be patched through to their suits. She knew if he was in a suit, he'd be in the field and not to be disturbed. Lilo was a news reporter. Calling like this might indicate bad news…

Griffin came hurrying back from the hallway, a hard look on his face.

"AIMI," he said. "Turn on the channel four news on the middle wall monitor."

One of the giant screens flickered to life. With it came pictures of a disaster unfolding in the municipal district of Cardinal City.

Sloan's whole world came crashing down.

"Looks like we found Max," Evan said.

twenty-nine

MAX JOHNSON

A WARM BREEZE tickled Max's face and arms. He was lying down. When he opened his eyes, blue sky peeked from the gaps between tall buildings. As his awareness began to focus, sounds of traffic, birds and conversation flowed over him. Frowning, he strained his hearing. It was more than conversation, it was panic. The whoop of a police siren had him jackknifing upright.

His head swam, his stomach rolled, and the weight of his body almost pulled him back down. Looking down at his torso, he knew why he was so heavy. There was a bomb strapped to his middle. Kilos of C4 explosives, wires, and a cell phone with a timer running.

Twenty-five minutes and counting.

IN THE LAZARUS BASEMENT HEADQUARTERS, pandemonium broke loose around Sloan, but she couldn't move. Couldn't speak. She was underwater, watching everything from a muffled distance. She could only watch the video footage, blurring in her eyes: Max sitting in a lonely courtyard in the municipal district, bomb strapped around his chest... bruised, beaten, about to die.

Then something surreal happened. A warbled ring penetrated her underwater doom.

Ring ring.

Ring ring.

Each shrill decibel grated down her spine and brought her closer to the surface of sanity. The sound came from Sara's old phone. Parker, Evan, Griffin and Sloan looked at each other.

"Answer it," Parker ordered her.

She hit the connection button and quickly put the call on speaker. "Yes?"

"You have twenty-four minutes and thirty seconds before the bomb goes off." The sexless timbre of the voice was unmistakable as their eldest sister. "If anyone but Sloth approaches him, I'll sniper shot them."

"It will take us at least ten minutes to get down there," Sloan said, surprised her voice wasn't shaking. "I need more time."

The call ended.

Sloan's fury broke loose. Red crowded her vision. She shook with bottled rage until it bubbled up and she screamed. She hurled the cell at the wall and watched it break into a million pieces.

Her brothers swiftly lifted their hoods over their heads for protection—hoping to insulate themselves from her ability, but screw them. She had it leashed. She did.

"Calm down, Sloan." Parker's dark brows drew together.

"Don't you fucking tell me to calm down," she shouted at him.

Griffin and Evan both tensed and shared a look.

She knew that look.

She goddamned knew it. They thought she was being hysterical. They thought she couldn't handle this.

Wyatt entered the room, stalled, and slowly tensed as he scanned them all. Immediately, he looked to her brothers for direction. Not her. He thought Sloan had messed up. She could see it in his eyes.

Screw them.

With a profound sense of deadly purpose, she stood, and she stood tall. She planted her palms on the cool glass table. She met each of her brother's individual gazes.

"You think I'm going to lose it again, don't you?" she accused through clenched teeth.

Parker lifted his chin slightly. "Your recent track record isn't inspiring, Sloan."

She gasped an almighty *motherfucker-you-did-not-just-say-that* gasp. Her eyes snapped narrow.

"You can all suck it." She rounded on Wyatt, slowly edging closer to her, and pointed at his face. "Especially you! I've spent the past fortnight training, working on my ability, and fighting to find my mate. That's the only track record you all need to worry about. No... you know what? How's this for a track record? How's this for control!"

She knew she had no time. She knew she was doing exactly what they accused her of, but she couldn't help it. Using the technique Tony had taught her, she conjured the vision of that nail file stabbing into her palm. Then she fired that pain at Wyatt. She fired it at Evan. And she fired it at Griffin and Parker. It all took mere seconds. Each of them grunted in varying degrees until one by one, they tensed, squeezed their eyes shut and groaned as they doubled over.

"And for the record, that's *not* me losing my shit. That's me teaching you mansplainers to *think* before you speak." She wrenched that pain reflex tighter, feeling satisfied at their grunts of surprise. "Next time you accuse your sister of being lazy or not pulling her weight, you'd better open your eyes first. If any of you had looked beyond your own male pride, you'd have noticed I'd been working my ass off to get my skills under control."

A slow clap came from the hallway and Sloan instantly let go of her hold on her brothers.

It got louder. And louder. And then Mary entered, a broad grin on her face. "*Mija*, I'm proud of you."

Parker cleared his throat and straightened his uniform.

Wyatt had the decency to look ashamed. Evan and Griffin avoided her gaze.

But Mary was the epitome of motherly pride. She stared her sons in the face, coming to land on Parker. "I think you owe your sister an apology."

A mumbled chorus came at her, then Wyatt came to Sloan.

"Mary's right. We all owe you an apology. Especially me. And I will—after we get to Max."

"You're right. Shit." Then the panic set in. Max. The bomb.

The truth was, Sloan's little display of power was full of false bravado. Yes, she could manage her powers, but she was out of ideas.

"Sorry," she bit out and braced herself on the table, breathing hard. How the fuck was she going to get Max out of this? What if she'd just wasted the precious seconds she needed to save him? She squeezed her eyes shut, but the sight of his despairing face was there, front and center. *Max.* "I don't know what to do."

"Signal jammer," Flint said, jogging into the room. "That will stop her remote detonating."

"Signal jammer?" But the hope was short lived as something came to her. "There's a hardwired timer on the bomb. That jammer won't work. It will disrupt everything within the radius, even emergency services."

"Can you hack the phone?" Evan offered.

"No," Parker answered. "The code on a cell is a minefield. It would take her months to find the relevant program that controls the timer."

"Oh my God." Sloan jolted with an idea. "My visual code program."

"What's this?" Flint asked.

"I've been working on a program that converts binary code into abstract visual patterns."

"You said the what now?" Evan scratched his head, but Parker understood.

"It might work." He nodded. "You can recognize the code in hours, not days."

"We don't have hours," Griffin pointed out the obvious.

"It's our best bet."

Evan lifted his moss green face scarf to cover his nose and mouth, then lifted his hood. "Right. While you two geeks do that, Griff and I will head down."

"I'll come with you," Sloan said, gathering her iPad. "I can work in the car."

"No," Parker replied. "You'll work faster here."

"Did you hear Daisy?" Sloan's voice was high. "I'm the only one allowed near him."

"That's what she wants, Sloan. It's a trap!" Parker replied, deep voice reverberating off the walls.

"Fuck you, Parker. I don't need your approval. I know I can do this and whatever the case, I'm not leaving him to die alone." She strode toward the garage. "Who's driving?"

thirty-one
SLOAN LAZARUS

PARKER ENDED DRIVING Sloan and her brothers to the municipal district. Night had fallen and time was running out. The mood was tense inside the black-armored Escalade as her brothers watched her work like a madwoman on her iPad, trying to source the frequency of the cell strapped to Max's bomb. It was a needle in a cybernetic haystack. But this was her jam. This was Sloan. A badass hacker who approached any hack with tenacity.

She found the frequency.

She connected.

"I'm in," she murmured, then continued her hacking onslaught.

When the vehicle rolled to a stop, she'd only been linked to the bomb-cell for two minutes. It wasn't long enough for her binary-to-visuals program to provide results. It had only just begun unpacking the data she'd received and, deep down, she feared there just wasn't enough time.

Zeroes and Ones.

If the program took too long to unpack, then she would not have time to find the offending code. Simple as that.

They'd parked down a side street—just outside the police blockade area. Griffin and Evan split and found high ground, hoping to combine their powers to create an electro-magnetic field to contain the blast... if it came to that. Wyatt got out and disappeared into the shadows. Without removing her eyes from her screen, Sloan allowed herself to be pulled out of the car by Parker, and in the direction of the municipal district. Toward Max.

The sound of traffic and people gasping bombarded her.

Eyes on the screen. Eyes on the visual code.

Someone bumped into them, and she vaguely noticed the thickening of bodies as they approached the event. Parker gave an animalistic snarl that scattered people, clearing a path. A jolt of panic surged through Sloan, but she refused to take her eyes from her running program. It was imperative she watched to look for the pattern that signaled the bomb timer.

Another jostle.

Another jolt of panic.

"Keep your ability leashed, Sloth," Parker murmured under his breath. It was purely meant to help. "I feel your fear."

If he could sense her, then she wasn't controlling herself. The next step could be a mass sleepover party for the citizens of Cardinal City... or worse. If they all felt her fear, it would be chaos. They'd evacuate en masse. *Remember your training.* She took a deep breath and exhaled, concentrating on the way her breath warmed the inside of her face mask. Compartmentalize. Deal with that fear later. *I've got this.*

Get to Max. Hack the bomb. Get him out. Don't hurt anyone in the process.

Easy.

Right?

When the two of them, disguised in Deadly suits and armed to the teeth, burst through to the main courtyard, people began to make way for them—they cut ominous figures.

Device in her hands. The sidewalk became overcrowded, and she couldn't stop the instinct to look up, for only a few seconds, but she caught glimpses of faces she knew. Street lights illuminated local cops desperately trying to hold back bystanders stupid enough to stick around. News networks. Lilo with a cameraman, and her bodyguard —one of Max's men. The big one with the red-tinged beard. Daymo, Max had called him. Flashes, that's all she received, and then she forced her gaze back to her program as they pushed through to come to the base of the concrete steps that led up to the Skyscraper court-yard where Max sat alone.

Her breath caught.

Three flag poles stood proudly behind him. One with the national flag, another with the state's and the third Sloan didn't catch, except that Max had propped himself against the base of its pole. His face was a Pollock painting of bruises and welts. His shirt, stained and ripped. The tape holding the C4 to him was wrapped around his torso like a bandage. His face was drawn, his skin color, pale. But his beautiful brown eyes... they were alive. He hadn't given up.

A white piece of paper pinned to his front lifted in the breeze.

Back to the program!

She forced her eyes to ignore everything else but her screen, only catching in her periphery a local police officer as he rushed over. "Is one of you Sloth?"

Parker must have indicated her because the officer addressed her next. "The note says only you can approach. The victim shouted it down, and when one of the squad tried to get close, he was shot by a sniper."

That meant Daisy was watching... or one of her Faithful.

Parker cursed and immediately relayed the information to Evan and Griffin through his internal hood communication. Griffin's power was metal manipulation. If a bullet was fired, he would sense it and halt its trajectory before it hit anyone approaching... but they didn't pass that information onto the officer. As far as the Deadly Seven were concerned, letting Sloan approach on her own first was the best option.

"Keep your officers away," Parker ordered. "Let us handle this."

"The bomb squad is on its way. We have men searching for the sniper. When they get here..." The officer didn't finish. He knew time was precious. He must have signaled for his squad to let them through, because Parker guided Sloan swiftly up the steps.

"Cover me, Greed. I'm taking Sloth up."

A mild panic twisted her heart. "You'll get shot."

"She won't shoot me."

"That's your pride talking. You can't be sure."

"You keep your eyes on the program." Parker continued to guide Sloan up the steps and mumbled observations about their surroundings, so she could keep her eyes on the program. Every second counted. "Liza's here, twelve o'clock, near the ambulance. An officer down. Must be the one the sniper shot. About five in riot gear approaching from the East." Almost at the top, Parker cursed. "Bomb squad. Damn. Arriving in full force, pushing through the crowd. One approaching."

Sloan's heart rate picked up.

"Greed. You on it?" Parker said.

"I still don't know where the sniper is. I can't say I'll feel the bullet in time." Griffin's voice came through their hood-microphones.

"He's going to get shot if we don't stop him. Do it, Sloan," Parker ordered.

"Do what?" she replied.

"What you've been training to do. We can't risk relying on Greed.

It's safer if you remove the squad officer from the equation. Let me take over so you can concentrate."

She shoved the iPad into his hands. "You're looking for a pattern shaped like an Atari Space Invader."

"Got it."

Sloan cast her gaze down the steps. It was as Parker had said. Already a man dressed in bomb-disposal protection was making his way up, despite the wild gesticulations of the officer in charge. Sloan didn't let him get far. She jogged down a few steps until she was sure she could target him specifically. She conjured the image of herself getting sleepy, of how she acted it out in the training room, and then with laser focus, she let her power loose.

Invisible energy whooshed from her body as she continued her descent. The bomb squad officer slumped to the ground. Sloan barely made it to him in time to stop him falling hard on his head. She guided him down gently.

"Night. Night," she murmured, and then launched back up the steps toward Parker and Max. A shout from another cop stilled her. She paused, looked back over her shoulder to see a row of police aiming their firearms at her. *"Greed?"* she barked into her hood-mic.

Within seconds, guns flew out of hands, hovered in the air and then dropped to the ground. Good. She raced up the steps to relieve Parker of the tablet. "You better go. We're pushing our luck with you here. Daisy still might shoot."

He made to leave before hesitating and turning back. His brows drew low over his eyes. "Obviously, I found nothing, and… there's a deadman's detonator in Max's hands. You can't cut the C4 off unless you've disarmed the timer, and then the bomb. I'll talk you through it when you get to that point."

Then he jogged back down the steps to haul the bomb squad

officer away, booming at the police, "Consider that a warning. Next time you pull a weapon on one of us, you won't get it back."

She couldn't let that new complication affect her, so shoved the panic aside and continued. As she crested the concrete steps to the platform, Max's eyes flared wide with relief. Then panic flittered, then anger. Before he had the chance to open his mouth to no-doubt admonish her for putting herself in danger, she sat down next to him.

"Shut it, Max. I'm here."

"You shouldn't have come. It's a trap." He lifted his hand, the one with his thumb trembling over a detonator wired to the bomb around his chest.

"Doesn't matter." Before she unpaused the visual algorithm, she finger-tapped the offending cell phone, just in case she could stop it manually. Nope. Didn't respond to her touch. Worth a try.

"Don't suppose you know the passcode on this thing?"

"Yeah, sure. *Five-five-five, this sucks.* How's that?"

She snorted, set her jaw, and then unpaused the iPad, zeroing in on the fractal images flashing on her screen. She sifted through them, looking for the identifying pattern that would point her to the timer program on the cell. "I'm hacked into the cell, Max, don't worry. I'm just looking for the timer program, then it's a simple thirty-second adjustment. Once that's done, I'll disconnect the deadman's switch. I'll stop this bitch."

While the algorithm worked, a few moments of charged silence passed.

"Heard about your little mishap with a bus," he said. "You good?"

"Let me concentrate," she snapped. "It's not the time for idle chit-chat."

A few more moments of scouring visual code. Nothing. Her heart-rate picked up and she had the irrational thought that she didn't want last words to him to be an angry snap. She knew why he tried to make conversation.

"Don't worry about me," she murmured.

"I'll always worry about you."

"I got this."

"I know."

Her throat closed, she held her breath, but she refused to look at him.

"I came," she said, words hanging in the air.

The two simple words made him tear up, she heard it in the tremble of his voice when he replied: "Knew you would."

She wouldn't let him down. Not this time. Never again.

She wanted to say something to him, to tell him she loved him. That she was going to sit right there and be with him, even if she couldn't get the timer to stop, but nothing came out. Time was ticking away. Instead, she immersed herself in the patterns forming on her screen.

Focus.

And then, suddenly, a recognizable pattern formed before her eyes. An Atari Space Invader. *Holy shit.* "I think I found something…"

While she narrowed down the offending code location, following the trail of Invaders, he kept talking, never once letting an iota of doubt slip into his voice. "Been thinking about where we can go after this… Gale told me about this little place down south… few hours away… been saving it… Waterfall…"

His voice became stilted, his breathing labored. Something was wrong. But Sloan forced herself to keep working. Like a drug, the closer she got to the prize, the harder she worked, the greater the pull. She came alive.

Three minutes.

A voice came over the speaker in her hood. "I'm here."

Wyatt. Must be close.

"That timer gets down to twenty seconds, I'm running up and smothering it."

"Fuck off, bras," she growled. "You get near this bomb, and I'll kill you myself."

"I won't let you die, Sloan."

"No one's dying, drama queen."

"What's the timer say?"

She shut her mouth. The man had a kid on the way, and he was being a dope. He was bulletproof, yes, but he'd never tested his invulnerability against a bomb. No. She shook her head. Not happening.

She must have whimpered, must have made a sound, because Max touched her wrist. She met his gaze and a jolt of fear passed through her. His eyes were turning glassy. A sheen of sweat spattered his forehead, wetting his hair. Something was wrong. Something *not* the bomb. He looked ill.

"She injected me with something," he said. "If you can't get the timer, run. I'm probably dead, anyway."

"What?"

"You heard me."

Her eyes burned. "Don't start doubting me now, Max."

"I love you, Sloan," he croaked, and then his head lolled on the pole. His body went lax, but his eyes moved rapidly behind his eyelids.

"Max!" she shouted, but he didn't respond.

Two minutes.

Fuck!

"You asshole. You asshole. Wake up."

I can do this. I can do this. She dragged her eyes back to her screen, heart pounding in her chest. *Follow the Space Invaders—look*

272

for the gap in the pattern. She scoured through the abstract visuals and then found a gap. The puzzle piece that didn't fit. That might be it. She dug further. Deeper. Opened up the binary. Hit a few keys, then looked at the cell and held her breath.

The timer stopped.

A burst of sound came out of her tight throat. "Thank God. Oh, thank fucking God."

"You got it?" someone said through the comms.

"Yeah, I got it. Which wire?" She tugged her knife from her boot.

"Where the detonator attaches to the main mechanism, there should be two wires. What colors?"

"Red and green."

"Green."

Without hesitation, she snipped the green wire.

Nothing. No bomb. No blast.

They were safe.

"We're good." She cut the tape around Max's torso, careful not to move the C4. He was out, completely. "Wait. Something is wrong with Max. He was injected with something. He needs medical attention."

"The detective is with an ambulance. Doc is on standby." Parker's meaning was not lost on Sloan. If their sister was there, she could commandeer the ambulance, and instead of taking it to the hospital, they could take it to their medical room in their basement headquarters. Grace, Evan's mate, was an excellent surgeon. But would surgery be what they need to help Max? He wasn't special like them—the safest place would be where the best quality equipment was...

"We should take him to the hospital," she said.

"Negative. We now have more knowledge at the base."

Barry. He meant Barry.

Sloan ripped the pinned paper note from Max's shirt in disgust.

Fuck Daisy. Why did she have to be like this? If Max died, she'd end Daisy. End that fucking cow... but as the thought formed in her head, she noticed something written on the back of the piece of paper, another sentence scrawled in blue: *The answer is in your blood.*

A strange nervous fluttering tumbled in Sloan's stomach, lifting her spirit. The note was from Daisy. It had to be. Could this be a lifeline? She scrambled the paper and tucked it up her sleeve.

"Let's get him back to base," Parker said, jogging up the steps to meet her, but she was already heaving Max's limp body over her shoulder in a fireman's hold. She was strong enough to carry him, and she wasn't afraid to show it. Not anymore.

thirty-two

TONY LAZARUS

TONY LAZARUS WAVED at the bartender in the nightclub, Hell. P-something-or-rather was his name. Pete? Paul? He couldn't remember. Too much booze in his system. A few hours ago, he'd been next door in Heaven with Sloan, having a celebratory drink after his latest training session with her. She'd gone to shower, he'd stayed on. Before he knew it, the dinner crowd started filing in, and it got busy. People noticed him. People stared. He moved across the way to the recently opened nightclub where it was less busy.

Behind the bar, the bartender walked over and raised his under-plucked brows at Tony. "Another bourbon, Mr. Lazarus?"

"Nope. All good." Tony checked his Rolex. The blurry watch-face told him it was either ten minutes to five, or ten minutes to... six? Maybe seven? The hand wouldn't stay still. Wait. It was after nine. That made sense if the nightclub was open. Parker had texted earlier. Something about Max. Didn't sound like he needed Tony's help, but he should probably go otherwise he'd never hear the end of it. He should. Maybe one more drink.

Nah. He should go.

Tony looked back at the bartender, still waiting for Tony's answer. The man had a smudge of something on his chin. Oh. It was a goatee.

Don't look at it. Don't look at it.

Tony lifted his gaze to meet the man's. "I got my marching orders, bud. Time to go. Put it on the tab?"

P-something nodded and flicked his dark gaze to Tony's right. "And what about the lady? Another drink for her?"

Tony blinked. Lady? He looked to his right and, sure enough, a woman sat next to him. He looked at the bar in front of her. French manicured fingers gripped an empty champagne flute. She was pretty. Blond. Typical model type. He'd probably had an entire conversation with her and forgot. He swayed back as he tried to focus on her face. Must be drunker than he realized. No matter. It would burn out of his system in mere minutes. That was the curse—and blessing—of his supernatural biology. He imbibed like a sinner. He also detoxed like a bitch.

That was Future-Tony's problem.

He looked at the woman again. She smelled like lavender. Did he like lavender? Forgot her name. God, he was drunk. He blinked again. But she watched him with *those* eyes. Loved-up-groupie eyes. She knew who he was, and she was up for it. Present-Tony could definitely get on board with that.

He stood up. "Nightcap—my place?"

The instant the words came out, he regretted them. He'd never invited anyone back to his place. It was too personal. Too encroaching. But it was literally around the corner. Lazarus House was between Heaven and Hell.

Purgatory. He snorted. Sounded about right.

She jumped up, firmed her jaw and widened her baby-doll eyes. She collected her clutch from the bar and curved those lips into a smile. "Absolutely."

Tony scratched under his ear. Right. Suppose he should live up to that reputation of his. He gesture-waved at the bartender. "We're out of here. See you next time, bud."

Tony curled his arm around the woman's shoulders and half leaned on her for support. One step. Two steps. He's all good.

Straight line.

Head outside. Eyes wide, he forced his vision to focus on the exit —a blast of soft light in the gloomy nightclub. Damn Parker for installing so many levels to this place. The architecture was set out like an amphitheater for the nine circles of hell. Steps everywhere. Not too many patrons this early in the night. His sense of gluttony was dulled from his own intoxication, but he felt the people in the club as they imbibed—like a worm wiggling in his gut.

He stepped. Wobbled. But he got it. He was good. Light shone from the vestibule of the exit, acting like a beacon for him. The vestibule led to the coat room. The coatroom connected to the street.

"The leg bone connected to the... something bone," he chuckled to himself, singing. The model giggled.

Of course, he was hilarious.

Sobering fresh night air blasted him in the face and he inhaled deeply. Purely. Heavenly. It was night. Sirens blared from somewhere. The city was coming alive. This was what he'd waited for. He paused and took a minute to appreciate the atmosphere. It was his city. He knew every dark street, every alley corner, and every filthy secret the underground had to offer. Some time later tonight, after his alcohol had burned off—mostly—Future-Tony would be trailing the shadows, wearing his Deadly battle gear, looking to pick a fight. And he'd get it. And he'd win.

And nobody knew he was Tony-fucking-Lazarus.

That's what he called heaven.

Cars whizzed by on the street, pulling his mind from the clouds.

People lined up to get entrance into Hell.

Customers walked in and out of the restaurant Heaven. A couple in love caught his eye. A short man and a tall woman. Strange combination, but they made it work. They held hands as they crossed the street to the taxi stalling for them on the other side. They smiled at each other and something in Tony's chest tweaked.

This amount of activity, it must be the weekend. He must have leaned on the woman too hard because she giggled flirtatiously and buried into him. He tensed. A bright flash popped—stupefying him —and then his brain caught up to why she'd suddenly become extra noisy and cuddly. The paparazzi.

Slowly, more sobering awareness crept in. Four men with cameras were camped on the sidewalk between a city trash can and a tree. From the looks of them all rugged up for the night, they'd been camped for a while and were prepared to wait longer for their payday. They knew he'd been in Hell. And now he was here, caught with this no-name woman, canoodling. Bitterness rolled in his gut, and he wanted to be annoyed, but this was his public persona. This was who the world thought he was.

"Tony!" one of them shouted. "Give us a grin. Show us The Smile."

Goddamn it. He winced, cursing under his breath. The Smile. That's how he'd been known in the media. Elle Macpherson was The Body... he was The Smile. If you asked him, his body was better, but whatevs. He was lucky he hadn't been duped The Diva, like a certain co-star he currently worked with. That would be rough.

He should have taken the secret backdoor from Hell to the neighboring Lazarus Apartments. Should have forgotten about the blond model and just gone home. It's what he usually did anyway, but for some reason, tonight he didn't want to be alone.

He winked brazenly at the paparazzi—decidedly *didn't* smile—

and dragged the woman toward the Lazarus House lobby between the two establishments. The place was secure, had a doorman and you could only access it from the inside, or with facial recognition. Lazarus Industries also had the security firm situated across the street on retainer. Their apartment complex was a safe haven.

Camera flashes reflected on the glass sliding doors before him as he walked up to the lobby entrance. For a split second, he was blinded. Then his eyes adjusted and saw someone waiting in the Lazarus House lobby. Someone *not* the sixty-year-old doorman. She wore a black pant-suit that failed to hide her luscious curves, although, from the masculine cut of it, she'd hoped to go for that look. Brown skin. Brown hair. Plump lips. Sexy, burning hot eyes narrowed on him.

Yes, please.

His pulse hammered. He couldn't look away.

The woman at his side made a movement, reminding him she was there.

"Um. Babe?" He untangled himself from the model. "Maybe we do this another night."

She pouted and ran a grabby palm across his chest. "Aww, honey, you don't mean that."

Now that pissed him off. "Yeah. I do. Forgot I had a thing."

Then he stepped away from her, waved at the doorman inside the lobby—Gus Magnus, a balding black man dressed in a bellhop uniform—and walked inside the air-conditioned lobby once the doors whooshed open.

Tony nodded at Gus, then made his way toward the elevator where the woman stood. Clearly, she wanted to talk to him.

He shot her a megawatt grin, eyes dancing over her face. Plump lips pursed. Her nose crinkled. She took a deep breath, then spoke. "Where have your people taken Max?"

Every cell inside him froze. "I'm sorry?"

"Max. Maximillian Johnson. Tell me now, or I swear to God I'm calling the police."

"I don't know what you're talking about."

She paused and narrowed her eyes again. God, he liked that. Was that bad of him? Was he mad to be thinking about her lips and eyes when she was clearly upset?

"Do you even know who I am?" she asked, hands on hips.

His grin widened. "That's my line."

"Ugh!" She threw her hands in the air and opened her mouth to say something else, but he cut her off.

"Of course I know who you are," he said, voice smooth, eyes darting down to the Nightingale logo on her suit breast pocket. He nodded there. "Nightingale Securities. You work with Max. You're female, and there's only one female in his employ, so you must be Bailey."

She jerked back, as though surprised. "So why are you being obtuse? Where is Max? I saw him on the news. He's not at the hospital. He's not—"

Tony frowned and held his hand up. "Wait. Rewind. What are you talking about? Why would he be at the hospital?"

"You don't know, do you?"

"Know what?"

Unease trickled in, casting a dampener on his drunkenness. His immediate thoughts went to his sister, Sloan. Was she okay?

"It was all over the news. They found Max in the municipal district—outside the courthouse with a goddamned bomb strapped to his chest. The Deadly Seven came in and deactivated it, but—" Bailey shook her head. Her eyes turned glassy. "Something was wrong with Max. They took him. I want to know where."

The blood drained from Tony's face. He pulled his cell from

inside his jacket pocket and checked. No one had contacted him since that first text from Parker. He opened the message, just to see if he'd missed a reply, or another message on the thread. Sometimes he did that.

Nothing.

He met Bailey's eyes. "You said the Deadly Seven took him. Why would I know anything about that?"

She stared at him, unblinking. That mind of hers revved a million miles an hour, and Tony knew in that instant, this woman was smart. Clever. Perceptive. She was cataloging every minute behavior of his and filing it away for another time. A distant memory came forth, reminding Tony of the conversation he'd had with Sloan about one of Max's staff being ex CIA. Not that Bailey'd officially told anyone else. That knowledge was supposed to be on the down low.

Well, Tony straightened. Bailey wasn't the only one who was perceptive. She wasn't the only one who flew under the radar. He knew how to appear not as he was too. He made sure to sway a little, slur a little, and even added a burp when he said, "Say that again. I may or may not have been thinking about your... b—" he glanced down at her chest pointedly. "Bootiful skin. S'really nice. What moisturizer do you use."

Bailey sighed laboriously. "Obviously, I was mistaken coming here. I don't expect you to know anything. I just know Max was on contract for Parker doing something top-secret. If you see Parker, please tell him to call me."

Tony nodded.

Bailey walked away. She smiled softly at Gus and he let her out.

Tony watched her stride across the street until she disappeared in the darkness. He stood watching for long moments and didn't know why.

I don't expect you to know anything.

281

He hit the down button on the lift. "Yeah, join the crew."

IT WAS a mad house when Tony arrived in the basement. He passed Griffin and Liza sitting morosely in the strategy room. Most of the action concentrated around the medical room and standing in the hallway, watching through the glass viewing window were his parents, Evan, Wyatt and Misha. Tony followed their worried gazes inside the medical lab and had a profound sense of déjà vu. Inside, laid out on a stretcher, was Max. Parker, Sloan and Evan's lifemate Grace were in there, as was the scientist they'd rescued, Barry Pinkerton.

It reminded Tony of when Wyatt had been sliced across the throat by his ex and was in there being patched up. Goosebumps erupted over his flesh, and he turned to check on Wyatt. He stood with his arms around Misha, holding her tight, eyes locked on Max.

When Tony brought his gaze back to Max, he knew why Wyatt looked disturbed. Something was wrong with Max. The whites of his eyes showed. His back bowed on the stretcher. Veins in his neck protruded. Foam spat from his snarling mouth. It was like the special effects team from a zombie movie had worked on the man. Parker used all his strength to hold down Max by the ankles. Sloan was holding his wrists, but not successfully.

"She needs our help," Tony murmured, catching the dismay in Sloan's eyes.

Wyatt cast a downward glance at Tony's attire—the loosened tie, the untucked shirt—and his lip curled with scorn. Then Wyatt gestured at Evan. "Let's go in."

Misha placed her palm on Wyatt's chest, lifted on her tip toes and whispered something into his ear. Wyatt's expression softened. He looked down at his woman and nodded. Then he shouldered into the med-room.

That love right there was something Tony would never have. As soon as the thought entered his mind, he saw the same love everywhere. Between his parents. Evan as he came up behind his woman in the med room. Sloan as she looked down at Max as if he was her life. What did people see when they saw Tony? Not even Tony knew.

He shoved his hands in his pockets, then stepped forward until his nose almost touched the viewing window.

Wyatt and Evan each took a wrist and held Max down. This only infuriated Max, and he strained more. It was as though his muscles expanded in diameter, as though his body was growing, getting bigger, stronger... like a monster. Like those beastly animals at the black site.

"Hold him steady," Grace insisted as she aimed a syringe toward Max's inner elbow. She had her surgical scrubs on, which meant she must have come straight from the hospital at Evan's behest. "If I can't draw blood, we can't test it."

Max was barely containable as he bucked.

Sloan shouted. "We just need his blood. The note said the answer is in his blood!"

Unable to get to his vein, Grace shook her head and quickly replaced her syringe with another. "We have to sedate him."

Then she plunged her needle into his right biceps and depressed. Max roared, bucked and threw at least two of them off him.

He should get in there. Max would want Tony in there.

"What happened?" Tony asked Griffin, who had come to stand next to him.

Griffin only gave him a sideways glance, then said: "You'd know if you came to the briefing when Parker called."

"He just said to get down to the basement," Tony muttered. "I didn't realize it was important."

Griffin's only answer was a grunt, because his wife also joined him at that moment. Flush-faced and fresh from the camera, her makeup was done. Her hair and smart dress was smooth.

She rushed up to Griffin. "Griff, honey. Is he okay?"

Griffin curled his fingers around his wife's waist and simply nodded toward the window. "We don't know what's wrong with him. They're trying to sedate him so they can test his blood."

Lilo frowned. "He looks like Donnie did when he took too much of the Greed Serum."

She was right.

Tony moved. He slammed his palm on the door to the med room, swinging it open. He strode inside and right to where Barry stood at the side, wringing his hands, eyes wide on Max. Tony clicked his fingers in front of the scientist's face to get his attention. "Lilo said he looks like Donnie did when he took too much Greed Serum. Does that mean anything to you?"

"I-uh..." Barry's fearful gaze darted between Max and Tony. He shook his head. "I'm sorry, Greed serum?"

"Out," Parker ordered from the table, face straining with his grip on Max's arm. "Get out, Tony."

Fuck that. Tony had to help. Max would want him to. He crossed the room to stand next to Sloan. "You want me to take over?"

Her eyes glistened when she brought them to his. "Parker's right, Tony. There's nothing you can do. We need to test his blood. The answer is in his blood."

"You keep saying that. Why?"

Sloan shook her head absently. "It was on the note pinned to his chest."

"You got that note?"

"Tony," Parker growled. "You stink like alcohol. Get out before I take you out."

Tony ignored his brother. Yes, he was still a little tipsy. Yes, he stank. But, no. He would not leave Max. He should have been there.

"Where is the note?" he asked Sloan.

"Tucked in my waistband."

Without waiting for permission, Tony lifted the hem of her jacket to reveal her waistband beneath. He saw the white crumpled paper wedged near her hip. He plucked it out. He opened the note.

"He's calming," Grace muttered. "It's working."

Tony read the note, eyes scanning across the words. *The answer is in your blood.* He repeated the words in his mind. The answer is in your blood. It was a note pinned to Max's chest. Whoever pinned the note knew what was going to happen to Max. They'd have known he wouldn't be in any condition to read.

The note wasn't for Max.

It was for Sloan.

"The answer is in Sloan's blood, not Max's," he said and then handed the note to Barry. "Does *that* make any sense to you?"

Barry's eyes suddenly focused, and he straightened. "In her blood. Yes. Yes, that makes perfect sense."

Max had gone lax, and Grace was drawing blood while Parker attached monitoring electrodes. Sloan chewed on her nails.

"We need to start a transfusion," Barry decided. "Sloan's blood"—he scanned all the Deadly Seven present in the room—"all of your blood. It's regenerating and you're all universal donors. Give the man a transfusion using your blood. Theoretically, it will purify the toxins from Max's system."

Sloan was already hitting the form-fitting button on her jacket chest, releasing the fabric's hold on her body. She tugged it over her head until she was only in her bra. Then she held her exposed inner elbow out. "Whatever you need, Doc."

Grace was ordering someone—anyone—to find her an intravenous transfusion kit. Parker dashed off to another door, yanked it open and disappeared into the darkness. He returned moments later with a long transparent tube with bags.

Don't ask Tony how the man could see in that pitch black room, but he had.

Parker handed the kit to Grace. "Field transfusion kit."

She nodded. "Good. This is good. Someone get Sloan a seat."

That's all Tony saw because Parker promptly shoved Tony out of the room, ordering the rest of the team. "Everyone out. Give the doc some space."

Seconds ticked by.

Minutes.

They all settled in the hallway, watching Sloan sitting with her sleeping man. One hand grasped his, the other was resting on a cushion on the bed as the blood drained from her body and into his.

Through it all, Tony watched quietly, trying not to pay attention to the cells in his body, already screaming out for another drink. At some point, Parker came to stand next to him. Both men stood stoically, staring. Hoping and praying that Sloan wouldn't lose her mate tonight.

And it wasn't because they were afraid of her snapping. It was because of the way she looked down at him with affectionately sad eyes. It was the way she gently wiped his sweaty hair from his brow, and it was the way her fingers trailed down to stroke his jaw before settling once again on his hand.

"You know, it's amazing what you can do when your mind isn't clouded by booze," Parker mumbled under his breath.

Tony's jaw clenched. He said nothing.

Grace shouldered her way out of the medical room. Evan went to her and clasped her on the shoulder. She smiled up at him fondly and then brought her gaze to the rest of them.

"The transfusion is done. Barry was right. As you're all universal donors, the blood seems to be taking. There's nothing left to do now but wait until he wakes up. Barry's taken the samples we took to his new lab. We should know more in the morning."

Everyone left, except Tony. He watched Sloan and her man through the glass, and he felt... he rubbed his chest. What did he feel? Something uncomfortable. Something that reminded him of the way Bailey had said, *I don't expect you to know anything.*

He didn't like that feeling. He was done with it. He pulled out his cell phone and dialed a number. Within two rings, a woman answered.

"Hello. Darling Greens Rehabilitation. How can I help you?"

thirty-three

SLOAN LAZARUS

WEEKS LATER, Sloan was hiking through the bush with Max, trying to find the place he insisted Gale had told him to visit. Now that Max was recovered, and she had her heart firmly back in her chest, this was the first place Max had thought to go. They both needed a break, but after hours of seemingly aimless trekking, it felt like they were chasing a ghost.

Gale had never been to America, so it didn't make sense he'd told Max about a certain camping spot... but she didn't have the heart to remind him.

The sound of rushing water took her by surprise, and she turned to him in surprise.

He grinned, dimples flashing. "I told you it existed."

"How did you—?"

He shrugged. "I called Gale's parents. They said they came here once when he was a child."

She smiled knowing he'd called them. It meant he was slowly coming to terms with what happened to Gale, and maybe, dare she think, forgiving himself.

Pushing through the overgrown bush and shrubs, they crested a clearing that ended in a small waterfall and a cascading narrow river. It wasn't big. It only had a few small ribbons of water that ran over rocks and boulders, molding them from sharp to soft lines before dripping into a stunning deep blue pool below. Big Aspen loomed on all sides, giving them shade and shelter.

While Sloan gawped at the stunning site, Max cleared the area of debris and twigs so he could lay the two-man tent. She turned to watch him, and couldn't help noticing the way he'd come alive on the hike. This was his element and, she had to admit, she enjoyed it too. Being miles from anyone but Max gave her empathic ability a reset, and she felt rejuvenated just by being there.

Lowering her heavy backpack, she sat on a fallen log near the river. Cool mist kissed her parched skin. Leaning down with her elbows on her knees, and chin in her hands, she watched her handsome man work. The weather was warm, and he wore a thin T-shirt that showed off his musculature—from robust biceps to neck tendons to manly forearms. Broad shoulders tapered down to a flat stomach and narrow waist where loose shorts hung low on his hips. God, she loved it when a man knew how to do manly things. The Max show was great.

So great.

And considering just over two weeks ago he'd almost died... even better now to be able to perv on him like this.

"Excuse me," she called out.

He had a cord in his mouth, and a frown between his brows as he concentrated on tying a knot around the base of the tent peg. Lifting his gaze, he mumbled through the rope. "Yeah?"

"I don't think you're doing that right," she said innocently.

"Oh really?"

"Yeah, I think the shirt is hindering your movements. It would work much better if you just took it off."

A lazy smile curved up one side of his face. Holding her gaze, he dropped the rope and tugged his shirt off. He lifted his eyebrows. "Better?"

She nodded, grinning.

He went back to his task, bending low as he adjusted the poles, heaved, and erected the tent in one smooth move. Then, just for good measure, he flexed. When he checked over his shoulder to see if she watched, his eyes twinkled. "I knew your prank with the thermostat was all about getting me naked."

Still grinning like a dumbass, she nodded. Wait. What?

She straightened, cheeks flaming. "No, it wasn't. I was just trying to make you uncomfortable."

"Sure," he laughed. "Whatever you say."

"No, really." She hopped up and strode over. "I was just trying to make you sweat."

"So you could get me naked."

Her mouth opened. Closed. He knew he had her. Then his gaze softened, and he nodded at his pack. "You want to put the bedrolls in the tent?"

She rolled her eyes. "You're all work, aren't you?"

"Got to be prepared. Make sure you keep the food double-bagged. We don't want to attract bears."

"Yes, Captain Bossy-Pants."

She turned to do as she was told, but Max took her wrist and tugged her to him. Their bodies clashed. He wrapped her arms around his torso and then ran his callused hands up her arms to cup her face.

He studied her. "I just want everything to be perfect."

"It was perfect the day you stepped back into my life."

Sloan's skin felt tight. Her heart pitter-pattered. Her eyes dropped to the curve of his lips and she licked her own. She wanted him... so bad... but had given him space. He was still recovering from his ordeal. At first, they weren't sure how he would feel after the serum he'd been injected with, then they weren't sure if her blood would have any side effects on him, then... it just became awkward. His physical bruises healed, but there were unseen scars.

Her sister had beat him and she wasn't sure she could do anything to help him get over it.

This was the first time they'd both truly been alone, and it was only for two days. That's all they could afford for a vacation before getting back to the city and getting back to work.

The Syndicate had remained silent, but they knew it wouldn't be for long. Both parties knew damning information about the other. It was mutually assured destruction, a Cold War. They didn't know what to do.

She flexed her fingers over his back. What if she just, let her desire slip, just a little... showed him how she was feeling? How she'd been so hot for him, watching him walk and take control of the hike, that her nipples had rubbed sensitively against her bra for hours and heat hung heavy between her thighs. But he kissed her gently on the nose and pulled away to resume setting up their camp-site. "Sun's going down soon. We don't want to be setting up in the dark."

For the next hour, as the light turned the cloudy sky from blue to orange, pink and purple, Max continued to fuss around the camp. Compartmentalizing her emotions—she was getting good at that— she set about to make a small campfire and heat some tinned food for them. By the time the night came, they were ready to sit on the log facing the river and eat. When they were done, he even got up immediately to clean the dishes, mumbling an excuse about attracting bears. She was beginning to think he was avoiding her, but eventually he came back to the log.

The small fire crackled quietly behind them, not that they needed it for warmth. It was purely for light. The weather was a tepid seventy degrees and beautiful. Crickets chirped and an owl hooted in the distance.

He took a deep breath and sighed, stretching his long legs in front of him, and put his hands on the log for support. The silence expanded until Sloan couldn't stand it anymore.

"How are you feeling?" she asked.

"Weird."

"Like, weird-weird, or funny-weird, or like, you're seven kinds of weird?"

"I don't even know what that means. It's been too long since I've needed to speak Sloan."

"Well, lucky you've got plenty of time to figure it out."

With a small frown, he picked up her left hand and fingered the ring he'd given her. "Yeah. I do."

"You okay?"

"Just can't believe we're here. You still have the ring. We made it back to each other. It's real."

She shifted toward him on the log and he lifted his arm around her shoulders, tucking her in to his regrettably T-shirt covered torso. He smelled divine. Sweaty, salty, and manly.

"She said some strange things," Max said, eyes looking off in the distance.

Sloan tensed. She knew he meant Daisy. She squeezed his hand and waited for him to say more.

"She said I'm stained. A murderer. A sinner. She said that I'm unwanted."

"Max."

"I almost believed her, and then… she started asking about our relationship, and they way she'd asked, it made me think she'd never been in one. This whole time, she's not known the meaning of love." His grip tightened around her shoulder.

With a sigh of her own, she melted on the exhale and rested her head on his shoulder. "I'm so sorry she hurt you."

"I'm not."

What? She pulled away so she could look him in the eye. "Why?"

"Because now I know something that can help you."

"What makes you think that?"

"It wasn't until I mentioned you'd set a place for her at the table that she really went to town on me. It bothered her so much. It made her *feel* something. And when your father ca—"

"Say *what?*" Sloan's voice peeped. "Father?"

"The man who was there with her, he's your biological father. I thought you knew that."

Sloan shook her head, throat turning to dirt. "I didn't. But it makes sense. Gloria was manipulated for years into creating us. Love will do that to you. Except, the love was only one-sided I guess. That man is a monster."

"No arguments from me there."

"Do you think Daisy is having second thoughts?"

"You tell me. It was her prompt that gave the antidote to the serum, right?"

Sloan nodded.

"And she argued with her father when he ordered her to inject me." He shrugged. "It might be nothing, but I have a feeling it means something. She's having doubts."

Sloan bit her lip. "We found out their base of operations is in the city. It's a tower facing the South-Side. We were going to infiltrate it to rescue you when we saw the news. We've set up surveillance and sat on the information for weeks. We have seen her go in and out multiple times."

"What will you do?"

"We don't know."

"If you can accept a murderer, a sinner like me, then she is redeemable."

The pain in Max heart leeched into Sloan and she whispered, "We've all done things we're not proud of, Max. I almost killed Barry. When you were gone, I snapped, and just like that, I almost killed him. No one was safe. If anyone is the monster here, it's me."

"I don't believe that."

Sloan didn't know how to respond. She wanted to believe it too, but after what Daisy had done to Max… if Tony hadn't put two and two together with the note, Max would be dead. He wouldn't be here in her arms. She would have no qualms exacting revenge on Daisy, just like Max had done for his friend.

It wasn't right. They both knew it, yet they were powerless to stop it.

They both lifted their gazes to the starry night, an indigo blanket someone had poked holes in. It reminded Sloan of something Tony used to do when they were younger. After they'd escaped the lab that created them, they would build forts made from sheets and knitted blankets over chairs and tables. While she was underneath, he'd stand outside and shine a torch through the blanket. Light sparked like little stars through the gaps in the weave and he'd tell her a story, making funny voices for each character. He'd been a showman even then.

It made her wonder what sort of professions they'd all have if it weren't for their DNA. Tony was an actor, obviously, but she wasn't sure if he really enjoyed it. It seemed like it was more of a means to an end—a reason for him to keep his other identity secret. Sometimes she wasn't sure if Tony was really Tony, or an actor in his one man show.

Shaking her head, she refocused on the stars.

"This is what life should be about," Max said.

"What? Us together?"

"That, and being out here in nature. No cars. No people. No tech."

Sloan bit her lip and he noticed.

His eyes narrowed with suspicion. "What did you do?"

She leaned behind the log and dragged her backpack closer. Opening it at the zip, she pulled out an iPad. "I brought games."

He gasped and held his hand to his chest with mock offense. "You don't think I'm entertaining enough?"

"No, I do. Of course I do. It's just that we used to have so much fun. You need to relax a little. Trust me, I know the consequences of being wound too tight."

For a moment, he frowned and turned back to the stars. She could sense his conflict.

"You know you want to." Sloan pulled out the second iPad and held it to him, waggling it in a teasing way.

He darted a reluctant glance at her and took it. "Maybe I do."

A full out grin broke across her face. "I even pre-downloaded Fortnite on there for you. And I set up your account."

"Okay. Now I'm scared." He took the device. "What username?"

"Oh, you'll see."

"Maxi-Pad? Are you kidding me?"

She shrugged. "What can I say, mess with the best..."

"Ha! Well, the joke's on you because we have to join some sort of group together."

"A squad."

"Right. Tell me more about this game."

Animated with the joy of her favorite game, she launched into an explanation, rattling off random facts until finally, they fell into companionable silence to play. Battle after battle, they fought, working together like old times. Sloan helped him pick up the finer details, teased him about being out of the gaming scene for so long, and helped him win a few battles. They did it as a team of two, every time. They were having so much fun that they didn't notice the rain clouds forming above their heads, or the first few drops of rain until it came down in a downpour, drenching them from top to toe.

Jumping up, screaming like children—her screaming like a child, Max mocking her in a high-pitched voice—they rushed to the tent, and crashed through, zipping it closed behind them. Trying not to drip everywhere, it was clear the devices were ruined. The water had leeched into the speaker gap and glitched the screen. Max was laughing uncontrollably, but Sloan wasn't.

"No!" Sloan whined. "This is all my fault."

"I think, maybe, it's a sign."

"A sign for what? Check the weather forecast before going on a camping trip?"

He took the device from her hand to place it gently down in the tiny gap between their bed roll and the tent edge. He dug around the bedding until he found his torch and turned it on. It was then she noticed the heat in his eyes as he looked at her.

"I think it's time for us to get out of our wet clothes," he murmured.

Suddenly the tent was incredibly small, and the little torch lighting their space was so very bright. Summer rain pattered on the tent. Max's body heat reached across the small divide to bathe Sloan's skin.

"And then what are we going to do?" she asked.

When his head dipped toward hers, everything inside her broke apart. Her breath hitched. He came lower, and then his lips touched hers.

The kiss started chaste, precious, but when she let a moan slip, he turned rough and demanding. He grabbed her face between his hands and claimed her until they were panting and gasping against each other.

"Shirts," she demanded. No more waiting.

He stripped her shirt from her body, only breaking the kiss to lift it over her head. She did the same for him, peeling his shirt off, and then went back to his mouth. For a long, suspended moment there was nothing but each other, their kiss, their skin, and then Sloan pushed firmly on his chest until he fell back on the mattress.

She straddled him. "I need to..."

"Look your fill, and while you're at it, take note of the silk sheets." He smirked and lifted his hands above his head in the perfect pose of male repose.

Cocky bastard.

As if she cared because she did want to look—she wanted to drink her fill.

He's real. He's here, and he's all mine.

The shadows cast his abs into sharper relief. A moan of appreciation slipped out of her mouth and she rubbed her hand over his velvety skin, sliding it all the way down to the brown fuzz near his waistband.

"I love it when you look at me like that," he murmured, voice low and rough. "Gives me fantasy fuel for years to come."

"Fantasy fuel?"

He turned away. "I didn't mean it like that."

"Like what?" He refused to meet her eyes and she wanted to reach out with her senses, to cast light on his emotions, but held back. He should tell her on his own terms.

"Hey," she whispered, and flexed her fingers on his skin.

His abs bunched, and his fists clenched at his side. A deep shuddering breath wracked his body.

"Max? What is it? You can tell me anything."

Slowly, he dragged his gaze back to her. "Any time I've been stuck in a situation I didn't want to be in—whether it was back on tour, or... being beaten by your sister... I used images of you to get me through. I'd fantasize about us being together. Over and over. Sometimes we were in a place like this. Now that we're here..."

"You don't want to wake up for it not to be real." She'd just thought the very same thing.

He nodded.

And her heart broke.

"Max, I'm real. I'm as real as any of these scars on your body. As real as that tattoo on your skin." She touched a raised line of flesh under his rib. "This looks fairly new."

"Was from a piece of shrapnel from an IED."

"And this?" She let her finger feather down to his belly button, where the hair tried, but failed to cover a round puckered scar. Not quite the shape of a bullet wound.

"Screwdriver."

"Someone attacked you with a screwdriver?" Then a fierce frown tightened her brow. "Was it Daisy? I'll mess her up if it was."

"No." He gave her a sheepish smile. "Daisy surprisingly never went for permanent damage. She only beat me in a way that looked worse than it was. I fell onto a screwdriver when I was putting together some Ikea furniture back in Australia."

She snorted and he laughed too. It was enough to break through the tension. Enough to relax her shoulders and draw attention to the hot male specimen, reclined before her. Her man was ripped. A body carved from rock. All ropy muscle and strength. His eyes, bright and filled with lust, watched her with intense heat.

"I have to say." She scraped her nails lightly down his front. "I think you look better in real life than on video."

"The view from here is bloody good, too. In fact, it's like a dream."

He kept going back there, back to his fantasy, and it worried her. She climbed up him until her hips met his. "Stop it. I'm very real, I can assure you." To make her point, she rocked her pelvis into his until he threw his head back on the mattress with a long, drawn out groan, fingers digging into her hips.

"Bloody hell. Keep doing that."

This was one feeling she'd never box up. She wanted it fresh and vivid. She grabbed hold of his shorts, only to tug them down his thighs recklessly before she got completely naked herself.

He watched with avid fascination, eyes like hot skewers burning right though her. No one had ever looked at her like that. Never. Only Max.

Flattening her body against his, she went in for a slow, languid kiss, melding their tongues together with hot, erotic strokes.

And, oh, it was good.

He tasted incredible.

He grabbed her thighs and positioned her with rough confidence until her core met his erection. Sparks ignited. Sensations bloomed. He was hard, so hard, and his ridge rubbed her in exactly the right way. He moaned and thrust upward, only the thin fabric of his briefs blocking their most intimate parts. She was damp, and he could feel it. But instead of going there, his fingers tangled through her wet hair while his tongue rolled against hers, savoring her taste. Then their bodies rolled—him on top, then her—until he broke free and kissed down her neck, to her ear, to her shoulder. He explored her body with his mouth, scratchy stubble, and expert hands. Confident hands. He knew exactly how to touch her, where to touch her, and it was fucking fantastic. Better than any game.

Stupid iPads. What had she been thinking?

Sitting up, they ended with her on his lap and him bracing her back with his hands. She almost passed out with pleasure when his tongue traced a pattern in the dip of her neck... and he hadn't even touched her where it counted.

Oh God. Where did it count?

Back down her front, he took her nipple into his mouth.

Yep. There. It counted there.

"Oh, shit. Keep doing that with your tongue," she gasped, arching into him.

He twirled and whirled until her limbs went liquid. She couldn't hold herself upright any longer, and he switched their positions so they were back on the mattress, and he was on top, in control. He took his pleasure all over her body, learning each inch of skin, each shiver of desire, and every desperate and embarrassing sound she made. She had the sense he was storing up the details, saving them, and it made her sad.

"Hey." She lifted his head to hers, locking fevered eyes. "There will be more times. Plenty."

"I know, I just..."

"Stop holding back. Just fuck me." She let the floodgates of her lust open and speared her desire into him. "I'm ready, Max."

His eyes glassed over as the sensation hit his system and he growled, nudging his hips into hers. "I brought protection this time."

"We don't need it anymore. I went on contraception while you were recovering."

He didn't wait for anything else. He dug his hand into his briefs, tugged them down half over his ass and pulled himself free. She widened her legs, giving him access, and then in a slow, torturous move, he entered her.

Fully sheathed in her, he lowered until the weight of his body crowded her. He clutched her head so she had nowhere to look but his scorching hot eyes. Then he pulled out, and in. Over and over again, he plunged, hitting her sweet spot, watching her reaction, soaking it all in. And, as she came alive, as the sweet pressure of bliss built inside, he knew. She let him feel it. His rising fever echoed in her soul with each, urgent movement until they came apart together, at the same time.

Afterwards, he held her. His ragged breath hitched. He made little sounds caught between a groan and panic. And he never let go.

"Hey." She lightly rubbed his back. "You okay?"

He nodded against her neck. "It's been years, Sloan. Fucking years and we're finally here."

Increasing the pressure of her embrace, she nuzzled into him. "I know."

"Finally."

"And it's going to be like this for the rest of our years."

The tension left him. His hot breath tickled her neck and then he took her hand and kissed her ring. His arm came up to brace over her chest, and she glimpsed the tattoo on his forearm. The nightingale bird, and the two dates.

"What's the tattoo about?" she asked softly.

"The bird is Gale. The dates... they're, um... the first date is when my parents died. The second date is when you first dropped into my Call of Duty game, I heard your sexy voice, completely froze, and then you shot me in the heart."

She looked over at him, frowning. "You want to remember the day I shot you in the heart?"

"It's never been the same," he answered. Her breath hitched, she planted a soft kiss on his pec, and then she leaned her ear right where the heart was, listening to it thud-thud with a strong, steady rhythm.

"Sounds good to me," she whispered.

"It is now."

"I love you Maximilian Johnson."

"I love you too, Sloan Lazarus." He kissed her lightly on the lips, and then he added, "Marry me, Sloan."

"I thought we were already engaged."

"I never actually asked you."

She smiled. "You know the answer to that, but in case you need to hear it. Yes."

A genuine smile transformed his face, hitting her in the heart, but she couldn't help herself. She added, "On one condition."

"Anything."

"Never put pineapple on pizza again."

His brows snapped together. "As if that will ever happen. Do I need to explain to you all the ways pineapple belongs on pizza?"

She grinned. "Please do. Right now, there's nothing else I want to hear about."

And her man actually did. The great pineapple debate raged well into the wee hours of the night, only to be interrupted by more love making. By the time Sloan finally drifted to sleep, she knew that life was more than ones and zeros. It was messy. It was gray. They might still have the Syndicate to deal with, but with Max, life was perfect.

The End.

epilogue

IN A DISCARDED dark underground laboratory of the Syndicate's black site, a small furred shadow darted about the legs of a white leather clad woman, gorging on meal scraps left over from feeding time. It scampered into open cages, sniffing the places the beasts left behind, cautiously testing for the scent of predators. Nothing remained except scraps of food, urine and the tang of blood.

The white woman went to cages containing fresh smelling plants. A clang happened. And then the woman left, leaving no sound in the room.

Until a scattering near the cage caught the rat's attention. Something moved, and a small piece of kibble rolled from beneath the cover of leaves. Scampering, small sections of the room at a time, the rat darted closer to the food and sniffed. Satisfied it was safe to eat, it nibbled, completely unaware of the vine tendril above its head, unfurling.

The rat was still nibbling when the vine wrapped around the furry body, tightened and contracted. The rat was no longer breathing when the plant pulled the rat's corpse into the shadow of its foliage and began feasting.

characters & glossary

THE DEADLY SEVEN

(Appearance in order of age from youngest to eldest)

ENVY: Evan Lazarus
SLOTH: Sloan Lazarus
GLUTTONY: Tony Lazarus
GREED: Griffin Lazarus
LUST: Liza Lazarus
WRATH: Wyatt Lazarus
PRIDE: Parker Lazarus
DESPAIR: Daisy Lazarus

Mary Lazarus: Adoptive Mother of the Deadly Seven and ex assassin for the Hildegard Sisterhood
Flint Lazarus: Adoptive Father of the Deadly Seven

OTHER CHARACTERS:

Dr. Grace Go: Surgeon at Cardinal City General Hospital. Mate to Evan Lazarus.

Lilo Likeke: Investigative reporter at the Cardinal Copy. Mate to Griffin Lazarus.

Misha Minski: Yoga instructor, exotic dancer and Mate to Wyatt Lazarus.

Maximillian Johnson: Sloan's mate and owner of the Nightingale Securities firm.

THE SYNDICATE

The Syndicate is a secret organization who believe the only way to save the world from its own harmful self is to eradicate all sinners, even if that means destroying half the world.

THE BOSS: Julius Allcott

SARA MADDEN: Ex-girlfriend of Wyatt Lazarus

FALCON/DESPAIR/DAISY: Enforcer for the Syndicate and lost eldest sister to the Deadly Seven.

THE HILDEGARD SISTERHOOD

The Hildegard Sisterhood are nuns with a history reaching back to medieval times when the original Sister Hildegard struggled against a male dominated clergy. Now the world know her as the founder of scientific history in Germany, but back then, her opinions were disregarded until she claimed to have visions from God himself. Belittling herself as a woman in order to be heard was only the beginning of the humiliation the woman faced.

So she started her own abbey filled with women. That same abbey exists today and is a place where women are celebrated and their education encouraged—minus the male influence. Records at the Sisterhood archives reveal they had a hand in the rise of many women over history from *Joan of Arc* to *Indira Gandhi*. From *Catherine the Great* to *Margaret Thatcher*.

Under the surface of the auspicious abbey lays the secret mission that no woman will ever suffer the same struggle as Hildegard and they condition a select few "Sinners" to enforce this mission. These Sinners are trained as assassins for the cause: Sinners like Mary Lazarus. A necessary evil.

In the prequel novella, *Sinner*, Mary Lazarus escaped the Sisterhood who wanted to use the children for their own gain, much like the Syndicate who created them. To this day, she is still on the run.

join lana's vips

Subscribe to Lana's newsletter and receive a free box set, first dibs on giveaways, special printable freebies and more. You won't want to miss out.

subscribe.lanapecherczyk.com

On Facebook? Join Lana's Angels Reader Group https://www.facebook.com/groups/lanasangels

characters & glossary

THE DEADLY SEVEN

(Appearance in order of age from youngest to eldest)

ENVY: Evan Lazarus
SLOTH: Sloan Lazarus
GLUTTONY: Tony Lazarus
GREED: Griffin Lazarus
LUST: Liza Lazarus
WRATH: Wyatt Lazarus
PRIDE: Parker Lazarus

Mary Lazarus: Adoptive Mother of the Deadly Seven and ex assassin for the Hildegard Sisterhood
Flint Lazarus: Adoptive Father of the Deadly Seven

OTHER CHARACTERS:

Dr. Grace Go: Surgeon at Cardinal City General Hospital. Mate to Evan Lazarus.

Lilo Likeke: Investigative reporter at the Cardinal Copy. Mate to Griffin Lazarus.

Misha Minski: Wyatt's mate

THE SYNDICATE

The Syndicate is a secret organization who believe the only way to save the world from its own harmful self is to eradicate all sinners, even if that means destroying half the world.

THE BOSS: Julius Allcott

SARA MADDEN: Ex-girlfriend of Wyatt Lazarus

FALCON: Enforcer for the Syndicate

THE HILDEGARD SISTERHOOD

The Hildegard Sisterhood are nuns with a history reaching back to medieval times when the original Sister Hildegard struggled against a male dominated clergy. Now the world know her as the founder of scientific history in Germany, but back then, her opinions were disregarded until she claimed to have visions from God himself. Belittling herself as a woman in order to be heard was only the beginning of the humiliation the woman faced.

So she started her own abbey filled with women. That same abbey exists today and is a place where women are celebrated and their education encouraged—minus the male influence. Records at the Sisterhood archives reveal they had a hand in the rise of many women over history from *Joan of Arc* to *Indira Gandhi*. From *Catherine the Great* to *Margaret Thatcher*.

Under the surface of the auspicious abbey lays the secret mission that no woman will ever suffer the same struggle as Hildegard and they condition a select few "Sinners" to enforce this mission. These Sinners are trained as assassins for the cause: Sinners like Mary Lazarus. A necessary evil.

In the prequel novella, *Sinner*, Mary Lazarus escaped the Sisterhood who wanted to use the children for their own gain, much like the Syndicate who created them. To this day, she is still on the run.

OMG! How do you say my name?

Lana (straight forward enough - Lah-nah) **Pecherczyk** (this is where it gets tricky - Pe-her-chick).

I've been called Lana Price-Check, Lana Pera-Chickywack, Lana Pressed-Chicken, Lana Pech…*that girl!* You name it, they said it. So if it's so hard to spell, why on earth would I use this name instead of an easy pen name?

To put it simply, it belonged to my mother. And she was my dream champion. For most of my life, I've been good at one thing – art. The world around me saw my work, and said I should do more of it, so I did. But, when at the age of eight, I said I wanted to write stories, and even though we were poor, my mother came home with a blank notebook and a pencil saying I should follow my dreams, no matter where they take me for they will make me happy. I wasn't very good at it, but it didn't matter because I had her support and I liked it.

She died when I was thirteen, and left her four daughters orphaned. Suddenly, I had lost my dream champion, I was split from my youngest two sisters and had no one to talk to about the challenge of life.

So, I wrote in secret. I poured my heart out daily to a diary and sometimes imagined that she would listen. At the end of the day, even if she couldn't hear, writing kept that dream alive.

Eventually, after having my own children (two firecrackers in the guise of little boys) and ignoring my inner voice for too long, I decided to lead by example. How could I teach my children to follow their dreams if I wasn't? I became my own dream champion and the rest is history, here I am.

When I'm not writing the next great action-packed romantic novel, or wrangling the rug rats, or rescuing GI Joe from the jaws of my Kelpie, I fight evil by moonlight, win love by daylight and never run from a real fight. I live in Australia, but I'm up for a chat anytime online. Come and find me.

Subscribe & Follow
subscribe.lanapecherczyk.com
lp@lanapecherczyk.com

facebook.com/lanapecherczykauthor

instagram.com/lana_p_author

amazon.com/-/e/B00V2TP0HG

bookbub.com/profile/lana-pecherczyk

tiktok.com/@lanapauthor

goodreads.com/lana_p_author